Yesterday's Enemies

Yesterday's Enemies

Erika M. Feiner

Five Star • Waterville, Maine

This novel is a work of fiction. Names, characters, places and incidents are either the product of the author's imagination, or, if real, used fictitiously.

First Edition
First Printing: March 2003

Published in 2003 in conjunction with Erika M. Feiner.

Set in 11 pt. Plantin.

Printed in the United States on permanent paper.

Library of Congress Cataloging-in-Publication Data

Feiner, Erika M.
  Yesterday's enemies / Erika M. Feiner.
    p. cm.—(Five Star first edition expressions series)
  ISBN 0-7862-4308-2 (hc : alk. paper)
  1. Americans—Germany—Fiction. 2. German American women—Fiction. 3. Women immigrants—Fiction.
  4. Pregnant women—Fiction. I. Title. II. Series.
PS3606.E37 Y47 2003
  813'.6—dc21   2002067514

In Loving Memory to my Father and Mother

Chapter 1

Germany, March 1945
THE VILLAGE

"That was our ferry! What did I tell you? Now you can swim across the Rhein if you want to get home before they come. If you don't mind freezing off your tail in green ice water, that is!"

Hearing this, I opened the window all the way, leaning out as far as possible, not wanting to miss anything. Only to learn, with a suddenly wildly beating heart, listening to a somewhat desperate looking young man discussing excitedly and right under my window the latest events with old Tulip Nose — a Village farmer the townfolk had rechristened on account of his angry-red, ever-in-bloom bulb of a nose — that the rumbling that had awakened me earlier and brought me to the window in such a great rush was the deliberate destruction of the beautiful bridge spanning the Rhein between Ludwigshafen-Mannheim, die Ludwigs Brucke. I learned that the German army, still on the other side of the Rhein, had blown up every bridge and ferry over the swiftly flowing river, that now we were cut off from the Germany across: the fields and meadow, the cities, our own Village. I heard them say the Americans were coming, today and for sure.

Standing there at the open window listening, I had become absorbed, unaware of the March wind's nippy cold breath mischievously grasping my long hair, pulling as with

7

invisible fingers at the frail material of my once-pink pajamas. I was not at all conscious at first of this willful, early messenger of spring, not until everyone out there under my window had gone and the street was once again empty and quiet.

Until I barely missed being hit with a careless good-morning greeting from the two pigeons living directly above my window in the overhanging eaves, where they had set up, without asking anyone for permission, their rent-free home.

I heard them quarreling up there, throwing insults at each other, getting into an outright fight. Fearing bloody murder, I looked up, and quickly down again, just in time to avoid another one. Both were cooing themselves silly now, playing their game of who was the better sharp-shooter, dancing a minuet on the broken-off flag mast. They were so ridiculous, I couldn't help grinning; then I stuck my tongue out at them, crowing, "Better luck next time!"

I stretched wide my arms.

Ah! It was good to be alive!

Boom, boom, boom, came the voices of the war, as if answering me. Reminding me instantly of the many who were not so lucky to see the sky, to breathe the air, to feel the wind and the sun.

The many who had died in the night past.

Suddenly I felt the cold wind cutting like a knife all the way through me, making me shiver. Making me tremble with the ever-increasing rumbling the wind brought to me from the west and the north. As if on their own, my hands came up to close the window. Resolutely I stepped back into the room and over to the couch in the corner, where I had slept these past hours of the early morning. For a moment I thought of going back to sleep for a little while longer, to snuggle under that rough blue blanket and warm up before getting dressed. But then my eyes saw the white featherbed lying there on top like a snowy cloud dropped from the sky. I remembered its fleecy warmth covering me. For a moment I felt puzzled.

The featherbed hadn't been there this morning when I slipped into this room — my father and mother's bedroom — and curled up on this narrow old couch, grateful for its springy, bumpy familiarity. My mother must have covered me with it when she got up, quietly, gently. I had not heard either of my parents rising.

For a moment I imagined their so-much-too-soon-aging faces — my mother was nearly fifty-five, my father close to sixty — as they must have looked at each other, finding me asleep once again there in their room on that bumpy couch instead of in my own bed just a wall away.

"Because you were afraid again! Hmm. Afraid of the dark, like a child. Is that why you came in here?"

Abruptly I stopped myself from thinking out loud, listening and hoping my father and mother had not heard me.

Surely I was not afraid of the dark! It wasn't the dark. Not even here, in this creaky old house with all its deep niches, hidden cupboard, and gaunt-shadowed high ceilings. I shook my head. I looked about, standing up tall and straight. I was past seventeen and when one was past seventeen — well — one was just not supposed to be afraid of the dark any longer. There! I made a face at myself.

Then I was unsure once more but if it wasn't the dark, the tall, gaunt shadows, what made me so afraid at times?

Was it the dead ones I remember having seen in the city?

Those all-too-quiet ones, so still?

The horribly dying ones I remember screaming inside

9

the smoldering ruins? Inside those just-made ruins, which were now but grey acres of emptiness where only ghosts lived? Or the rats, real ones and human ones, slithering about in there creeping up stairways leading to nowhere, gazing out through empty, staring, cavernous holes with all those dead, dead eyes?

God! Oh, God! Sometimes I wished I would not remember. What good did it do? The dead stayed dead and the ruins remained ruins. We were lucky indeed to have come through the war alive.

"Poor as the sparrows in the fields, but alive!" My father's own words. And he was certainly right. Thinking now of my father and mother, I felt the corners of my mouth lifting with a smile, my heart beating with gladness. I touched the imprints of their heads still visible in their pillows.

"She is a queen, she is! And he is a king! A real king!" I whispered up to the ceiling looking down at me with cracks for eyes. As if in answer to my thoughts, I heard their voices floating up from the yard — my mother asking my father why he would not paint, as every year around this time, her wooden geranium boxes, which she had evidently brought up from the cellar this morning for that very purpose.

"Because there isn't a drop of green paint left," he explained to her.

"You've got plenty of blue paint. Blue will be just as nice for a change," she answered him.

"You really mean that?" came his astonished voice.

I, too, was surprised, thinking this would be the first time indeed that my mother's precious geraniums would look out from blue boxes instead of green ones. Their voices receded, became fainter, then got lost in the garden that began where the cemented part of the yard ended.

I picked up my clothes, holding up my underthings, looking them over critically, wondering whether I should exchange them for the other set — just as often washed and just as worn — that I had carefully folded and put away in my room in one of the empty drawers of my dresser. Standing there, goose-pimpling all over with cold, for it was certainly as cold inside the house as it was in the street outside, I gave a sigh. To be warm was all that mattered. I took no time at all to get into just anything.

And how I hurried washing my face and hands. I skipped my neck without a second thought. The icy water was enough to turn away a polar bear. Shivering, I brushed my teeth, sporting quite a grimace into the mildewed mirror above the tiny, old-fashioned, iron-and-enamel sink, catching the girl in the glass promptly grimacing impishly back at me: brown eyes a crinkle, long chestnut hair wild and unkempt, lips pursed from the bite of rough salt on the blue toothbrushes we both were holding.

The war was evident even in such simple things as toothpaste. I certainly had not seen or tasted any kind of toothpaste for many months. I had convinced myself I would never get used to brushing with salt, no matter how long I had to use it, which I did daily and faithfully, preferring it to the wood ash my parents used. Ah, well, so long as it kept my teeth healthy and clean. And it did do a good job, this rough salt. Two rows of white assured me of that.

Another day that began in the kitchen, clean and oh, so empty, without even a whiff of any real cooking having been done in it since heaven knew when. Always the optimist, I peeked into the gaping void of the cupboard for something to eat. As usual, nothing much was to be found there this morning, except for a crust of stale bread left over from a stone-hard loaf of comis bread moldy when bought, the shelves were empty as if licked clean.

I picked up the crust of moldy, hard bread, poured myself a cup of the bitter black ersatz coffee sitting on top of the wood stove, chewing and swallowing as I did every morning throughout the week and on Sundays, too, telling my outraged taste buds to shut up.

"Pfui! Ugh!"

I could never have said which was the more disgusting of the two — the blackish-grey brew of ersatz coffee or the greenish-black lump of what-not bread that even the mice had scorned hungry as they, too, surely must be. Maybe they had moved to greener pastures — I hadn't seen any around for some time — or they had simply died from disappointment.

Almost sadly I peered into the mustard jar. Even that was empty. The little remaining along the sides and the bottom had dried up and looked a ghastly yellowish-brown almost like — "quoting my father" — baby diarrhea. Ugh!

One day, plagued by my ever-lively imagination, and always and forever hungry, I had discovered that one need not eat bread dry simply because there was no butter, margarine, meat, preserves, or jelly around any longer. I had discovered that one could always toast bread whatever there was of it, salt it, sprinkle it with parsley and horseradish, rub it with garlic or vinegar, dip it into ersatz pepper, ersatz sugar, or ersatz anything. Or cut it into cubes or other fancy designs topped with mustard, which I had discovered one day was halfway satisfying, teasing my stomach into accepting my forced dieting. Maybe because mustard could still be found on the almost bare shelves of the grocery stores — and without food stamps, wonder of wonders! And wasn't it simply amazing what such a spartan diet did for one's figure! I, for instance, was slightly more than streamlined, to the distress of my mother and to the salty ribbing of my father, who had more than once consoled my mother and assured me, "Fat is good on cows. Girls need only a little padding here and there."

Promptly each time my mother had asked back, "But what about girls who look as if they are boys?"

"Ah! Not this girl! Never this one!" my father would always say, smiling at me. "This one has too much hair. That's what makes the difference. Besides, her name is Lisa, isn't it?"

Ah, how I loved them both. I could almost taste my affection like honey on my tongue.

With near-heroic effort I began once more to chew on my tasteless breakfast, all the while aware of the ever-closer-sounding booms of the war, reminding me what was here and now.

The war. I reached up to the shelf where the radio sat and switched it on.

". . . Our beloved Fatherland! Long live our *Führere! Sieg Heil! Sieg Heil! Sieg Heil! Sieg —*" I shut it off again, wincing. And then I was grinning, hearing my father's voice from outside and drifting in through the open window.

"Listen to that! 'The Fatherland', he says. The devil take it already, and the mustache-snapping bellyaches! The Fatherland indeed! *Donner wetter noch einma —*"

"For heaven's sake, don't speak so loudly." My mother's voice stilled, as usual, my father's outburst. Then, hushed, as she continued, "You will get us arrested yet. And at the very end of it all . . ." She whispered. I heard her, but I wasn't listening any longer. I was busy chewing.

For a time now I had stopped wondering why my mother whispered when she begged my father to keep quiet — for the sake of us all. I had always known my father's private opinion of Hitler and his Third Reich. I'd heard him speak about it often enough. The first time I had ever heard him in a hot argument with his older brother, Johannes, from behind the closed kitchen door in our house in the city. Before it burned down. I can still remember the bitterness, the disgust, his voice had held. And I can hear still my mother's voice begging him, "You have a family, Joseph. Think of us."

And at another time, when my father's friend, the funny, curly haired, fat little Oscar, had almost overnight decided to go and live with his sister in England. My father had bought from him a whole box of dog-eared old books, many of them written in strange dots and lines — Hebrew — which, listening to my mother, he couldn't read or understand, yet which had cost him nearly our last savings.

"Can you see little short-legged Oscar walking all the way to England?" my father had said back to her, a gay twinkle in his eyes. "All right, then. So I helped him to take a train!"

"And a ship!" my mother had told him, laughter coloring her voice. "Oh, you fool, you! You wonderful old fool!" she had said.

Yes, that had been a while before the war started.

We had lived in the city still, in a comfortable brownstone house with many windows and doors, and I had been less than eleven years old. The word war had meant to me little then. And planes. Planes were something to look up to, to admire. Now they made me instantly think of what they could do, of what damage they did. Reminding me of hiding in dark, musty cellars, of smoking ruins, of pain and sudden death. And were they not the reason for our being here in this house, in this village, which I still could not call home after all these many months? The village, so cold, so unfriendly seeming, and from which I dreamed to escape one day — where to and how, I never knew exactly.

Still, it was also true that this crumbling house we lived in gave us shelter and warmth. The four small rooms over the first floor, with the entrance at the back of the house and up a flight of stone steps sided by an iron railing, were the place we called home now. Where we slept and lived and hoped — ever since that unforgettable night when our house in the nearby city had burned to the ground in an air raid, taking with it everything that had meant peace and security to our close-knit little family.

In one hell-fired moment — or so it had seemed afterward — the sprawling brown house, the friendly, light-filled rooms holding the real and imagined treasures of my childhood, had become rubble, a mound of broken, twisted things. And destroyed with it was my father's workshop, his machines, his tools, all so very necessary for his family's well-being, leaving his hands suddenly idle and empty. Those good hands, which were so very able to transform the smooth substance of wood into graceful furniture, into works of art his mind's eye had designed long before his hands touched the wood.

Now he was getting old. Still, he called himself lucky, holding a job in the carpenter shop of a nearby factory, driven as if he were but another machine to keep fed the ever-hungrier beast of war. He usually got up before five in the morning, returning home again by seven or eight in the evening, hungry, tired, dirty. Solemn-faced and quiet, he would come home almost every evening looking as if he was returning from a burial. From the burial of a good friend.

I am glad he is home with us today, I thought.

Thinking about my father, I looked out the window, I could see only his face and shoulders. I couldn't see my mother. She had left, surely seeking something for my father to fix, since he was home and willing. For a moment my gaze caressed the shock of silvery hair, the high broad forehead, the thin face with its clear skin stretched over high cheekbones. I was his earnest, thoughtful eyes, more green than brown, warm and understanding and not so common any longer in a world gone strangely selfish and cold.

I touched his chin with my eyes. His chin — just ever so faintly a little weak.

Each day I love you even more, you dear old man, I thought with sudden tenderness, the corners of my mouth turning up. For all these reasons and many more.

I took a mouthful of the cold coffee I had not found worthy to warm up over the wood fire now glowing low in the black iron kitchen stove. While I sat there by the cracked window, my eyes fastened on the horizon, on the blurred skyline over Ludwigshafen, the closest of the two cities on one side of the Rhein, where suddenly the low-hanging clouds exploded with every color imaginable. I watched, till the angry, untimely sunset faded away.

It was but one of several of the city's chemical factories on fire. Set aflame by the constant stream of planes that seemed, like harmless-enough-looking silver beetles, to own the sky. It was nothing new. I had seen the sky look that way many times before.

But I could not ignore the ever-close-sounding rumbling of heavy artillery fire, the far-off spitting of machine guns.

I covered my ears, letting my eyes linger instead on a small, perfect watercolor of a lofty Bavarian Alps meadow. Pine trees, green moss, wild strawberries, blue and yellow wildflowers bending in the morning breeze. Melting Alpine snow, soil moist and crumbling in my hand. Old Christian

Hoffmann lived up there, near his own star-ceilinged Alm.

Boom! Boom! Boom! came the voices of the war, interrupting my dreaming. It was just not possible to ignore them. That fair mountaintop of mine — it was as far away as the moon. As was peace on earth. Only the war was real. Being hungry and cold and scared was reality. And soon, now, all would be over. That, too, was real. Abruptly I turned away from the little painting of the pine-crested, peaceful mountaintop, aware now of the sounds coming close and more urgently.

For weeks now the Americans had been advancing steadily eastward, driving before them the crumbling German army, chafing the heels of what was left, running and defeated, most of the German soldiers now caring only to make it back alive, to return home to their families from which most had been separated for months and years and, many, through the entire length of the war. I know. I had heard them talking in the night past, dropped down by the sidewalk in front of our house, too tired to go on, only to be driven on once more by their own fear, by those few who still felt themselves defenders of their country, threatened by the idealistic diehards of the Third Reich who would shoot anyone on the spot who dared to show signs of revolt or of having had enough.

One grey-haired soldier, his bandaged arm curiously foreshortened and resting in a dirty grey sling, had said to Frau Berger — she, out there in the street with a pot of steaming tea made of wild peppermint, hot water, no sugar — that he had in mind to walk right home the minute he knew the Rhein was behind him. And to hell with it all, even if that made him a rotten deserter. "You see this bloody fool head?" He had pointed to his head. "Tomorrow it will be resting on my own white, soft pillow!" "Or hanging purple, with its tongue sticking out, from a tree, you stupid old bastard!" one of his comrades told him.

No one had laughed or denied that.

Yes, I and many of the Villagers had heard and seen the trucks rumbling by. I had seen the clumps of fatigued, worn-out German soldiers on foot, all streaming eastward across the Rhein into Germany, while I sat there on the top stoop of our house watching. Sitting there through the long hours of the dark night, feeling very young . . . and very old.

"The first American tanks have reached Ludwigshafen!" someone shouted in the street below, pulling me abruptly from my dreary thoughts of the night past with this electrifying news.

Suddenly I had to get out of the kitchen. Dashing into my room, I snatched up from the wardrobe my white woolen sweater, leaving open the door, my red Sunday dress peeking out after me with two silver button eyes as I shrugged into my sweater. And I ran out from the house and into the restlessly seething street to become but one more Villager waiting. Waiting, like all of them, for that which soon would come.

The end of the war.

They were all there, the Villagers. All of them out there in the street. The children and the women. The men — yes, there were even a few men, now that I looked more closely. Old men, few youths. And none of middle age at all. The old men's sons and grandsons were all gone to war, or dead in the war, or crippled and maimed. Worse off than the dead — too many. So I had heard the "Old Ones" say to one another whenever they came to sit together on that paint-peeling wooden bench ringing the Wasserturm there in the middle of The Village. When they came to sit — a grey row of winter-shriveled, trembly-cheeked human crow, warming their aching bones in the sun, discussing the war, the future, the past. Mostly the past.

Leaning back against the cool smooth stones of our house, I let my gaze wander over the Villagers mingling about, standing together in pairs and clumps, talking and gesturing excitedly to one another. I saw them suddenly curiously alike. I blinked, separating one from another, individuals now, some young, some old, and some quite ancient.

There were the smooth, innocent faces of the children not yet shaped by disappointment and grief, by passions and failures. There were the ones crinkled and wrinkled and carved by life, marked by years of knowing what these young, smooth ones could not even imagine yet. And somehow I knew almost all of them and their life stories, for one cannot live in a place as small as The Village and not be aware of her people, of the various happenings under the big and small roofs.

There, just across the street from me, stood Herr Bach and his tiny wisp-in-the-wind, always-on-the-verge-of-tears wife. Three of their four sons had put on uniforms and said good-bye. Only one had returned — bitter, aged, with all ten of his toes frozen off in the merciless white hell of a Russian winter.

Leaning against the door of his house, bent with the illness that surely one day must carry him off to a kinder place, stood Herr Meister. Once he, too, had a son. Tall and handsome, the Villagers said whenever they talked about him. An only child he had been, and Frau Meister had died bringing him into the world. Now, for these three years, he lay buried deep under the rolling ice-green breakers of the North Sea, with only an occasional fish thumbing its nose at his rusting iron coffin, then drifting

19

away again, no longer surprised by the mute presence.

There, not more than a stone's throw away, stood Frau Stein, her work-roughened hands folded across her bloated stomach over her faded-blue much-repaired, but thoroughly clean apron, her two youngest children clinging to the folds of her worn black dress. Her oldest son: shot through the head by a plane while he was on flack duty, outside the city, operating a searchlight. He had been barely sixteen when he died. Frau Stein's husband: a prisoner of the war somewhere in North Africa. Was he still alive?

Looking out a window of his narrow, three-story gingerbread house just a few meters down the street was "Grandpa" Hausmann: youngest son missing in action since the beginning of the war. Second son in hospital for months, blinded, his nose and cheeks burned away horribly by an exploding phosphor bomb while he was, ironically, at home from the Russian front, visiting his girl in the city across the Rhein.

I turned, looking at other faces. There was ancient Frau Waldhausser, gabbing away in her amazing sharp young voice to the nearly deaf barber from down the street. Frau Waldhausser's only daughter had been somewhere in France the last time she heard from her, away in the war as a nurse. Her oldest son had, more than twenty years ago, emigrated to the United States of America, where he owned now a fine restaurant in Philadelphia or Pittsburgh — I can't remember where exactly — doing well, according to Frau Waldhausser, with a family of his own: two sons, both old enough to be in that very army rolling closer with each passing minute.

How strange a world indeed we are living in, I thought, stifling a sigh, feeling indescribably saddened.

Sgt. Krauss, our one-in-all police force, quite advanced

in years — as he had to be for a man still to be found at
home at this time of the war — had come riding down the
street on his squeaking red bicycle, shouting to everyone
within hearing distance not to panic, not to do anything
foolish to endanger The Village and the people.

All listened respectfully, looking gloomy, falling silent.
Even the children hushed their voices, edging closer to their
elders. And the butcher's black-eared bitch dog, lying there
by the curb not far from me, felt the sudden silence, lifting
her head in alarm, looking around warily, her nostrils wide
and probing the threatening stillness, sensing, beginning to
tremble with all the tumultuous emotions hovering so
thickly around her, becoming suddenly excited, not understanding why.

Above the rooftops the ever so willful March wind had
now succeeded in pulling apart the clouds. The face of the
sun appeared, golden and warm, smiling down upon the
still-brown fields, upon The Village with its red roofs, its
pointed church steeple, its flowing green river. Almost as if
she were saying to the world below: Cheer up! Spring is
here, and so am I.

The sky turned a sharp blue. As if by magic the clouds
began to blow away in flocks of white and grey — sheep of
heaven! — driven by the heavenly shepherd, the wind.

All the while the people waited.

I waited.

The butcher's dog seemed to be waiting, too, standing
by the curb with her ears cocked, her body taut, sensing, listening — until suddenly she gave a strange, frightened yelp.
Turning on the spot, she bolted and vanished through the
open doorway of the butcher shop, beyond which was her
own helpless brood in need of the comfort of her swollen,
outsized nipples dangling below her floppy belly. But then

the strange silence settled once more over The Village, interrupted only now and then by the bomb-shocked clock in the Wasserturm.

It was almost noon when the first Americans reached The Village. They came from off the highway, from the city beyond, from out of a dust cloud by the edge of the fields.

Incredible!

Chittering noises! Clanking, howling sounds! Then suddenly, three tanks: menacing, lumbering, oily-smelling monsters, whining and growling, leaving in their wake the cruelly mauled pavement of the street, their gun turrets turning, pointing, without doubt ready to fire on anything even slightly suspicious. They passed by. And then, closely following these armored monsters, vehicles loaded with soldiers, all with guns pointed, each on guard, prepared for any attack from the windows above, all looking darkly alert at the seemingly petrified Villagers. The old men, the women, the children, standing huddled together, staring, wide-eyed.

I stood and stared from among them, barely aware of my father and mother but inches away from me, with my arms hanging by my sides, with my tongue like a foreign thing glued to the roof of my mouth. I stood there staring . . . wanting to feel bitterness, resentment, disappointment. I thought surely one must feel nothing else — only that. For a moment I thought of those other soldiers passing by in the night, their hopeless, tired eyes, their pain. I thought of how much we all had suffered. How very much we had lost. Of all these ruins, all the many dead, who must be turning in their graves, just now closing their eyes for good.

I wanted to think only that.

Instead, I felt an overpowering sense of stillness, a clear

knowing of all being over now, at last, spreading through me like a tonic, like hands touching me. And suddenly it was as if I stood all by myself on a point out in space, seeing all clearly yet as if from an enormous distance. Hearing all as with ears not my own yet my own, removed, remote, but not to be forgotten. Seeing with these other, knowing eyes history marching by — on — through the tunnel of time, and the past like a gigantic thunder cloud towering above following behind step by step.

From all around me came not even a whisper, soldiers and Villagers equally silent, on guard, not trusting the other — the enemy. Staring. Staring. Until the vehicles had passed by. Infantry, soldiers on foot, now followed, one man after another in two lines flanking the street, walking close to the stony-eyed Villagers, watchful, dust-covered, their rubber-soled boots hardly making a sound.

My eyes seeking among them. Barely able to breathe, I saw the strange soldiers.

And I saw this One.

Saw him as if my very soul had jumped into my heart, and my heart was looking out from my eyes, seeing only him.

He was taller than most of the others. His stride was graceful and light despite the gun in his hand and the packs hanging from his belted middle, despite the dust of long miles powdering him with grey. He carried his head high, proudly. From under his netted helmet his face showed clearly with easy strength and quick intelligence. I saw his nose, straight and well shaped. His mouth firm and strong, his eyes — his eyes were blue. Deep blue, and remarkable, like the sky on a clear, sharp winter morning, with tiny crinkles around the outer corners made by laughter, by smiles. And they were looking into mine, looking into mine —

with recognition? Beginning to smile at me. The most wonderful, warm, incredible smile, which I — which I — I —

With a start I realized that I was gazing back at him.
Seeing him only. None of the others. Instantly I felt shy,
closing my eyes, tightly, not daring to open them again until
he had passed me by, not daring to question this incredible
something trembling inside me, left there ever since I had
gazed so into the strange soldier's blue, blue eyes.

For a long while I just kept standing there, feeling
pounding inside my trembling heart. Then, not saying a
word, I walked past my father and mother, walked back
through the yard, up the stairs into the house, and into my
room, closing the door behind me softly.

I was very quiet for the rest of the day, filled with
strange, disturbing thoughts of a pair of blue, very blue
eyes. . . .

Chapter 2

Since noon American soldiers were occupying The Village. After a thorough search through every house for hidden weapons or soldiers of the German army, the Americans had been satisfied and left us alone. The Village was quiet, unbelievably so, with enemy soldiers all about. So very much would I have liked to discuss with my father the day's events, but, strangely, we now had little to say to one another; we were as if numb, without words, emptied of all emotions. My mother was the one who finally spoke, voicing rather wistfully her apparent relief.

"Now surely it will be peace." Yet she looked at my father with questioning eyes, almost like a child in need of assurance.

"Yes. The war is over." He answered her, avoiding her eyes while bending down to untie his shoelaces, taking off his black half-boots and setting them exactly side by side underneath his chair.

We went to bed early with the fall of night, after having listened to old Sgt. Krauss announce, with the help of a loudspeaker mounted on his red bicycle, that the Villagers were not to leave their houses after onset of night, were to stay indoors until sunrise. We didn't mind going to bed early. With no electricity and very little to eat, going to bed was the only sensible thing to do. And sleep — sleep was a welcome thought. It had been a long day. We all were tired. I was dreadfully tired. All I wanted to do was to sink into my pillow, into dreams, where everything would be all right and whole once more.

In no time I was in bed with my eyes closed, my heart safely tucked away inside me.

Only to remember the day's happenings vividly. Finding myself looking once more into those very blue eyes. Seeing once again the smile appear in the sun-darkened face. To be suddenly awake indeed and dreaming with eyes wide open.

Dreaming of happy times, of another time and place, when we still lived in the city, in that other house.

It was a happy house. Flowers growing from green-painted window boxes. By the wooden fence, in back of the house, stood a great, beautiful, weeping willow tree. The ground under the silver-tipped, constantly trembling branches was never entirely dry. I didn't mind. It was a wonderful hiding place for my rock collection, for the horse chestnuts, and little green apples and acorns a small girl gathered and kept there. And sometimes it became a tent, a cave, a meeting place much favored by the little girl and her friends, human and otherwise.

Yes, it had been a nice homey place, that house and its small garden. It had been a happy time while we lived there, long before the war came. So many happy hours had revolved around my father: he taking me places, showing me wonders and treasures in museums, strange birds and animals from far-away lands in the zoo. Always teaching me, showing me, making me open my eyes wide. And we had many laughs together — my father laughing at me and with me and, sometimes, I laughed at myself.

Ah! Those long, shiny Sunday mornings. I can never forget them. My father and I started out with a bag of peanuts for the squirrels roaming and owning the Stadtpark in Ludwigshafen — peanuts in brown paper bags I so happily carried and which sometimes we ate ourselves. When we drifted across the Rhein to Mannheim instead. To a place definitely more exciting.

At the dinner table, hours later, I always had a difficult time not giving away our secret place, not talking about the swift, beautiful creatures I had visited with my father in their stables after the race was over and where a friend of my father's let me sit on one of the horses he owned, giving me one apple for myself and one for the horse.

I could not understand why I must not talk about having watched horses run so swiftly, nor why my mother would not like them, as my father did so obviously. She did like the puppies and all the neighborhood cats and kittens I brought home to feed and to hug so frequently, so enthusiastically.

As I grew older I began to guess that my mother's dislike for such places as the racetrack in Mannheim had something to do with that mysterious time when my father was not yet married to my mother, when he traveled a lot, seeing places, spending the money left to him by his family, accumulating his own rich kind of wisdom in those years of roaming. He had liked watching horses run in his carefree Wanderjahren. My father's older brother — my well-nourished Uncle Johannes, who lived with my father's sister and her family in the lower Bavarian Alps on a large farm, home for many generations to my father's people — had asked me more than once and with a sly wink if my father still liked horses. I always answered steadfastly and honestly, "He loves them!" And he would say back, mysteriously, "I hope he can afford them."

Getting older, I never gave away our innocent secret; for innocent it was. Papa didn't bet now, not even on a "sure one." He couldn't afford it. And since he was a good father and a conscientious husband, I helped him after such Sunday mornings with the horses to shake out my coat and pick clean my hair of the straw before we came into the house. The smell of the stable, however, was not that easy to lose sometimes, and my mother would twitch her delicate nose and wonder out loud if squirrels smelled so or if I had mistakenly picked up a skunk. A couple of times I came home with strange words added to my vocabulary, picked up in the stables and definitely not learned from either skunks or squirrels.

Ah! Then my father had been quite tall and certainly handsome, with his hazel eyes so clear and happy-looking and with his hair full and nearly black above his broad forehead, his voice rich and warm and alive in the rooms of that other house.

How his voice rang when he laughed, becoming gentle when he explained something to me. And how it could boom when he scolded me for some kind of mischief I was guilty of, for a mischievous child I certainly was at times.

Still I was never afraid of him.

"Lisa, *Du kleine laus*," he more than once shouted after me. "Did you take a straw to my beer stein, trying to make it look full underneath all that foam?"

Deep inside myself I know he shook with laughter, thinking it a clever trick of his fledgling. After all, was he not the inventor of this very kind of nonsense? And had he not told me with a grin that this is what he had done to his father's beer as a boy in Bavaria on their farm?

And I could be quite a willful little devil in those days, when in the early-morning hours of a Sunday, tired of waiting for my father and mother to wake up, I would climb the pear tree growing by the side of the house, inching out on a gnarly limb as far as possible and as close as I dared to my parents' bedroom window, taking a deep breath and letting go of such a blood-curdling yodel my poor mother would bounce upright in her bed, knowing that the sleeping neighborhood would be asleep no longer, was indeed plotting to stuff a certain someone's mouth and send her to the moon without a return ticket. But my father would instantly recall that he had promised me the evening before to take me fishing, blueberry hunting, May Käfer catching or whatever, in the mist-covered hills of the Oden Wald across the river.

And then there were those glorious, unforgettable summers when both of us became gripped and carried away by the *Wanderlust,* exploring the stony, stark country of the Eifel, the romantic mountains of the Hunsrück, the Mosel Valley, the Lahn, and the Neckar Valley — the whole singing, shimmering, lovely Rhein land. We started out with rucksacks on our backs, hobnailed shoes on our feet, rugged clothing to rough it for one glorious week or so, with *"Das wandern ist des Müller's lust"* and *"Muss Ich denn zum Stadtele hinaus"* on my father's lips, I yodeling along on my harmonica.

We would come home to my mother — she did not share our Wandervogel enthusiasm — sunburned and so very much richer in body and soul.

I wore my hair in two pigtails then, and I had exactly three freckles sitting daintily astride my nose. My eyes were brown — or green, depending on what I was up to or what I was dreaming about — shining with the joy of being alive, with seeing everything, missing little.

"My curious little monkey," my father often called me in those glorious days past, watching me climb with him the ruins of one or another of the numerous castles, time-battered towers and moss-covered ancient dwellings our countryside seemed to abound in. And "My Liselle," he would say, affectionately and with a warm smile, the two of us sitting side by side in the deep shade of an ancient oak tree, I, listening, spellbound, to the many stories he knew and told so well. I would question him, grill him. Had the war destroyed this castle? And that tower overlooking the Rhein, the Mosel, the Neckar? Hearing him answer me with a yes most times.

Next I wanted to know what he did when he fought in World War I, near Verdun and in the Argonner Wald — on the mountain they called The Dead Man because not even a blade of grass grew there after all the shelling and fighting. Full of concern, I would ask him, how big was the bullet tearing a path through his right arm? And had it hurt much?

One day — I couldn't have been more than six or seven — we had stopped to rest on a hilltop overlooking the invisible border between France and Germany. With his hand my father made a sweeping gesture from west to east. "That is France. And this is Germany." I followed his hand with my eyes, bewilderment and disappointment beginning to flood my small eager face. I stretched my neck and stood on my toes: "I can't see it!"

"What can't you see?" my father asked.

"The giant wall all around and all the way to the sky!"

"A wall? Oh, I see what you mean." He smiled, amused. "There is no wall. Nor is there a rift marking the ground." Suddenly his eyes changed, gazing over the lovely meadows, the flaming autumn hills, the green and brown fields — the whole beautiful land stretching away from under our feet. Then he spoke aloud his thoughts.

"Look again. See how the earth is one. A mysterious beautiful lady. With a bunch of troublesome children unable to see that the roof above them is also one. That they all have one mother after all. One home."

I looked up and all around. The world seemed to be one, just as he had said: one sky, one earth under my feet. But then my father spoke often in a language not yet understood by me, though I could sense his words meant more than they were saying. For a while I kept quiet. Then I asked, "When there is a war, do we all build a wall around ourselves?"

"We do build walls when we go to war," he answered, and he did not smile now.

I thought awhile about the meaning of it all, greatly interested.

"When you were fighting in the war, were you a brave soldier? Never afraid of anything?" I wanted to know, wide-eyed, tongue wetting lips gone dry. "Did you almost get killed?"

"Almost," he answered me. Letting me inspect once again his arm, where the bullet had torn a ragged line through the flesh. "Sometimes I was very much afraid. I did not want to die just yet."

"I am sure glad you came through alive," I exhaled.

But my father smiled sagaciously to himself and answered, "I am glad, too. I could not have you otherwise."

That made me think of yet another mystery. "Where do we go when we die?"

"Why, I thought you knew. To heaven, or wherever."

"I think you are not so sure yourself!" I was pouting, not satisfied with his answer. "One day I heard Uncle Johannes arguing with Father Paul after church. He said, 'When you're dead, you're dead. And nothing happens afterward, not in heaven or on earth. Except the worms get you after awhile.' That's what he said."

"Your Uncle Johannes doesn't know it all either. He has

31

no children, no little girl, as I have. To live on in afterward. I like to think that's how I may live on. You understand?"

"I am sure glad we don't have to be dead for years and years yet," I whispered, taking a deep breath, leaning my cheek against his hand.

Wrinkling his brow with the effort to make me understand, he chose his words carefully. "You ask why is this and why is that. I try to explain what you cannot yet understand. Later, you will know, you will ask instead, 'How? How?' Then you are grown up, world-wise, never to be a child again." For a long moment he looked at me seriously, imploringly. Then he added, "How I wish, though, for your sake, that you will never completely forget to ask, at least once in a while, the little word why."

I had felt goose bumps on my arms, a kind of holy feeling squeezing my throat.

I went everywhere with my father. The hours we spent together are as if painted in my heart. Once in a while, though, my father could not take me with him, for grown-up reasons, I supposed. To help me over my disappointment at such times, my mother would take me out. To a Kasper Theater, to one of the puppet shows always performing somewhere in the city or in the city across the river. And sometimes to the zoo, to the Hindenburg Park, to visit the monkeys, the wild pigs that stank up the place for miles around. On our way home my mother would treat me to a giant pretzel and a sprudel wasser, which only made mule-headed me remember what I was missing by not being with my father.

My father was so special to me in those years.

Always there was this warmth, this quick response between us. As no other he was aware of my vivid imagination, my need to know, my search for learning, to discover.

When I was seven, knowing already how to read, he began sharing with me his astonishing collection of books. For our circumstances, it was astonishing — I know that now. We had certainly more books than anyone in the neighborhood. These books were his treasure, proudly kept in sight in cases and on shelves in every room. Within the magic of their pages we flew together through time and space, meeting prince and pauper, God and man, the poor and the rich. And many times we forgot the world around us, even became deaf to my mother's calls for aid with the dishes, blind to the red dish towel flying through the doorway as a last warning, only to lie crumpled in a heap on the floor, forgotten, while clever Faust outwitted old Mephistopheles, brave William Tell shot an apple off his son's head, and the golden-haired Lorelei sent a ship to its doom on the Rhein of long ago while I got lost in the tender beauty of Rainer Maria Rilke, von Fallersleben, Uhland, Heine, and many others while I looked through magic windows, feasting my heart and my soul.

When I finished a book, my father always found time to sit down with me for a discussion. "Having a bite off The Tree of Knowledge," he called it, a twinkle in his eyes. And he'd add, "chew it well so you'll digest it and it won't become a problem," he would jest before becoming serious again. "Sometimes the fruit from the mystical tree can give you quite a headache, my girl. Too much may swell your head, make you wing from the tribe, from the world all together. Or make you stumble and fall in between, so you'll wish you had never tasted a crumb. That is, if you're not brave enough, or if that knob between your shoulders is not bright enough."

So he had said then.

Now. . . .

Now my father had never much to say anymore. Now he often just sat with a faraway look in his eyes, making me wonder what it was he was thinking of, so evidently sad.

Atop the Wasserturm — down the street and but yards from our house — the clock struck out a shattered, cracked midnight. I listened, to hear once more the rumble of far-off guns coming south with the wind, bringing with it dreams, memories I feared so, making me cry out with vivid nightmares of days and nights past.

Of one night, that one night. . . .

The planes had gone; Ludwigshafen was burning from end to end. Burning was the city of Mannheim across the Rhein — blazing, smoldering, nightmarish, fantastic, making invisible the very stars in the sky. The air itself was hot and dry and burning in our nostrils, tormenting our lungs and eyes. The road running away in front of our partially upright garden fence was lit brightly enough to read in — lit by the burning bell tower of the church at the end of the street, burning like an enormous uplifted finger of God's wrath.

There was our house, now a smoldering heap surrounded by the dug-up, rubbish-strewn earth that had been our garden not long before. There was a large pit made by the bomb that had caved in the house like cardboard.

And fire. All around. Everywhere I looked.

Flickering lights, flames hungrily devouring what was left, sounds, smells, cries, and the hooting of fire engines. Strange, how the ear, nose, and tongue remember.

How I remember. Walking in a daze around the ruins of the house, coming suddenly upon Black Peter, my beloved cat, half buried in the garden by singed stones and blackened chunks of timber. Sickened to my innermost heart, I knelt to push off all the rubble pinning him into the ground, only to find him horribly burned and broken.

Peter! His eyes glowing up at me, green pools of pain, Peter! Oh, my Peter!

A sound bubbles up from the crushed chest. . . . He knows me . . . is trying to answer me even while he is dying . . . and I can't do anything to save him . . . nothing.

Don't die! Oh, please don't die! You can't! I won't let you!

He died just the same, while I begged him not to, childishly, a terrified girl of fourteen. Death took him away, leaving behind this slack, frightfully still corpse showing open jaws and many teeth.

I remember squatting in front of it for some time, with my head upon my knees, sobbing.

Black Peter had been with me as far back as I could remember.

I was three or maybe four when my father brought him home. Smiling fondly at me, Papa had put him into my eagerly outstretched arms, saying, "Take good care of him. He is only a little fellow, and he needs a friend!"

Woolly-haired and cuddly as he was, my heart had gone out to him in a flash.

We were friends in no time; I and the bemustached one. The fur-coated one, who from that day on, walked with me, played and did homework with me, came to sleep in my bed the minute my light went out and my mother's footstep had gone from the stairs.

He was the hero who protected me from lightning and thunder, from all harm. For ten years he had been my friend — through most of the years of my life.

And now Black Peter had left me forever . . .

By the broken walls of what had been her home, down at the end of our street, sat Frau Muller, with terribly dry eyes. Under a coarse blanket marbled with strangely spreading designs lay the mangled body of her father, the torn shell of her husband.

A street away, by the broken window of her kitchen, tightly clutching to her childish breasts a small bundle, sat young Irmgard Hoffer empty-eyed, far removed from the cruel world, rocking back and forth, back and forth, in her chair. Back and forth . . . humming to the dead child in her arms already as cold as her husband, he lying in an un- marked grave in a Russian cornfield.

In the city, all over Europe, all over the whole suffering world, was dying and tears.

I was crying. For a cat. For an animal I was sobbing.

And then I was horribly crying for the hell of it all while I buried Black Peter under the biggest stones I could carry. When I finished piling his grave tall, the tears on my cheeks had dried. With the death of my friend, at least part of my childhood had come to an end.

An eternity later we were on our way to The Village, hoping to be taken in for at least the next few nights and days by longtime friends of my father, trudging the seem- ingly endless miles through a night that never seemed to end, through a grey morning hidden by a veil of steadily falling rain, cold and pitiless, the road never ending and like a tunnel into nowhere. And all of us so tired.

It was only yesterday when I had slammed our front door behind me, calling to my mother upstairs, "I'm home!"

And she, laughing, her words a happy tinkling cascade, responded, "This I can see — and hear — you firecracker, you!"

And a little later that last evening, my father had once more shown me the splendidly colored wood-block prints in his oldest, most treasured book, and my mother and I had made plans for a visit to her family in the Black Forest.

Determined not to think back again, I lifted the hem of my stained, torn blouse and wiped away with it from my face the rain and the grime of the night past. Then I caught up with my father and mother, walking between them, suddenly aware how old and bent and shrunken they seemed now.

"It was only a few years old, and the best ever made!" my mother said, her voice heavy with tears.

"What?" my father barked back, asleep on his feet while we walked on and on.

"My cooking stove! That's what I mean!" my mother said, sounding now as if she was explaining something to a child.

My father and I looked at her, incredulous that she could think about her stove now, when she had no kitchen to cook in, not a whole dress on her body nor another to her name. But then my father's face began to break into a strange, slow smile from under all the dust and soot covering it like a mask.

"I'll get you another stove one day," he promised bravely. And then he laughed while tears streamed down his cheeks, standing there in the middle of the road with his hands blackened, his eyebrows singed, his eyes red and swollen and half shut. He had helped a neighbor rescue his wife and children from the cellar under their caved-in house.

Then, incredibly, he laughed out loud. "We're alive, dear wife. All of us! That is surely enough for today!" He took my mother's hand and mine, and we walked on together once more through the drizzle and the smoky-white fog of another day coming.

In The Village, my father's friend, Herr Bauer, welcomed us with open arms. His good-hearted wife could not do enough to make us feel at home and comfortable. Still, it seemed hours before we could overcome our shivers and our weariness.

That very first night in The Village I experienced for the first time one of the nightmares, when I woke up feeling I was choking, burned and buried alive in the cellar, under the house. Screaming in terror, bathed in cold sweat, I sat up in bed, finding my mother beside me, holding me as if I were a small child. "Don't be afraid," she whispered.

The night always ended. Day came and went. Weeks and months passed by.

I soon came to learn that life can be cruel as well as kind. I was getting used to the house and The Village, though I never felt truly at home. Something like homesickness had come to lodge inside me. A kind of longing, for a place permanent here today, tomorrow, and always. A place to be happy in, to live in, in peace, a place where one could speak up and not be afraid. For I had also learned that fear comes in many shapes. That fear now lived in many a heart and soul. It seemed strange for me to feel so, safe in a house, in a country where I was born, with my father and mother who loved me.

Several weeks after our arrival Herr and Frau Bauer had left The Village, glad that now they could at last live in a more peaceful place, with their son's family in the Alps of Bavaria, eager to rent to us the second floor of their two-story house for as long as we wished to stay.

We stayed, thankful to have a roof over us, grateful for each kindly given piece of furniture, for every used garment that showed possibilities of becoming a dress or a skirt through the skillful, thrifty hands of my mother, knowing well how lucky we were after all in these harsh times. There were now many who lived huddled together in one room in hurriedly constructed shelters, and in the cellars of all endless ruins, with only the barest necessities and little to eat.

The planes kept coming; the nights were either very dark, without even a glimmer of light, or brilliant nightmares set to a hellish chorus of bursting bombs. After years of war, years of growing up in great, painful jumps and leaps, peace meant the time when we had enough to eat, when indeed we had several kinds of food at one single meal and leftovers to boot. Now, real peace had become but a memory of birthday cakes inches thick with icing, Sunday roasts, and, of all things, freshly baked bread.

Real peace was vacations in the Alps and in the Black Forest. Peace stood for a house with lighted windows surrounded by a small garden smiling with a thousand flower faces. Peace was a magic word, a holy, sacred word.

Our world had changed.

All that had once seemed bright and shining was now turned to rust. The glory had worn thin, so many mighty words of conquest shamelessly shown up as lies. Then, even the rust crumbled, leaving gaping holes, and the truth was bitter as gall.

Now there were many who had learned to speak softly. Many who were not heard from at all. There were now too many mothers and wives without husbands and sons, too many children without fathers. There were endless hospitals filled with the heartbreak from the battlefields of Russia and North Africa. And many now were afraid and tired and not sure of anything any longer.

Our neighbors had changed. They talked now only of their losses and disappointment, and, consumed by self-pity, they soon knew only bitterness and hate.

Food had become all-important.

It made the selfish more selfish and the kindly out-standing, as if they were a special breed. Big bellies became fewer shrinking into yellowed bags of skin, and thin people became skeletons in rags. The glory had indeed worn thin.

There were always planes now. Night and day they came, leaving fire and smoke behind. And that other smell I could never forget — that strange, sweetish smell of burning flesh as a dozen horses burned to death in the city's brewery. The screams, the horrible screams, tearing out from one of the Konrad boys — Herbert, it was — trapped in their upstairs kitchen, slumped over, pinned down on his belly on the red-hot stove by a heavy beam caved in from the roof above. He had screamed for a full minute before death released him.

The planes were here and gone.

One day, on my way back from the city, after having been caught in an air raid, I had seen dug out from under the charred ruins of their house the pitiful, heat-shrunken body of my friend Hanne.

I cried every time I thought of the small wooden crate in which the firemen had carried away her body.

I cried this night, too. I cried and I whimpered and I couldn't seem to swallow, to breathe. I felt myself choking, dying horribly, as Hanne had died . . .

I couldn't stop moaning until my mother's voice opened to me once more the door to consciousness, begging, "Stop it. Everything is all right."

And I recognized her hand softly stroking my hair.

And it was good. Yet I was glad when she returned to her bed.

I was ashamed to have cried aloud again. For a time now I had become childishly ashamed to be found crying. Even in my dreams.

Chapter 3

The morning after the Americans arrived I awoke late, with a ray of sunlight slanting across my face, golden and warm and startlingly alive.

From outside my window came the daily garbled quarrel of our two renters: the pigeons. I heard my father sawing wood in the yard. Hushed a bit by distance came the barking of a dog, then the angry, high-pitched voice of Frau Keller promising the dog a good hiding. I stretched my arms straight up into that shaft of sunlight, making a million dust-motes dance wildly. I sneezed. And then I laughed aloud as I realized why Frau Keller was so angry with the clever dog, who had figured out how to befriend the Kellers' not-so-clever few chickens so he could dine on an occasional egg.

I thought of how funny the furry thief must look after having dined in the forbidden dust of the hen house, surrounded by a bunch of nervously cackling hens, his hairy visage dripping with egg yolk. I laughed again, and suddenly I was inexplicably happy. A kind of joy made me kick aside the featherbed, sit up straight, then fall back into the pillow. Somehow, indisputably, I knew something wonderful had happened. I knew the world was different today. Different from now on.

For a while longer I lay there, letting my gaze wander over the varying shades of yellow and brown in the room. My room, I thought with a sudden sense of ownership for the small, narrow, rectangle crammed tight with its few pieces of chipped, mismatched furniture.

Yes, it was my room. I had put it together with what I could find: the wardrobe my father had built for me, which I had painted a faint yellow; the bright yellow curtains my mother had sewn out of an underskirt wide as a wagonwheel and loaded with ruffles from a costume from another time. On one wall, right above my bed, I had hung a primitive little painting of Till Eulenspiegel. It was a happy, funny picture done in sharp yellows, reds, and warm browns on stiff ivory-colored linen, evidently painted by someone with great care. From the other wall, across from my bed, smiled down the cherubic faces of six, pinkdimpled nymphs dancing a circle around the flute-playing Earth god Pan. His beautiful, dreaming face was touched with such sadness, it captured my imagination as did his shaggy hair, his upper body that of a man, and his contrasting bony shanks and cloven feet of a goat.

In the small space between the door and the window I had nailed the picture of a young girl sitting in a chair by a window, looking out into a place mysteriously veiled, her eyes wide and curious, longing. In my imagination I knew she was unable to walk; her poor feet crippled, laced-up into crude, ugly shoes.

One day my mother had come into my room, and, having looked at my choice of decoration, which I had found in the attic underneath all kinds of junk unloaded by the former owners of the house, she remarked, "I suppose the clown is for the child you still are. This goat god and his little playmates . . . Hmm. Well. You like it. But girl! Why would you pick such a sad-looking child from all the cheery pictures we saw lying around up there?" Puzzled, she had looked at me.

"It's me! Can't you see? Sometimes I'm her," I answered, trying to grimace in self-mockery revealing instead a glimpse at the sadness, the loneliness hiding inside me.

A short while after dressing I came upon my mother in the kitchen, looking over a pair of my father's woolen much-darned socks, eager to share with me the latest news.

The big sprawling house next door — empty these past two weeks, its owners having fled into Austria for reasons of their own — was now occupied, since last night, by American soldiers.

Listening to my mother brought back instantly and vividly the memory of the tall, blue-eyed soldier. Suddenly, though I could not have explained — not even to myself — why this was so, I was certain that he had been the reason for my earlier joyful feelings upon awakening. The reason for the expectancy I felt at this very moment. As if she was able to read my thoughts, my mother thoughtfully looked into my eyes while her fingers closed the top button of my dress, taking her time, before she began voicing her own thoughts.

"You must stay away from the house next door. Do not go close to any of the foreign soldiers. All soldiers are alike, and you are a young, pretty girl with yet a lot to learn."

But then she found one more reason for me to keep my distance, quite amusing to me. "Don't go near the Big Cannon or even look at it!" She pointed out the window.

The "Big Cannon" was a harmless enough-looking mortar thrower when in action, and the Americans had set it up in the neighboring yard.

With a flippant wave of my hand and a silly smile I promised not to venture into the firing line of any kind of cannon. Due to my age, I suppose, I thought to myself, *"Why in the world would they want to shoot me?"*

I did stay out of sight and away from all danger lurking

about visibly or otherwise until I became bored looking at our cracked, bomb-shocked walls. Until my ever-present curiosity began painting pictures of our new neighbors. My mother left for The Village, and my father was busy in the cellar, stacking wood for our hungry kitchen stove.

At first I just peeked through the cracked window in the kitchen facing the house next door. Then I thought of washing the few pieces of my forever-being-worn-and-washed clothing. This would give me something to do — and an excuse to go outside to the clothesline in the garden.

I had to hang my wash to dry. Did I not?

And so I washed clothes, and when I had finished, I picked up my basket and walked into the garden and to the clothesline, determined to run at the first sound of danger from the house next door and its mysterious new inhabitants.

I had just finished hanging my wash when a low voice called to me from close by, "Hello there! Good morning!"

I looked up. And then I blushed so fiercely I could feel it pinking my cheeks all the way up into my hairline. For there, just across the low fence, stood the tall, blue-eyed soldier from yesterday, bare-headed, clean-shaven, and washed, his shirt open at the throat, almost as if he had dashed outside in a great rush.

I stood as if nailed to the path, forgetting that only a minute ago I had meant to run at the slightest sound from over the fence.

Now I could only stand there, filled with wonder, thinking instead, how very black his hair is, how deep blue his eyes. Forget-me-not-blue . . .

He, too, was gazing at me intently, as if he was touching with his eyes each detail of my face. I meant to turn away; I could not. Something strange and inexplicable was holding me captive with invisible strings. As if he could read my thoughts, he stepped closer to the fence, holding out his hand, speaking softly.

"Please don't go just yet. I saw you — yesterday. You were standing out in front of your house." With his chin he pointed to our house. His voice was deep and warm, his eyes gentle and expressive. I could understand him perfectly even though my English was limited and rusty since my school days — and since those weeks shortly before the war when I had made friends with two American children on vacation with their parents at their grandmother's house in Ludwigshafen. Against my promise to my mother, I began to smile, shyly, but I could not seem to speak.

He smiled back at me, and for one incredible, hushed moment we stood there, smiling at each other.

Until close by a small boy began shouting, a high female voice scolding him. Then the Kellers' dog — tongue lolling, barking madly — came charging through the Waholder-berry bushes in a wild chase after Frau Schäfer's black cat, Sophie, giving her the first exercise for the day. From the house next door came a shrill whistle and the shout, "Get a look at that! Our big Sarge-the-Wolf and Little Red Riding Hood!"

Instantly the magic of the moment was lost. I turned and fled through the garden and up into the house, closing the door behind me, hugging to me the image of him, the sound of his voice forever imprinted on my heart. Hearing him say, "Please don't go just yet . . . I saw you yesterday . . . I remember you. . . ."

I had been dreaming — daydreaming — when all around me the air filled with a hundred screaming devils and fiends, my ears ringing with the bursting of shells. The walls, the very floor beneath me, suddenly reached out for me, pressing me down, brutally as with invisible hands. A cloud of dust and a shower of dirt and plaster followed . . . then someone was screaming . . . drowned out by the howling of the answering American mortar thrower only yards away . . . the bursting of shells . . . explosions . . .

I crept under the big white sink, the only thing seemingly steady enough to protect me somewhat, where I crouched, huddled into a ball, in its darkest corner for I don't-know-how-long-hell-lasts.

Until all became still again, the sudden quiet almost ominous.

Lifting my face from my knees cautiously, I opened my tightly closed eyes — to see red brightly smearing my right hand, dripping down to the floor and into the new dust at my feet.

Blood, I thought in stupid surprise, staring at it while I crouched, frozen, then hearing from outside the excited voices of my parents and a voice I recognized as the one of our other neighbors, Herr Keller.

Then I heard a shout in American from one of our new neighbors. I got off the floor. I stumbled out through the crazily-hanging kitchen door into the brilliant sunshine and right into my mother's arms.

It was over!

We were alive!

Everything was all right!

There was a funny feeling in my right hand. . . .

I held it up and saw that my middle finger was dripping blood like a leaking faucet. My father and my mother tried to stop the bleeding; however, very soon we could see that my finger needed to be stitched by a doctor. Only there was no doctor any longer in The Village; the doctor had been drafted a month earlier in spite of his advanced years, into the army.

The nearest hospital was in Ludwigshafen, some miles away. Since the bus would not be running for a while, I would have to bicycle there. Under the prevailing circumstances I did not relish the thought of the trip. Getting my bicycle out from under the porch stairs, I looked about me dubiously.

Our roof looked certainly more shabby than ever. Most of the holes my father and I had closed after each air raid had opened once again, the old patches blown all over the yard, mixed with the glass from several windows. Carefully I pushed my bicycle across the mess and out into the dazed village. Past the dumb pain of human sorrow, past the old rubble and the new.

Aware of the presence of the Americans, the retreating German artillery still across the Rhein had fired into The Village in a last frenzy of insane rage.

But I was off and on my way to the hospital, pedaling away, steering with one hand, my heart and thoughts still back in The Village.

Where the road met with the shadows of a clump of tall fir trees, the halfway mark to the city, I found myself suddenly halted by two men I thought immediately to be Russian prisoners of war from one of the outlying farms, where many had been forced to work up until a few days ago. Most now roamed the countryside, waiting to be returned to their homeland, while, to my surprise, quite a few wanted to stay in Germany.

The two made it clear to me that my bicycle was what they wanted. Pulling and pushing, they tried to throw me off, only to have me hang on, stubbornly, and foolishly, with all my strength and regardless of the pain in my finger.

I would have lost surely in the uneven struggle had it not been for the sudden scream of auto tires and the angry, authoritative shouts from the two soldiers in the vehicle, demanding in English to know what was going on.

The two road agents didn't take time to answer. They let go of my bike and ran like a pair of frightened hares toward the trees, vanishing into the thick underbrush, leaving me standing there shaken, looking at my two rescuers. Immediately I recognized one as the tall, blue-eyed American — the very one so disturbingly in my thoughts since my first glimpse of him.

Then my two angels spoke, both at the same time, in tones of astonishment, for they, too, had recognized me and asked if I was all right and where I was going on this dangerous road.

In my limited English I explained, holding up my bandaged hand for them to see. To my relief, both seemed to understand my somewhat hesitant talk without difficulty and immediately the blue-eyed soldier promised they would watch out for me on my way to and from the hospital while they were patrolling the highway for the next three hours — a promise the handsome red-headed soldier seconded with a nod.

I felt warm and flushed at my two gallant, supposed-to-be-enemies' gracious offer to protect me. Incredulously, I felt they were friends.

Gratefully I thanked them. But when I turned to ride away, I found myself halted once again by the curious voice of blue-eyes.

"Please. What is your name?"

"It's Lisa. Lisa Forster," I told him.

He smiled. When he repeated my name, it sounded beautiful, different. Never before had anyone said it the way he had just now — almost like the beginning of a lovely melody.

Tipping back his helmet, his smile wide and just a bit sheepish, showing two rows of strong white teeth, he said, "And I am Andrew Morrell — Andy, for short." He pointed at his even taller comrade. "This here is my friend John, John Starbruck — better known as Red."

The cheerful-looking giant promptly removed his helmet, letting fly into the enthusiastic March wind a flaming shock of red hair.

"I'm a boy, all right, but I couldn't find a barber lately," he said, grinning largely and just a bit awkwardly with eyes bright and almost as blue as those of Andrew, twinkling at me out of a face as strong-boned, high-cheeked, and square-chinned, as that of a Viking.

Suddenly the three of us laughed aloud at the wonder of it all, and to me it was the most wonderful sound I had heard in a long time.

Andy and Red proved true to their word: They passed me every three kilometers or so, coming and going, until I had reached the safety of inhabited neighborhoods.

My luck held also in the hospital.

There were many injured people waiting, but a tiny bird-like nurse briskly pointed me and my bleeding finger through a door into a makeshift operating room.

With my stitched finger swaddled in white and looking like a stuffed sausage, I left the hospital, impatient to reach once more the countryside to search for a jeep and two American soldiers named Red and Andy.

For a moment a fleeting thought crossed my mind: what would my mother say now, could she hear what I was thinking? Was it truly only this morning when she warned me not even to look at the strangers?

Where the fields seemed to become one with the horizon I saw a small but fast-growing daub coming closer, closer.

It was Andy! And Red!

With still a distance between us, Andy began calling, "Are you all right?"

"Yes! Yes, I am fine," I answered back feeling truly just that at seeing them. We waved, and I rode on, and when I reached the first houses of The Village, their jeep passed me once more.

"Good night, Lisa!" I heard Andy calling. Then, from farther off, riding on the wings of a frisky wind, came Red's call mixed with mischievous laughter. "Good night, Fraulein Lisa!"

A couple of minutes later I reached the house — to fly breathless into the kitchen, where my mother took one look at my flushed face and shining eyes and instantly became worried, thinking I had surely developed a fever, an infection, reaching for her box of homemade teas.

Come night, I did not mind going to bed early. Bed was the only place where I could be by myself and undisturbed to think over the exciting happenings of the day. It was rather strange that I thought of the morning's attack for a moment only, while for a long time I dwelled deliciously on the raven-haired soldier named Andy. . . . And for once I did not worry much, either, about the coming day, which must dawn on our once more broken roof, on our empty pantry, on the cracked walls, on the mess everything was in.

Just now I couldn't care. Not really. Not just now.

Tomorrow would be a new day. A new beginning!

We would fix the roof as we had so many times before.

Only this time it would hold. The war was over. The planes had gone!

Tomorrow! Ah, tomorrow would be another day. A great day!

Chapter 4

"They're going to raise the ferry from the river next, I heard!"

"The Americans have almost finished a wooden bridge across the Rhein right where the old one used to be," my mother answered my father. "It seems a miracle, building a bridge in less than two or three days."

She went on talking about this new bridge floating on pontoons over the Rhein. I tried to follow her words while I swallowed my uninteresting breakfast, listening with one ear to my parents, having my other ear turned in to the happy chirping of a flock of birds outside in the bright sunshine, my eyes and my thoughts on a patch of fantastically blue sky, winking at me through the broken pane of the window.

Ah, how I loved the color blue.

It was a fine morning. A beautiful day!

A most perfect day for fixing the roof, my father and I had decided on upon getting up.

"Do you have enough nails?" my mother wanted to know.

"What I have left will have to do," my father answered.

"How is your finger? Does it still hurt much?" My mother had turned to me now.

Everything is made of blue and gold, of silk, I almost said out loud, my gaze wandering over the unbelievably blue sky. I managed to say, "It just itches a lot. Don't worry. Excuse me."

Then I was off my chair and leaving the table, suddenly convinced I could not wait another minute to be outside, to be up on the roof, to feel the warm sunlight, the eager breeze. I found just enough time to call back, "I'm fine! I never felt better!"

In my room I got busy pulling on a pair of old slacks and a monster of a sweater with no color, struggling to stuff my long hair under a boy's cap I had found this past winter hanging forgotten on a nail in the hallway.

Dressed, I emerged again into the kitchen and let myself through the trapdoor and out onto the roof, not waiting for my father to finish his cup of peppermint tea and come along, ignoring the puzzled looks on my parents' faces, the question in their eyes, as they sat there watching me disappear while whistling a sassy tune.

I had a secret, and only I knew!

A secret so wonderful it was dancing inside me, a bubble rising and swelling, 'til I felt lightheaded and ready to fly off and away, no matter where.

I had felt like this since last night, after I had seen Andy again, talked to him.

At first I had felt miserable that morning, when I had looked out the kitchen window at the sprawling house where the Americans stayed now. With an incredible sense of loss, I had found the large yard nearly empty of vehicles and soldiers.

Andy! Had Andy left, too? I had to make sure.

The only way I could think of was to go to the garden fence, to the clothesline, where I had talked to him earlier.

I slipped my mother's rubber gloves over my bandages. With speedy fingers I dipped into a bucket of water anything explainable to be hung up on the clothesline, my newest friend, stretching so patiently, so conveniently between the gangling poplar tree and the stout fence post in the garden.

I had been outside not more than a minute when Andy appeared jumping right over the fence.

He was still here! I let go of my breath with a whoosh. He was still here, smiling, talking. . . .

Then we were both talking, laughing in open joy, for now, now we knew each other, already for a long, long time.

He held out his hand to me, and I took it. He said, "I'm staying in The Village for a time. As military police, Red and some others are staying at the motor pool." Then he added, "I am so glad."

Spontaneously and before I could feel shy I told him, "I am glad, too." While my heart was beating fast, doing a *purzelbaum* — a somersault.

"I will wait for you here by the fence tonight," he said before we parted. "Will you come?"

I nodded, suddenly convinced that something momentous had happened, changing the world all around me into a friendlier, more beautiful place.

"And where would you be going?" my mother asked later that evening, watching me running through the kitchen to my room, flitting from the bathroom to the small mirror over the sink and back again, scrubbing my face and arms, my neck and all the rest of me with my father's last, carefully hoarded piece of shaving soap, which I had confiscated on account of its far superior scent over our rough, ugly-smelling soap.

Quite nonchalantly I tested the heat of the old-fashioned curling iron on a piece of newspaper, toasting, in one of the pictures, Hitler's face and mustache a smelly brown. Grinning wickedly, I thought.

How do you like that? Now you're not so white any longer.

Casually I told my mother, "I am going to see Inge next door." Inge was the daughter of our neighbors, the Kellers, a friend for these years since we came to The Village.

I could not have told my mother where I was really going. She would have kept me in the house, forcing fate to change its plans for me — perhaps forever, I was convinced. This I could not let happen.

"To see Inge you must wear your best shoes, curl your hair, redden your lips, and darken your eyelashes?" My mother had marveled at my sudden vanity. "Bah. You look better without it. You're a pretty girl, and you don't need that junk."

"Times have changed. Girls wear makeup now. Anyway, I feel like looking interesting for once." I decided to leave it at that, to avoid stirring my mother's suspicions.

I hung around for a while, 'til my mother and father had settled down for the evening, my father with a book, my mother with her never-ending darning. Then I slipped out and winged down the outside stairs into the yard and into the garden, where soft dusk was veiling the bushes and the trees, the first shy flowers peeking out from last year's leaves.

So much loveliness all about.

Which I could not see clearly just now because my gaze was running along the fence even faster than my feet could follow — only to find the fence standing there with no Andy in sight.

I felt disappointed. Crestfallen, I walked on to the very end of the garden, where the field began, where my father had built a small shack to store firewood for the winter. All hope vanished, I looked up sharply — for sitting there upon a fallen tree trunk, his back against the unpainted shack, sat Andy, arms folded across his chest, watching me, having done so ever since I came down the porch stairs, seeing my eager and then so disappointed expressions. A slow smile spread over his face, turning into laughter, happy, infectious laughter. The both of us were laughing, each knowing the other's thoughts, delightedly. When Andy stood up to approach me, I had to look up. He was indeed tall.

"You came! I was worried you might not, that you were afraid, perhaps, to come into the garden at night to meet me."

"I often walk in the garden. Even at night," I answered him.

Then we stood there looking at each other, not knowing what else to say at the moment.

"Would you like to sit down?" He pointed at the logs piled against the shack. I bobbed my head, sitting down on the nearest one. He sat down beside me, so close I could have touched him without stretching my arm. Much aware of his closeness, I looked at him, then looked away again, shy.

He was wondering what to say; I saw the effort in his face. Then his eyes lit on my bandaged finger.

"Your finger, does it hurt much?"

"Not much now. It's beginning to heal already. See? I can touch it, and it doesn't hurt!" I touched my finger to show him, feeling a bit silly.

He took my hand, holding it. "You must be careful so it won't bleed again."

I looked down at his hand covering mine, and slowly, reluctantly, he took it away. Then we sat there in silence, a silence so loud, I could hear it pulsing in my ears.

"That shell," he began after a little while, "did it do a lot of damage to your house? I saw your dad working up on the roof this afternoon. That was your dad I saw?"

"My dad? Oh, yes. My father."

"He has white hair and wears glasses?"

"Yes. That was him. He is getting old. He is almost sixty."

"That isn't old." Then he asked, "Have you brothers and sisters?"

"No. There is only myself, my father, and my mother."

And then we were off, talking about all kinds of things. He was full of questions, which at first I answered in short, carefully thought-out answers and with long pauses in between. Then, after a time, I forgot completely about being afraid of not pronouncing accurately each word — after I discovered Andy understood and spoke French. Even better than I did. So whenever my English became too weak or threatened to collapse entirely, I used a convenient word in French, in German, using my hands to help explain. Andy seemed to guess quickly anything I could not express in any language.

"You are a very pretty girl," he said at one point.

I didn't know what to say to that, and blurted, "And I think you are a very beautiful man!"

He laughed at that, much amused, and said, "A man is handsome. A girl is beautiful."

I should be flattered, though I suppose. I thought a moment. "Your friend with the red hair — Red. He is nice, too."

Andy looked at me thoughtfully. "He is very nice. They don't come better anywhere."

"Red is your friend for a long time?" I wanted to hear more about his tall, red-haired companion.

"For a long time. For years, since our college days. We

enlisted together, and we've been together through Normandy, the Beach. Before the war, Red lived for some time at my home, with my family."

Curious, I asked, "Where is Red's family?"

"Red has no family of his own. No one. They died in an accident just before we became friends."

"Red is older than you?"

"Yes. By four years. He's twenty-eight, and I'm twenty-four." He looked at me. "And how old are you?"

"I am nearly eighteen."

Somewhat self-consciously, I mumbled into my chin, thinking how grown-up he was and how naïve and young I must seem to him. Quickly I said, "You must be from New York!"

He laughed at that. "No. I'm not from New York. I come from Texas. From out West."

I felt instantly excited. "Then you are a cowboy? Or maybe an Indian? I've read books about them."

He shook his head, smiling. "I'm not a cowboy — and not an Indian, either; do know, though, how to sit a horse, if that helps any." He was chuckling now. "You see, I was raised on a horse ranch, and so —"

Suddenly the sky in the northeast lit up in a kaleidoscope of brilliant colors, that then faded away into the night. The faint boom of guns — the ugly voices of war sounding once more out of the dark — making me shiver, made my imaginings of cowboys and Indians vanish instantly.

Andy felt me shrinking into myself. He took my hand gently, assuring me of his presence. He put an arm around my shoulders, pulling me closer to him until my head rested against his inner arm. "It's far away. Don't be afraid."

The guns stopped. The war retreated once more.

I never thought to pull away from Andy. He was warm. I

felt safe with his arm around me. He smelled of a nice shaving lotion, and I liked him. Maybe I loved him, had loved him always, and for a very long time had been waiting for him. . . .

He laid his chin atop my head. Slowly he began to stroke my long hair. "What lovely hair you've got." He was fondling it gently. "How very soft it is."

I closed my eyes, listening to him talking quietly.

"I liked you since that first moment I walked by you — when I saw you that first time, standing there — small and lost, among all those staring faces."

"I saw you, too. I knew you were looking at me," I whispered up into his face, so close to mine. Suddenly the world around us vanished, eclipsed by his lips finding mine. The garden was now an island up in the clouds, where God Himself had taken up a harp and was playing heavenly melodies never before heard on earth.

"Do you like me?"

"Yes. Like no one ever before . . ."

My father's voice suddenly broke into my daydreaming of the night before.

"Let's get on with the job and not waste time." He stood by my side, one rough, work-worn hand on my shoulder pressing down affectionately. "It is rather pretty, isn't it?" he said, both of us looking out over the awakening land, over The Village and across the brown and green countryside to the Edison Power Station down by the river toward the north, the many rooftops of the widespread pharmaceutical plant to the northeast, the outline of the city across the river. The softly rolling meadows and the woods. The Rhein, a dark-green band like molten glass nearly touching the outlying houses of The Village. And beyond it, toward the south, the swamp of the Old Rhein, with its numerous strange forms of life.

The Kingdom of Erlkónig, I had named it secretly, that first time I wandered into it, coming upon a hauntingly beautiful hidden clearing, where I found a tree growing, a giant, awe inspiring and tall. An oak tree, majestic and ancient, the heir and keeper of the forgotten place. My tree. My secret garden.

"Well, come on girl! Let's snap out of it and start fixing this sick old roof so it can keep out the rain!"

I took the box of nails my father handed to me, and he picked up his tools and boards. Then we started to patch up the sick old roof as we had done before and many times in these past years.

However, we never got too far. For barely had we started our banging and hammering when Andy's voice had floated across the yard, interrupting our work.

"Hello there! How is your boy doing his job? Is he worth his keep, Mr. Forster?"

Then Red's voice, followed Andy's with a cheerful "Good morning, sonny!"

Surprised, I looked up. Then I stood to call my own impulsive good morning to Andy and Red standing in a wide-open window of the neighboring house. For a moment I forgot the presence of my father. He had to inquire for a second time, "What are the soldiers saying to us?"

"They wished you a good morning, and they want to know if your 'boy' is working out all right," I explained, glowing all over.

My father smiled, and it made him instantly look years younger. Andy was right. Father wasn't old at all. Then I remembered how well my father spoke French, and suddenly I wanted them to speak to each other, have my father say something friendly to Red and Andy — to Andy, whose lips I could still taste on mine, having kissed him back but hours ago, there in the garden by the shack.

I said, "Why don't you answer him yourself? The tall dark one speaks French very well."

Soon words were flying across and back.

"It is a boy? Is it not!"

"My boy and my girl all in one!"

"I bet he can't hold a hammer straight, this 'boy' of yours!"

This I answered with a shout of indignation, "Who said that!" I got back a wave of laughter from Red.

For several short, carefree minutes our words flew back and forth, in French and in English, until Andy and Red had to leave to patrol the highway and the roads along the river and into the city, leaving us once more to our work.

Then, with surprise showing in his face, my father looked up and right into my eyes. "How could you have known that the one with the black hair spoke French? How could the one with the red hair have known I am Mr. Forster?"

I realized, in my eager happiness at suddenly seeing Andy, I had given myself away and good.

"Oh. The two asked me some questions yesterday, while I was hanging wash in the garden. I discovered I could answer that black-haired one in French." I defended myself, blushing a deep crimson I could feel. "I also told him my name when he asked me. He guessed through that, that you were my father," I stammered, aware of how much I had left out and changed around, feeling guilty that I could not tell my father all about Andy.

"You don't do so badly with your schoolbook English, I must say," my father said, looking at me shrewdly. "I never thought you remembered that much."

I shrugged. We began once more our hammering and sawing.

The morning went fast. With the stroke of noon by the clock in the water tower, I saw far out on the highway beyond The Village, Andy and Red returning in their jeep from patrol duty.

My father and I had nailed and patched the roof together as well as we could, and now we stopped, put down our tools, and climbed down into the kitchen through the trapdoor, where my talented mother had managed to conjure up a lunch for us, consisting of a couple of wrinkled potatoes, boiled, and a kind of chopped spinach that was not spinach at all but the first tender shoots of the brennessel plant — poison ivy — which was nutritious, with lots of vitamin C, prepared like creamed spinach.

We could trust my mother in such matters of the stomach! She had been born with this instinct, with the knowledge that made her recognize plants and leaves, mushrooms and seeds. And no one knew that better than I, the many times in these past meager years when she had filled my empty stomach with Mother Nature's blessings, when nothing much could be found in the stores or anywhere else. How many times had she quieted a feverish body, a sick stomach, with tea made from herbs and leaves she had carefully selected and hung to dry under the roof in the summer and fall.

Lunch over, my father and I went on to put glass into the window of the kitchen. This we did from the outside, standing on the porch. The warm sun of spring and the fresh air of our morning on the roof had made me a bit sleepy. I almost dropped the can of putty I was holding for my father when Andy's voice sounded so close to my ear.

He had come up the stairs and surprised me once again

with a cheerful, "Hello there!"

And right off he began talking to my father in fluent French, making him think he was only interested in what he was doing and not at all in his blushing daughter. My father looked as surprised as I. Not for long, though. Soon he could not help but smile, too, answering Andy's interested, sympathetic questions about the damage to the house. Very soon I could tell my father, too, liked the handsome, tall American.

While they talked in elegant French, I suddenly remembered my not-so-elegant appearance. With heat rising all the way up into my hairline, it occurred to me what a fine sight I must be at the moment. Maneuvering around a little, I managed to see myself in the new glass of the window. Now I truly wished I could vanish into the ground. There were dirt smudges on my cheek, my hair hidden under the ridiculous boy's cap. My slacks, too large, were hanging from my hips like empty potato sacks cut off and sewn together at the top. Even my sweater seemed to be borrowed from one of the scarecrows in the fields, worn by them for at least two wet seasons.

I was never more ashamed than just now, being seen by Andy! By Andy! Of all people!

He seemed not at all disturbed by my workingman's appearance. When my father turned away for a minute to cut out a piece of glass, he snatched my hand, dirt and all, and whispered "Snow White," under his breath, his dancing eyes making me feel even more aware of my looks.

When my father invited Andy to come over in the evening for a glass of wine, Andy accepted — with a twinkle in his eyes in my direction — leaving soon after, taking three steps at once of the steep stairs whistling a happy tune, whistling all the way down and over the neighbor's fence.

That evening both Andy and Red came a-visiting.

My mother opened the door and invited them into the kitchen — the only room almost wholly repaired — after having looked up at both of them uneasily, two giants whose talk she could not understand, two strangers, soldiers, who had come not long ago into The Village with guns in hand and fire in their hearts.

"Come in, please," she had stammered in German. Then she had called to my father, "Joseph? Joseph, come! Two are here!"

I began to get a little worried, standing behind the closed door in my room, comb in hand, waiting for what would follow next.

"Come in! Come in and feel at home," I heard my father say in the same friendly fashion he would ask any neighbor in.

Now I knew it would be all right. I wanted to giggle when I heard Andy say, "This is Red, my friend," and my father replying in German, "Pleased to meet you, Mr. Red. Let's find a chair large enough for you, and let us sit down."

I went out to join them, and we all sat around the table a bit awkwardly at first being polite. But I remember my father's excited face, his smile — it had been long since he had seemed happy — as he filled Andy and Red's glasses from a slender bottle of Rauenthal 1937, one of a kind, which had miraculously survived the fire and the bombing, perhaps protected by cobwebs and dust in the ruins of our house in the city. The bottle was one of but a very few left to my father at this time, prized highly and, as I knew well, hoarded throughout the war years like liquid gold. Yet for Andy and Red he had brought up from the cellar this wine.

A few months earlier, when my Uncle Johannes had come for an overnight visit, Father had filled his glass with but a nameless tropfen.

Red seemed to recognize and appreciate the superb quality of my father's wine, wanting to know all about the making of wine in our part of the Rheinland, how it was bottled and stored and enjoyed with which kinds of food. Even I knew a lot about that, having been born and raised in the Rhein Valley, close to the bountiful vineyards of the Weinstrasse and the Bergstrasse, so I was able to contribute to our conversation, which we held in three languages.

My father spoke French and just a little English, Red spoke only English, and I translated into English for him and into German for my mother. It was almost like attending an international convention, but a friendly one to be sure, for soon even my mother had begun to lose her uneasiness.

"They both seem very nice. And they certainly have good manners, their being soldiers!" she managed to whisper to me.

I could have hugged her for that. I certainly agreed fully with her.

Then Andy discovered my father's interest in horses. His voice took on a longing as he spoke about his own family, about the wide expanse of Texas where his father raised and bred horses on their sizable ranch.

My father became all questions, which Andy answered eagerly: about life in America, about ranching and livestock and the weather. And my father, born and raised on a farm and familiar with such a life, soon admitted that there was much indeed he had not heard of before tonight.

From horses and living on a ranch they went on to discuss history — my father's true love. I felt very proud of the amazing man who was my father, this man who could fix a roof, reglaze windows, sew buttons on his own shirt, and equally well talk in fluent French about history and horses with two strange soldiers who seemed not strangers any longer.

Red, however, had become interested in our old-fashioned electric system, not in use just now, our only light coming from two kerosene lamps. Part of the wiring had been torn loose from the wall when the shell hit, and it looked as if we would have to get along for quite some time without electricity, since this was one of the few things my father did not know how to repair.

"I think I could fix it," Red volunteered, "since the wiring is outside the wall and showing. I'd love to have a try at it," he said to my father, his gaze eagerly following the run of the visible line.

"Red is a very fine electrical engineer in civil life. When it comes to anything in need of fixing, he's a regular wizard," Andy assured my parents. "I've seen him more than once rig up the most impossible-looking wreck."

I thought I'd take another look at this clever wizard, but he had already disappeared.

He returned carrying a heavy bag spilling over with tools and cords and wire. And he accepted the help of my father and Andy in checking first the circuit-breakers in the cellar, working by himself from then on silently immersed in the job before him, making me wonder if this was more fun than work. And I swear only one hour later, Red threw a switch, and the lights went on like magic.

My mother couldn't thank Red enough. It meant so very much to her, to all of us, to have real lights again, not having to see these cracks in the ceiling and walls weave and creep like snakes in the flickering light of a candle or lantern, making one wonder if they were alive and ready to spring.

Light. Was it not true that even God had first of all created light? So He could see what had to be done first and next? And only then, much later and on second thought, according to my father, God gave to mankind Edison — for having left us in the dark so long, my father explained with a wink. Then he all but ran to the cellar to bring up his very best wine — and the only bottle of its kind, the last one he owned, preserved "for a very special occasion."

This now was his very special occasion! My father was more than pleased to have us all toast this latest of the light-makers with his Schloss Johannisberger — a toast we all delivered with much enthusiasm; our light-maker's face turned nearly as red as his hair.

And he had won the heart of my mother completely, a fact neither of them fully realized just then. Tremulously happy, I wished I had a tail so that I could wag it with pleasure over the way the evening went.

Still, best of all that evening was our saying good night at the very end — when I had discovered Andy's cap right after he left our house, where he had cleverly forgotten it.

Surprised at my sudden haste, my father and mother wordlessly watched me snatching up the cap, slamming the door behind me, making the curtain over the glass pane do a fluttering dance, and ran out after Andy.

I didn't have to run far.

In the dark under the porch stairs by the entrance to the cellar, Andy was waiting for me, and he pulled me into his arms eagerly kissing me until both of us were glad for the support of the cellar door.

"I've wanted to do this for hours," Andy whispered into my ear. "Actually, ever since we said good night yesterday in the garden."

"I brought you your cap," I stammered, suddenly not knowing what to say, trying to quiet my racing heart.

My father and mother could not understand how it was possible to have forgotten to give Andy back his cap — the very reason for my flight after him — for when I entered the kitchen minutes later, I still held it in my hand, my cheeks on fire, as if they had been rubbed with rose petals.

Chapter 5

From that night on, the days and nights seemed to fly by.

Spring was fully here at last and in all its ever-new magic. A pair of storks had arrived at The Village, taking over the empty nest atop the Metzes' barn, busy from dawn to dusk making it ready for young ones soon to leave their eggs. The swallows, too, had returned from their winter quarters on the Nile, just as busy now as the stork couple and with the same intentions.

Almost overnight the trees had broken into bloom, scenting the air with the perfume of a million cherry and apple blossoms. The garden had become a paradise to Andy and me — for it was there that nearly every evening we managed to meet behind the shack, in the softly glowing darkness, in the friendly concealment to the night.

In the daytime hours all was different again. We did see each other then, too, but we could touch only with our eyes, hands carefully restrained so as not to give away the night's secret of having held and touched one another so intimately.

Andy would come across the low garden fence at all hours of the day, whistling up the stone steps to spend a few minutes with me and my parents. Red would come along most times, shielding us with his comfortable presence, with his quick laughter and easy talk, helping me hide the joy I felt at seeing Andy, being near him for even a few stolen moments.

Thinking back, it was certainly Red, not Andy, who had

first quite effortlessly attached himself to my mother and father. Actually more so to my mother, as I remember. He seemed to be happy just being able to sit there in our big kitchen, watching my mother and me do the cooking — whatever there was to be cooked at this time — watching us wash the dishes, doing whatever chores women do around the house the world over. When he discovered one day my mother had a headache, he left and returned quickly with a bottle of Alka-Seltzer. He had shown her how to dissolve the tablets, waiting around until she could tell him that nothing ever had helped her so fast and so well. When he discovered that my father was smoking his pipe outside on account of the stink his own homemade mixture of leaves made — there was no tobacco to be had anywhere — he gifted him with a pack of golden pipe tobacco. His eyes reflecting the pleasure my father showed just smelling the princely gift.

And it was Red who repaired our electric iron, sitting down right on the kitchen floor amidst his tools and wires, telling my grateful mother it was his pleasure. Next he fixed our waffle iron, and he showed my father how to put into the outer wall of the house an outlet for his saw. He forced our ancient, battle-scarred toaster to do its popping-up job once more, shrugging off our thanks and striding red-faced from the kitchen, not letting us say another word of thanks. He did return, though, in the evening with a whole loaf of white American bread under his arm — such lovely, snow-white bread we had not seen since before the war. He stuck a slice into the toaster, and, turning to me with one of his happy grins, he said, "What else is there to be fixed?" I brought out my alarm clock, which had refused to tick for ages. Red made it work in no time.

My mother began to feel guilty about not being able to

thank Red properly. She wanted very much to do something for him in return, but she did not even have enough flour to bake a cake.

Then, one day, at last, she found her chance — when she discovered that Andy and Red were doing their own laundry. My mother easily convinced the two that she could do a much better job of it and that it would be no bother whatsoever.

From that day on our clothesline in the garden held out to the lustily blowing spring wind a fluttering assortment of GI shorts and shirts and male apparel at least once a week, and certainly every morning two pairs of white leggings, white MP gloves, and two MP belts. Red and Andy went overboard with praise of my glowing mother whenever she asked them if everything was all right.

"We are the two most clean-scrubbed soldiers in this here army!" Andy would say.

"The pride and joy of Uncle Sam!" Red boasted.

At first my mother staunchly refused to accept anything for her work. But Red and Andy insisted — even more than she could refuse, being daily confronted by her empty cooking pots — on bringing her "just a little something."

Both were aware of our sad circumstances, though my mother and I had tried heroically to hide from them our gaping, empty pantry, many times waiting patiently to eat our meager supper until they had left, my mother sadly aware it was too little by far to invite a sparrow, self-conscious because our poor fare was not good enough to even let them see.

My father always ate cheerfully anything put before him. Even this certain kind of a pea soup over which I shut my eyes and told my stomach to shut up, stop protesting, and to be thankful instead. That didn't always work, though. I couldn't help thinking that some of the peas held tiny maggots, so small they looked to be the peas' first tender sprouts. According to my father, who tried his utmost to convince me, "Just something to put into your shrunken stomach, girl. This is better than nothing, anytime!" So he would say of the soup my mother boiled until it was mush, running it through a strainer many times. After my first disgusted outcries I never mentioned again what else these peas might contain. Hunger is a mean customer and not too choosy.

There was nothing to be found anywhere after the war. It was just as bad as during the war, if not worse.

We wouldn't even have had those disgusting peas if not for my father, who had gone one day into the factory where he had been employed after losing his business in a bombing raid, to see when work would start again. The machines stood still, though the place was not deserted. Russian soldiers from the Ural and Siberia — former prisoners of war — had been there, waiting to be transported home. Also the same men with whom my father had worked and many times shared his own meager lunch — an apple, a bit of soup from his small canteen, a sandwich, perhaps — had still been there. And they had not forgotten. So now it had been they who shared with him. Calling him Joseph and friend, they poured into his pockets dry lentils and beans and peas — all they had themselves to eat, as much as his pockets would hold. He had come home that day and stood before the kitchen table, pouring from his packets the humble seeds. Nuggets of gold to us at this terrible time.

Standing there, tears running down his cheeks, he told us how these men had remembered when he had shared with them, and how they had now shared with him. I almost cried, too, seeing my father's tears, knowing I had never seen him show such emotions.

But we never touched the few bottles of wine we still had left. We ate but a very few of the first strawberries from our garden when they finally ripened, glad that now we had at least these sweet berries to offer, proudly hearing Andy exclaim his joy and pleasure over the deep-red berries I placed on my mother's one and only surviving Rosenthal dish. He never noticed that the three of us did not eat any.

Even now, years later, I swallow with difficulty remembering Red coming to pick up a clean bundle of clothes, leaving on the kitchen table without a word cans of meat and milk and fish, blocks of brown soap, and other important articles.

But Andy, just as thoughtful as the down-to-earth Red who knew life was not always easy, put into my mother's big blue apron wonders long vanished though not forgotten: chocolate, coffee, and cookies, reckoning them just as necessary for human comfort. And he would bring exquisitely scented soap to wash his socks with, grinning disarmingly at my mother, who thought it a shame to waste such preciousness on dirty socks.

To me this soap was amazing: to think there was such a fine thing left after all this warring! One day I made my mother laugh when I said, "I could bite into this wonderful soap, it smells so good! I love washing clothes just because of it!"

"You don't remember the kind of soap we had before the war?" my mother had asked me gently. "It was just as nice."

"It couldn't have been this nice!" I shook my head.

"Then you have forgotten. The war was much too long."

Yes, we appreciated Red and Andy's thoughtful generosity, their understanding, their concern for our present circumstances.

★ ★ ★ ★ ★

I thought of Red as the kindest, most unselfish human being anywhere — but I loved Andy. Loved him body and soul.

The nights seemed long, waiting for morning when I could see him again, hear him speak and laugh and whisper into my ear, hug me and hold me in his arms. And I found many ways to be with Andy.

My best excuse was quite abominable in a way, I admit now. But to me it was foolproof in getting me out the door any time I wished to.

Since the pipes in our bathroom had been so badly damaged by bombing, we had to make use of a neglected outhouse, for a time, whether we liked it or not. This contraption now stood — so conveniently for me — in the far corner of our yard. One can be sure I took great advantage of this necessary evil indeed. My mother became openly worried over my frequent trips. Reluctantly I had to become slightly "better" at times so as not to rouse her suspicions agreeing with her wholeheartedly that unripe fruit should be left on the trees. She remained much concerned, however, and could not understand why none of her remedies worked.

She could not know that I had no need for them in the first place, that I poured them into the lilac bush under the window by the porch, to have it blossom in a sharp, uncommon purple that year and as never before, to the great amazement of our neighbor Frau Keller, who begged my mother for some cuttings from the gorgeous bush to plant in her own garden.

These symptoms of mine developed usually after lights-out; however, only Andy and I knew when my "trouble" would plague me — usually by ten or eleven, or sometimes at midnight, when Andy had officially returned to his own quarters after a quiet evening spent with us. I would need only hear the zip of small pebbles on my window to feel instantly the need to go outside.

Had my parents already gone to bed, I would quickly throw my housecoat over my pajamas and softly open the door. To avoid even the slightest noise I would slide down the banister to Andy's delight: the wicked witch riding her broom! Once he called my inelegant decent Paul Revere's midnight ride.

"And who was he?" I asked curious.

Andy mumbled back into my ear, "I'll tell you some other time when I'm not so busy."

The night was kind, protecting us in her dark mantle when we came to sit behind the shack in the garden.

There was one other, though, who knew about us and our secret place, but he never told on us.

Usually our cat, Uncle Max, came along with us, stretching out close to us, not moving, except for his tail and eyes. He was our self-appointed lookout.

Uncle Max was an especially clever cat, a big, handsome tomcat, he was. One morning, some years back, when we had first come to The Village, I stepped out onto the porch and there he was, dressed in an apricot-marmalade-colored fur coat and white fur boots, green-eyed, worldly wise, and evidently well traveled, washing the dust of the road off himself with his tongue for a facecloth, using the morning sun for a towel.

As if he was long familiar with me, he followed my invitation into the kitchen for a saucer of milk, eating with dignity and good manners, though he was very hungry indeed. When he finished, being a gentleman and of a polite nature, he rubbed his handsome head against my legs as his thank you until I told him it was all right should he want to stay. He didn't stay, but he did insist on singing me a song in a deep, rich tomcat voice. Then he left — vanished through the open window and out into the garden — only to return a few hours later, watching me set the table with a clatter of spoons and dishes, to stay from then on. He became Uncle Max to us for no known reason, except that he needed a name.

Now he was a favorite with Andy, who would take him across to his place to feed him at least twice a day with rich American food, which seemed to agree fine with Uncle Max. He gleamed with good health, his eyes shining, and he purred with affection and gratitude, following Andy and me around like a dog.

All things were changing for me.

I was happy as never before.

Where the brown waters of the Old Rhein joined the glassy-green of his bigger, younger self, where it was quiet and far from The Village and her people, where my friend the ancient oak stood — head in the clouds, feet firmly planted in the soil — there Andy and I became as one in our love for the first time.

In the deep shadow of the giant, in the very place where Roman legions had rested weary feet on their way up the Rhein to England, where Napoleon had twice crossed the Rhein, where deep under the water lie buried the fabled treasure of the Nibelungs — there Andy and I became one. I became his with all of me.

Gently, ever so gently, he held me to himself, whispering softly, "I love you. I love you so much."

I looked up into his dark blue eyes, feeling his arms holding me close, thinking *I loved you before I was born, before I could feel and touch and know.*

"This first time, it might hurt. Are you afraid?"

"I'm not afraid," I murmured.

And gently he came down to me, into me all the way, burying himself inside me at last, stilling our hunger for each other . . . for a little while.

Never let me go. Never leave me, I thought.

Later, much later, we drove back through the peacefully dreaming fields, through the sleeping Village, to say good night at my front gate for the first time. I wanted it so. I wanted the world to know. I wanted to shout with my unbearable happiness. I could murmur only, "I love you. I love you so." I whispered up to the star-filled heavens above, "I love him. I love him so."

In the big house next door Andy opened the door to the room he shared with Red, closing it softly behind him so as not to awaken his friend.

But then, from the darkness, came Red's voice, sounding wide awake, as if he had been lying there in the dark, unable to sleep.

"I'm awake." Then, after hesitating, he said, "You've been with Lisa, as every night, I suppose."

"Yes, it got late and —"

Red interrupted, "Her family — the Forsters are decent people!"

"Yes. They certainly are that." Andy readily agreed.

"Lisa — she is very young."

"She is a woman. The most wonderful woman alive! I love her! I've never felt like this before!"

"Then you . . . know her now. . . ."

"I know her, now and always."

A silence followed. When Red spoke again, his voice was strangely rough. "Don't hurt her, Andy. Don't play with her."

"What are you saying, friend? Red!"

"I'm reminding you that I've seen you with many women. In England it was a blonde, with fabulous green eyes. In France it was a tall brunette. You loved them all — and you forgot them all by the time we landed in Normandy."

"This time it's different. All different. Don't ask me how I know. Those others . . . yes! I've forgotten their names, their faces. But Red, I want to marry Lisa! I would marry her tomorrow if not for that stupid law just passed. How long do you suppose we'll have to wait?"

Red remained silent.

"Red . . . my friend . . . you . . . you like her, too! You love her!"

"I . . . like her. But she loves you."

Very soon after, Red was recalled to his company, stationed near Frankfurt on the Main, and was promoted to master sergeant. He was to supervise the company's motor pool, maintaining the vehicles, their motors, their engines, which seemed to speak to him; I was convinced of that.

I felt sad when Red left The Village. But with me was my beloved Andy. Every day he was with me now . . . and often through part of the night.

Chapter 6

In the city, in the towns and villages, a black market had sprung up overnight with the ending of the shooting war, and like a bloated mushroom it was ever growing in size. Anything could be bartered for — by those who had something to barter with, that is. Seldom was it money. At least not at first.

In the neighboring village the butcher had been discovered trading skinned dogs as young lambs, the carcasses of fattened cats as rabbits, to unsuspecting, meat-hungry city dwellers in exchange for bed sheets, cigarettes, and sugar. I heard talk about a woman in the city opening a can of meat bought from the black market and finding in it what looked like regular veal a whole human finger.

In The Village, Frau Weisser's oldest son had returned one day from no-one-knew-where and was promptly arrested and taken away for crimes committed in the war. Outside Ludwigshafen a compound filled with German prisoners of war had been dissolved, most of its inmates discharged to go home.

Frau Waldhauser's grandson from Philadelphia had come to The Village visiting. He was a blond young American soldier, looking amazingly like the rest of the Waldhauser family, like his cousins and uncles. Frau Waldhauser was very proud of him. She brought him over to our house, introducing him to Andy as her grandson von Amerika, her own "Willies Bubbele"! Her Bubbele had blushed at that so furiously, he had to think twice where he was stationed when Andy asked him.

One day all the trucks and jeeps were gone from the yard next door. Andy was sure that any day now he would be re-called to the rest of his company; our side of the Rhein had become the French Zone now. My heart beat faster when I saw the nearly empty yard.

But then, like a miracle, a prayer answered — or was it our guardian angel, who had found a reason? — Andy was to stay on in The Village for just a while longer.

Several miles west of The Village lay a deep, dark green lake overgrown with water roses and frogweed, known to all as the Teufel's Loch — the Devil's Hole. One morning a group of army specialists arrived there and began to set up prefabricated huts, preparing to dive for the wreck of an American plane lost in the murky water shortly before the end of the shooting war. The plane had carried documents of value to the Allies. Andy had been requested to stay on with several others of his company still left in The Village as M.P. guards to the divers and all their ponderous equip-ment.

Do I have to say one word more to explain our jubilant feelings?

It was fully summer now. Every day the sun climbed the horizon in a glory of warmth and golden showers of light, while the nights were tender and starlit, bewitched with an unearthly beauty. How aware we had become of the night's tender beauty, the day's shining hours.

One afternoon I was showing Andy our family album. He had returned earlier than usual from guard duty by the Hole and found me sorting out the contents of a green-with-time-and-mold chest — rescued, like my father's wine, from the cellar under the ruins of our house in the city, miraculously with most of its treasures untouched. It was dear to us indeed now.

Bending over the open pages of the album on the kitchen table, we giggled over the often ridiculous snapshots of my childhood years, snickering at the stiff, forced, and sometimes fierce expressions on the children of schooldays past.

In one photograph I looked like a tomboy of six or seven, front teeth missing due to my age, with bangs out front and stiff, curled pigtails sticking out over my ears. This one Andy thought the funniest of them all, and he took it from its page to add to his collection of pictures of me.

Andy was an eager picture-snapper, often developing his own, surprising me at times with an unexpected click and flash of light.

With his arm around my shoulders, hugging me affectionately every so often, we stood laughing and giggling as if we were not much older that that imp in the funny picture. Until suddenly, out of the corner of my eye, I saw my father standing in the open doorway to the living room, a look of puzzled bewilderment quickly changing to one of surprised knowing. His lips had parted, then closed again, leaving a sadly mellow look about his eyes and mouth. His hand came up, as if he was going to speak, but let drop limply to his side, just gazing at us. Not saying a word, he turned away, going back from where he had appeared, closing the door behind himself quietly.

Andy had not noticed his presence. But I, I could only think, HE KNOWS! And I felt glad and relieved.

For it had become nearly impossible to hide that which seemed to cry out with a voice of its own, refusing to be denied, to be kept hidden any longer. For so long now I had wanted to shout out my love to the two people I had loved and respected from the beginning of my life, so I was glad and relieved to think, *Now he knows, and he will understand,*

and so will my mother. She likes Andy. She had liked him from the first evening. . . .

However, I soon discovered that my mother saw things differently, living in the reality of our world now, not wearing rose-colored glasses. She didn't wait long to let me know her thoughts. The very next morning she had a talk with me.

"I couldn't fall asleep last night," she began, looking me in the eyes directly. "I came into the kitchen for a drink of water — to find you and Andy sitting out there on the steps, whispering as if it were day and the sun out bright, not the middle of the night. Tell me, just what was so important that you had to leave your bed and sit out there in the night on those stairs? I lay awake waiting 'til I heard you coming into the house. But then I couldn't sleep, after all. I had to think about all kinds of things . . ."

"I — I couldn't sleep. I got up again and stood by the window. I saw Andy out by the fence. He looked so lonely, I wanted to talk to him for just a little while." I shrugged. "I — I —

"He is not a stranger." I sounded lame even to myself. "He's told me even more about his home in Texas. America," I answered my mother, tenderness stirring inside me as I thought of Andy. "He told me about the prairie, the grasslands, about the cities with all buildings nearly touching the clouds. Can you imagine? In the American West there are corn and wheat fields the size of small countries. Americans are brown and white and black, descended from Indian, Spanish, Chinese, and European stock — all of them Americans of the United States of America. Can you imagine a country as large as all of Europe?"

"You are a dreamer, just like your father," my mother said.

But I went on.

"He told me about an ancient tribe of Indians who dwelled long ago in caves high in the cliffs. Cliff dwellers, they are named now. I asked him about all kinds of things. He is so nice. We laughed together, and he didn't even mind when I told him you thought he has the biggest feet, washing his socks."

"You told him that?"

"Yes. He just laughed and said, 'I come from Texas, where all things come big.' Oh, Mother, Andy is the nicest man I've ever met. If you could only know him as I do!" Not waiting for her reply, I went on eagerly, needing to confide in her now. "Sometimes I think I've known him for years. Forever!"

A soft light had come into my mother's eyes. For a moment her face opened with tenderness, quickly to close again.

"He is nice. A nice stranger, a soldier here today and gone tomorrow. You, like a child, believe anything. You see only what is immediately in front of your nose. I am your mother. I have lived longer than you. I must think of you first. I want you to grow up happy, to one day marry a man right for you. Have children, a good life."

"No one can say who is wrong or right for another." I attempted to ward off my mother's words, spoken from her love, her concern, for me, muttering more to myself than for her ears to hear. She heard though. And she called after me as I hurriedly attempted to depart.

"You keep your feet on the ground, girl. You hear? Young sparrows should try out their wings in their own yard before they explore the world!"

But the following day I did not get away that easily.

That day my mother became angry with me. She caught

me smearing shoe polish instead of glass wax onto her bedroom window, my eyes and my thoughts on a fast-moving
fluffy cloud, rubbing away dreamily, flying away with it over
the roof tops and across the fields and meadows to where
Andy was. That day my mother put aside my father's good-
natured excuse for my distraction, what he had jokingly
called "growing pains." My mother called my present state
of mind "one-hundred-percent goggle-eyed daydreaming."
By evening I had had quite a day, and I went to sleep both
goggle-eyed *and* hen pecked.

For several days after it was rather quiet in the Forster
household, as I tried hard not to create waves, another
storm.

Then it started all over again, in spite of my efforts and
careful tactics.

My mother left early in the morning, on the first bus
going in to Ludwigshafen, to visit with our old neighbors
still living in the city. She returned in the early evening,
seemingly more determined than before that nothing but
harm could come of my seeing so much of Andy. Unfortunately, as it happened, the instant she opened the gate into
our courtyard, she saw the two of us standing close together
by the fence where the garden begins and the yard ends.
Not hearing her enter, we were kissing each other good-bye,
as if Andy was leaving on a long journey, not for but a few
hours of guard duty down by the Hole.

Humming one of Andy's little tunes, I came into the
kitchen minutes after, to find my mother sitting at the table,
her best black hat still pinned to her hair.

"How was your trip into the city, Frau Forster? How is
Frau Brand and all the little Brands?" I greeted my mother
gaily, for my thoughts were still with Andy, his kisses, warm
and tasting of lemon candy, still lingering on my lips.

"It's about time you and I have a serious talk together," she answered me quietly, ignoring my nonsense, sighing audibly, and shaking her head. I stopped short, seeing the gloomy look in her eyes, letting myself down slowly onto the edge of a chair by the window, carefully putting distance between us, whisking my bubblegum out of my mouth, since my mother had an abhorrence for this kind of chewing.

"I've been thinking all the way home on the bus," she began. "One child we have. A good girl, pretty and intelligent and healthy. She is also very young and too inexperienced to know what is good or bad for her at times. All the way home I worried about you, about all manner of things, after having bumped into Frau Rabhoff. Remember Frau Rabhoff and her daughter Lotte? Lotte is your age. You went to school together. I still remember her as the prettiest little girl, blond with big blue eyes.

"Well, now. Frau Rabhoff seemed terribly upset with something — I could tell just by looking at her. She looked sick, actually. I walked home with her. We had a cup of tea together while she opened her heart to me, spilling out her troubles. She was crying, and I felt like crying with her. Her husband died last month, and she and Lotte are alone now. Their handsome house, the store — everything gone. They live in a nearly bare, dark room in a house more like a ruin on the Schiller Strasse — close to where the Schneiders' married daughter used to live, remember?

"Anyhow, this very morning the Rabhoffs' family doctor had called in Frau Rabhoff and told her now that he had seen Lotte, and had found her pregnant more than three months. From this American soldier, leaving her behind with his child. The poor woman is sick with worry — with that little baby coming and not knowing what will happen with Lotte."

My mother stopped for a moment, then went on. "These silly, foolish young girls." Her hand came down on the table hard enough to make me jump. "And you! Don't you look at me so. I come home saddened unto my heart, and what do I see first off! You and Andy shamelessly smooching! That's what!" She took a deep breath, composing herself, trying to control her turbulent emotions. "What can I do to have you see straight again? Ask Andy not to come around anymore? Send you away from here? Tell me! Tell me!"

I left my chair to stand now by the sink, my hands deep in my pockets. I was suddenly sweating with fear, thinking my mother might send me away — to our relatives in the Black Forest, to Bavaria, my father's people.

I forced myself to sound calm. "Andy is the finest, kindest, human being I've ever known. He wouldn't do anything to hurt me. He is not like Lotte's soldier. Believe me. I know what I am doing. Don't worry about me. And don't ever say you would send me away! Don't say Andy can't come here," I begged my mother with my very heart in the eyes, going to her, taking her hand, and pressing it to my hot cheek while she sat there as if she had suddenly lost all answers, turned to stone.

Then her hand came up to her hair, to find the hat still pinned to it. Slowly she took it off. "I want you to be happy. That's all I want — for you to be happy."

"I am happy! I am very happy. As never before I am happy now!" I assured her as if my life depended on it.

She shook her head at me, at herself. For a moment she looked at me as if she had trouble remembering why we were sitting there. Then, as if she realized her own helpless feelings, she got up off her chair and heavily walked past me, closing her bedroom door behind her, shutting me out gently. Leaving me kneeling there beside her empty chair, looking at her closed door.

For a time after that we talked like polite strangers to each other. I tried not to show my feelings for Andy around her, while we met daily as before, my mother looking at Andy thoughtfully, unable not to like him.

And now we met in the lush fields of sugar beets and tall corn stretching far beyond our garden.

We found each other by the twinkling waters of the old Rhein, under the green and gold shadows of the whispering forest. And we came together, underneath our oak as if drawn there by our giant friend, to share precious hours in the deep grooves between his strong, gnarly roots, under the shade of his many greensleeved limbs, which protected us, too, from all curious eyes. We spent many hours, there in our secret world, where, freed from human sin and shame, we discovered one another anew, delighting in each other like two children in an Eden all our own.

Until one day, when our dreams of paradise were invaded, when the world knocked on our rainbow door, making me open my eyes to stare back, unflinching, my hand secure in Andy's hand, his love, my trust in him my shield. Our love at last was to be out in the open for all the world to see.

I had come walking home from the edge of the forest, where I had said good-bye to my love, seeing him off on his way to the Hole. Near the Kellers' house I came upon Inge standing as if waiting for someone, for me, her hands rammed into her pockets almost up to her elbows.

"Hello, Lisa. Out for a walk already, so early in the day?"

"Yes, out for a walk," I replied. "It's such a lovely morning."

"In more ways than one," Inge answered, and I could sense more was to follow.

"It depends on what you expect to find," I said, watching the flicker of impatience in her eyes, hearing the edge in her voice.

But she could not contain herself any longer. "Do you really believe that you can keep a secret in The Village?" and then she was off, informing me of all the vicious gossip circling The Village about Andy and myself, about the Forster girl and that tall, blue-eyed American soldier. Gossip, which old Frau Moll — better known as the busybody who lived in the last house at the edge of town by the fields — delighted to trumpet to anyone wanting to hear. "That Forster girl's shameless behavior with an Auslander. Going for walks with him, holding hands, smooching."

The Villagers liked nothing better than throwing dirt, especially at one not born in The Village.

Inge shrugged. "They call you names behind your back, things you are certainly not."

I watched her kick the wall behind her. For a fleeting moment I felt touched that she should be angry and concerned about me. But then I could not care who in The Village was saying what. Indeed I felt like laughing, and, suddenly angry, I snapped at Inge, "Let them talk. I couldn't care less for The Village and its narrow-minded ways. You see, I love my American!"

Inge stood stiffly against the wall, her eyes filling with tears. "He is very handsome, your soldier. I saw you two yesterday. He was helping you bring in firewood. You were both laughing. So happy. You wore a green ribbon in your hair. I thought it looked nice with all your beautiful hair."

Her hand wandered over her own mousy hair, pulled back severely into a shapeless bun at the nape of her neck. She shook her head. "What you said about The Village . . . You're not the only one stuck here, wanting to be away at times." She was flushing, taking a deep breath to go on. "The Villagers, they are good and bad, concerned and indifferent as anywhere else, I suppose."

She stopped, then added, "I always thought of you as a friend, ever since you came to The Village. Today I wanted to talk to you because I am your friend." She swallowed. "When he leaves here one day, you will still be here. The Villagers won't forget so easily."

I could only shake my head at her.

"In Mannheim," she went on relentlessly, "it is still called fraternizing with aliens! Do you know?"

I had left her, walking away without looking back.

But I took the stairs to our kitchen in giant strides, feeling suddenly sick.

What indeed would I do if Andy had to leave, to return home across that immense ocean, so very far away?

Abruptly I felt frantic with fear. I wanted to run and find Andy — shout his name until he would come and tell me that nothing could take him away for long, not ever. I wanted to rush time. I wanted it to be evening, night. But the clock on the wall insisted I had hours to endure before he would return from duty.

My mother came into the kitchen, from the droning heat in the garden, which she daily weeded and planted, happy to have a garden of her own again.

Thoughtfully she looked at me, as if sensing my emotions. She took off her blue apron carefully, so as not to loose any soil onto the clean floor, folding it and putting it away. Then she washed her hands, slowly, carefully, scrubbing under her nails with a small brush.

I couldn't stand her silence any longer. "Why aren't you talking? Is something the matter?"

She began drying her hands, and only when she finished

did she turn to me, seeking my eyes with her troubled ones.

"I asked your father to talk with you. It seems to me he has more influence on you," she said. Then she turned away, leaving the room just as my father entered.

He faced me. I looked into his eyes, boldened by an edge of defiance at what it was he needed to discuss. I cut through the silence, asking him, "You wanted to see me?"

His lips parted, and he looked at me, then looked away again. "Yes. We must have a talk." He seemed to be groping for words, his hands opening and closing. Once more he looked at me, then gazed out the window at the house next door.

"I don't know how to begin with this, which I should have discussed with you long before today," he finally began. "I should have known from the beginning, when I saw Andy coming here, so unmistakably in love with you. And you with him. It was all so obvious, so predictable." He paused, then went on, "I am to blame for not saying anything, for keeping my eyes closed as you both fell in love. But seeing you, like a flower turned to the sun, awakening, forgetting your nightmares of all you had seen in the war — I was glad to see you smile again, becoming curious once more, mischievous once more, as you were before, when you were a happy child. Still I know you are young, and easily hurt. I am your father. . . ."

He shook his head. "You must not blame your mother for worrying about you. She wants your happiness, what is best for you. She loves you. She knows what is good for you." He stopped, as if aware of the lameness of his last words.

I sat listening, waiting for him to go on.

"We must not forget that Andy is far from home and lonesome. You are a very pretty girl, easy to be with. He is a man with needs, a soldier, but he will go home again one day, you staying here."

"Don't say that! Don't!" I cried out, unable to listen to another word. "You cannot mean it! How could you? Andy loves me. I love him! He is not only lonely. I thought you would understand. Andy loves me! He loves me!" I buried my face in my hands, crying with unbearable agony. "I would rather be dead than without him!"

My father came quietly to me, stroking my hair as he used to do when I was a child, and he murmured, "I do know. From the very start I have felt your happiness, and I hoped, wished, you would never have to know disappointment or despair. What can I say now when —"

But I slipped out from under his hand to run into my room, slamming the door behind me. I threw myself onto my bed. Then, in bitter silence, I began raging inside at The Village, at the whole world. Slowly, my rage made room for a new fierceness inside me.

I will fight the world for Andy, I decided. *No one can take him away from me!*

"I don't care what they are saying about me in The Village," I mumbled into my tear-drenched pillow. "I don't care about those self-proclaimed saints. I'll show them all," I told the uncaring pillow. "Why can't they leave us alone?"

Exhausted, I fell asleep at last. The Village, the world, retreating, not daring to invade my dreams, where, surrounded by Andy's love, I was safe.

My father and my mother wisely left me to myself.

It was hours later when I woke to a short knock on my door. Before I could answer or sit up, Andy stepped into the room, closing the door behind him, holding in one hand an ivory-white rose. His other hand he kept behind his back, as if he was hiding something. Something important, it seemed, for he wore a big grin, his eyes dancing with joy.

"What is my sweetheart doing in bed on such a fine day?" He clucked his tongue at me, shaking his head.

"Andy, you're back! And early! I'm so glad!" Heavy with sleep, I thought I might be dreaming still. "How did you get past my father and mother?"

"Ah! I received special permission. I heard that you were boo-hooing about the world in seclusion, with your door closed, keeping out even Uncle Max!" He bent down to me, pushing the rose playfully over my ear into my hair. Dropping a large white envelope by my pillow, he sat down on the bed.

"Now, what is this all about, sugar?" he asked, taking my hands between his. I looked down at those hands holding mine so firmly yet gently. How safe I felt being held by those hands.

The last light of the waning day had found us, wrapping us in a cloak of red and gold, reminding me once more of my day's misery.

Trying hard to hide the tears welling up in my eyes, I blurted out my heartache. "My mother, my father — they are worried about us. Worried I will get hurt one day, when you leave here, and go home and I never see you again." The tears were running down my face now. "They don't understand how very much I love you!"

Andy put his arm around me and lifted me to lie against him, stroking my hair back from my face, holding me close.

"I know you love me," he whispered, his voice hoarse with emotion. "And I love you — more than I can say in words. And I'll always love you — never forget that!"

I lifted my face to him. "My mother — she is very worried that I could get into trouble, have a child. A child with no father. That you would forget us . . ."

"Oh, my God. My poor darling! I could never leave you, never forget you. I love you more than my life!"

We fell silent for a while, holding one another. Then I began once more. "The Villagers — they say that I am a . . . whore. And that terrible Frau Moll is telling everybody that my hide should be tarred and feathered and my hair cut off so that all could see and know."

Andy's face suddenly lost all color. He clamped his teeth together, making the muscles in his face stand out. "God! They wouldn't dare touch you!" And then I heard him swear for the first time, low and fierce. "The dirty-minded swine. The sneaky skunks! God damn them all to hell!" He hugged me to himself so fiercely that I felt the air rushing from my lungs. Instantly he gentled again holding me in his arms, putting his cheek atop my head, slowly rocking me back and forth as if he were holding a small child in need of comfort and protection.

"I'll never leave you. How could I, now that I love you as I have never loved anyone?" He gave a deep sigh. "Listen! Listen to me. Soon, the day will come when I have to go away from here, but you must not worry. Promise me you will trust me when that time comes. I'll be back for you, come hell or high water. I'll find a way for us to be together. One day soon all this will be in the past. Then I will take you home with me, to my family, as my wife. This I swear!"

I curled up in his lap, my arms wrapped around his neck, my face pressed into the warm skin of his throat, The Village left behind on our way to the future.

Until Andy remembered the letter he had dropped on my bed. He reached for it now and opened it, all the while talking eagerly.

"I have written to my family about us, about you. Many times I've written letters in the middle of the night when you could not be with me, when I could not fall asleep for thinking of you. My family knows how very much I love you, how very much we love each other."

His eyes almost violet, smiling, he went on. "I told them all about you in my letters: the way you smile, how you put one finger on your nose when you think up some mischief, how your eyes seem green or brown or flecked with gold, depending on what they see, how your hair is the color of ripe chestnuts and soft as silk."

"You told them all that?"

"More, much more!" He grinned, laughter dancing in his eyes. Then he grew serious again. "Now, honey, don't feel bad, not even for a moment. At first my family felt they had to talk some sense into me. My mother thought our love was just for the moment and soon to be forgotten. My clever sister, Ann, wrote me a long letter, reminding me of the carefree years I am passing up. But I kept on writing that you are the one, the only one!"

I felt his arm tighten around me as he went on.

"I sent home pictures in every letter. Soon they changed their minds about us. Indeed, now my father wants to know all about you. One day he wrote, 'I like the girl in the pictures. Send more!' A month ago I sent the ones we took in the garden. Here is his answer."

I sat up quickly to hear what Andy's family wrote about me. Andy gave me a reassuring hug and began to read, often putting down the long letter to explain his family as clearly as possible.

"You'll like my mother," he said at one time. "Her grandmother — my great-grandmother — came from a small town in the north of Germany, near Hamburg. My mother often talks about her grandmother — of how she came west in a covered wagon, married to a Dutchman, settling the very land we live on now. My mom is American mixed with German, English, a bit Irish, a pinch of Swede. My father's people, on both sides, are French descendants. He's a great guy, too. Mountain-big in all ways. Before he married my mother, settling down on our ranch, he was a cowpuncher, an oil-driller, a horse-breeder one day rich, the next poor again. I know you'll like him. The two of you will get along fine and dandy. But see for yourself what he writes."

"How could I blame you for falling in love — it took but one look at the girl in the picture to understand why!"

"You see?" Andy grinned roguishly, giving my nose a little tap with the tip of his finger. "Like father, like son, as the saying goes!"

Andy's mother invited me to write to her, and she asked Andy to give her regards and her heartfelt thanks to my parents for being so kind to her son far from home.

"And here is my sister Ann's letter." He put down his parents' letter and brought out another from his back pocket.

"Write more, dear brother! My ears are open for anything concerning you. I'm in love myself — getting married soon, I hope. Give my love to Lisa."

Andy put down his sister's letter to hug me. And I felt ashamed for having let the slightest doubt influence me.

He took my face between his hands looking deeply into my eyes. "Promise me you'll never again think that I would forget you. Remember, wherever I must go I will find a way to be with you. I can only be happy when you're with me, when I can hold you like this." He smiled, his very heart peeking through his eyes. "My silly little woman!"

How fortunate I was to be loved so. I began to wish time would stand still and nothing would change for us, ever.

But nothing ever remained the same for long.

Soon we became aware of my father and mother in the kitchen, knowing how worried they must be after my stormy disappearance earlier.

My hand in Andy's, we walked out together, the happiness in our faces telling it all. We sat at the table, eagerly sharing our plans for the future with my parents. Soon my mother's eyes were shining again, trusting, my father's laughter ringing like the church bells on Sunday morning.

The days passed fast from then on.

Some of the Villagers still talked about us, but we didn't care, and most began accepting our love.

Red came to The Village often at first, having joined his company across the Rhein in the American Zone. But his visits became fewer and shorter after the afternoon he came across the river on the ferry and up to the house to find us out.

"They went swimming somewhere upriver," my mother told him, glad to see him.

Red had waited patiently for us to come home until evening, falling asleep for a time on the couch in the living room. He had a bite to eat with my parents. Then, with the clock striking six and us nowhere in sight, he had said goodbye to my father and mother.

He was driving toward the ferry when we saw him, we were on our way back from our secret place under our giant oak tree, our eyes glowing with fulfillment.

I saw Red first, but both of us called out to him, Andy's voice as glad as mine. We tried persuading him to return with us to The Village, but he looked at his watch several times, avoiding our happy eyes and insisted he had to get back to camp.

Chapter 7

Maybe I remember that one evening so clearly because it was raining, a gentle, constant rain after a long dry spell. Or because that evening my heart opened its very last door . . .

That evening Andy and I had driven all the way to Ludwigshafen, to the street where I was born, to the ruins of the house where I had lived. We drove to the playground where years ago I had created my first mud pies. We drove by the rebuilt schoolhouse where I had learned my ABCs, by the marketplace where my mother and I had shopped every Friday and Monday.

And we drove through the streets I still remembered with mixed emotions: lit by many candles set into red glasses in the house windows at night on national holidays. Red as if dipped in blood, then red-glaring in the war years from the fires of the endlessly falling bombs, which had finally left behind a Stygian darkness, replacing all that red with a silence and emptiness just as terrible and even more frightening.

On the street where I had lived the first fourteen years of my life, I saw old Herr Wenz, hunched over, bony, and sallow-faced as I had never before seen him, but still hanging on, seemingly a little surprised with himself for having outlived his three strapping sons, all dead in the war.

I called out to him. "How are you, Herr Wenz!" He stared back, not recognizing me.

When we drove by the burned-out shell of what had been Capt. Friedrich's house, I had to chuckle at a hundred memories suddenly springing alive inside me.

"What's so funny?" Andy wanted to know.

"I just thought of this crazy old parrot living over there when the house still had a front porch. He would sit on the iron railing, ruling the whole street with his extraordinary use of language. He belonged to Herr Friedrich, a retired captain of a merchant ship, who brought him home after they roamed the oceans together.

"The parrot's name was Solomon. He was so foul-mouthed, Capt. Friedrich was forced to move back to Hamburg with him to escape the wrath of the citizens. Solomon had insulted one too many with his swear words."

Andy was intrigued with my story, so I went on. "Every morning on my way to school, I relished his undivided attention, hearing him call me snotnose or baldhead — this with all the hair I had. He kept it up 'til I got down the street and into the schoolhouse. I learned some very colorful expressions from him, but when my mother heard me shouting one of them after Fritz, one of the neighbor's boys, after he had won a fist fight, leaving me with scratches and scrapes, she did not believe that a parrot had taught me such filth. Lucky Solomon went merrily on, shouting insults, calling the butcher who drank like a sieve a *Schnapsnase,* and the mailman a *Wasserkopf* — the man did sport an extraordinary skull. When I told my father what Solomon had called the mailman, he couldn't help laughing.

"Later I heard him telling my mother the latest about Solomon. And she grinned. 'That Solomon is the only one on the street brave enough to speak the truth. He's right about the mailman.' "

The mailman was known to all as a man with little humor, seen only in his mailman uniform or his Party uniform.

I could tell that Andy enjoyed my stories.

"What became of Solomon?"

"Solomon moved to Hamburg with the captain, shortly after he gravely insulted the astonishingly fat Frau Eberhard, the dentist's wife. He couldn't keep his beak shut, seeing her walking by his porch: she was so enormous, she waddled like a duck. And, thanks to Solomon, she became the number-one joke to the neighborhood. One fine morning he was overheard calling after her, loud and clear, like a drill-sergeant at training, 'Chest out! Belly in! Tail up, old cow!' "

For a lighthearted moment we both laughed aloud over a parrot articulate enough to ridicule a streetful of respectable citizens.

Then we arrived at the remnants of a fence where a rusted plate creaked in the wind, showing the number 32.

Strange, how shrunken the place looked, how even the garden seemed so much smaller now, almost obscured by weeds, so different from the garden I cherished in my memory.

I looked for Black Peter's grave, but it had vanished. Only the willow tree had survived, barely, sad somehow, with the rain dripping like tears from its silver spears of leaves.

How very lovely it used to be. Now it seemed lonely and sad.

It was good to walk back to the jeep with Andy by my side. I was glad to snuggle close to him, to drive away. I felt lighter, knowing that the nightmares, the terrible dreams I had taken with me from the burning house, the burning city, that night years ago, had vanished, dissolved, dislodged by Andy's love.

We drove aimlessly through the darkening streets so

much like vales of rubble. Then, in the Kaiser Wilhelm Strasse, across from one more ruin made by senseless hate, I asked Andy to stop.

The street was sparsely lit, almost totally destroyed.

"I'll show you where God lived once, to many in this city." I answered solemnly the question in Andy's eyes, beginning to speak of things I had thought locked away deep inside myself. I wanted to talk, to tell. And to Andy, I could.

"Before the war, these heaps of stone were a house of God. A synagogue, where my friends Ilse and Franz Ostemann prayed."

I remembered standing there, with a loaf of bread under my arm. I had come from the bakery when the yelling had started, the smoke and the flames. Instead of running home, I ran towards the commotion curious to know what it meant, what was happening in that unobtrusive house where God lived, where men in shiny boots were throwing into the flames scrolls and books. Books and scrolls about God, Ilse had told me years ago, showing me where they prayed on Shabbat, on Saturday. In turn I had taken them to the Luther Kirche to show them where I prayed on Sundays.

It had all seemed very uncomplicated. We had no difficulties understanding each other.

Standing there behind the screaming mob squeezing in my arm the freshly baked loaf of bread, not really understanding what I saw happening, I became frightened. I ducked into the doorway of a house, but someone was already there, pressed against the wall, shuffling his feet, weeping, moaning, heartbrokenly. Scared, I turned to look into the face of an old man. He had silver-white hair and a great white beard. There were tears running down his cheeks, his thin lips trembling and moving in silent prayer. I can see him still — and myself staring at him, at his long black coat, the sidelocks dangling from under his wide-rimmed hat, with silver curls cascading to his shoulders.

He never saw me. He would not see me in his pain. I wanted to say something to him — anything to have him stop shaking and quivering so, but a sudden fear seemed to be squeezing my throat. Very much a child, I backed away. I ran home as if I had gazed into hell, hearing the shouts, the moans, of what seemed like damnation, haunting me.

Somewhere along the way I fell. I remember dropping the loaf of bread into a puddle, skinning my knee, tearing a hole in my long cotton stockings.

When I reached home, I found my father in his shop, working still. My mother was talking over the fence with a neighbor while she took off the clothesline snowy-white sheets. The windows were lit and the door open. All seemed to be as it always was. What was happening in the inner city did not reach here. But I still felt the terror. I still saw the old man crying and praying. I saw the house of God burning and His books being burned. And why did God not put out the flames?

When we sat around the supper table decked with sparkling glasses and rose-rimmed Bavarian china, filled with soup and salad and roast meat, with vegetables grown in our garden by my mother with the help of heaven above, I wanted to talk, to tell what I had seen. I started out quietly, but I could not fight down the fountain of grief gushing up into my throat, into my eyes.

My father's and mother's eyes met and parted again, my mother not yet understanding it all. Then she did understand, and her eyes looked shocked, full of grief. "They burned down a temple? A house of God?" And she seemed to hear the stirring of a monster, and she looked very much afraid. Then alert, a lioness needing to protect her young from the hunter, no matter the cost. "Don't go there again! Stay away — just stay away! Do you hear me?"

My father picked up his spoon, and, staring into his bowl, he began to eat his soup, his spoon moving up and down like a piston.

"No one tried to save the temple. I saw a policeman laughing! The fire engines sprayed the neighboring houses only!" My voice still trembling, I turned to my father. He didn't say a word, just kept on eating his soup, his spoon rhythmically striking the bowl.

"The books, too, they burned!"

He didn't answer.

I tried once more. "I saw an old man crying!"

No answer.

"Maybe he is still there. Maybe no one helped him. I ran home . . ."

"Dear child. I wish you hadn't seen this," my mother sighed.

"Maybe we could help him, that old man. Maybe he is still there."

"Animals! That's what they are! They went and did what they were bragging about, in the *hetz* paper, *The Stürmer*. I wouldn't wipe my arse with it if one was handed to me. The swine!"

"Joseph!" my mother cried out, reaching across the table to my father, grasping his shoulder to make him stop. "Joseph, Joseph, you must not ever speak out loud like this! Think! The new people across the street — the man wears a party button when he is not in uniform. Oh, my God. He is standing in front of his house. What if he heard you? He would report you. I know he would!"

My father looked as if he had much more to say. But then he picked up a piece of bread instead, stuffing a large chunk into his mouth. It got stuck in his windpipe, making him choke and pull for air. I sprang off my chair to pound his back, but he pushed me away, coughing and choking. "Damn! Damn it all to hell!" And rushed from the room.

My mother followed him into the bedroom, where they talked in whispers for some time, his voice like rolling thunder, my mother's cajoling, convincing. I sat there, left to myself, seeing as if for the first time, the tapestry my mother had embroidered and my father had framed, and hung on the wall right across from me.

Mag draussen die Welt ihr Leben treiben.
Mein haus soll meine zuflucht bleiben.

Let the world out there go about her business. Here in my home I'll be safe from it all. I read it over and over until it burned into my eyes. Until it made no sense any longer. Something was wrong with it. . . .

The world outside had come into our home.

That old man . . . was he still there in that doorway crying? The temple had been Ilse and Franz's place of God, the Ostermanns' temple. It was. . . .

Dr. Ostermann!

Maybe he didn't know what had happened! I would tell him. I had to let him know! Now!

I got off my chair, left the room, the house. I walked down the street, down another street, another. I had to tell him.

I came to the Ostermanns' house. I knocked on the door with my fist, then with both my fists.

A relative of Dr. Ostermann's wife, known to me as cousin Lina, came to open the door. She looked frightened.

But when she saw me, she seemed relieved. She said ever so strangely to someone in the dark hall behind her, "It's only Lisa, the little goyem."

Her voice seemed different than usual, her eyes cold and strangely hostile, cutting into me as if with knives. It hurt. I remember still how it hurt, standing there in front of the familiar door on the green rubber mat with GRÜSS GOD printed on it in bright letters.

Then the door opened a little wider. Dr. Ostermann was standing there.

He looked older, smaller then usual. He was coughing nervously when he spoke. "It is only you. I thought it was . . ."

He seemed so different. Not at all like before, when I had come to play with Ilse and Franz. Quickly I said, "I came to tell you . . ."

"What! What? Speak up. Did someone send you?" His voice and eyes seemed suddenly eager.

"I just came by myself. I wanted to tell you . . . about . . ."

Cousin Lina was mumbling something behind the door. Dr. Ostermann gave a sigh.

"It's very late for you to be out. I can't let you in. My wife is ill. Her heart —"

"But — but I came to tell you your temple was burned down." I had begun to stammer.

He said, "I know. How could I not know?" And, urgently, he added, "Go home, quickly. Straight home you go. Do you hear?"

I didn't move.

So he said even more urgently, as if very much concerned, "Run! Run home quickly, child! Good night!" The door began to close.

Suddenly I became frantic, seeing that door close, watching the friendly house shut itself away from me. I threw myself at the slit, crying, "Wait! Oh, please wait! You must write Ilse and Franz about it! You must!" Both his grandchildren had returned a week earlier to Vienna.

The door opened wider once more. The tired voice behind it came even lower now, sadder. "They know already, I'm sure. Please go home, dear child." Then the door had shut with a final click.

I stood looking at the closed door. It seemed suddenly forbidding, not a sliver of light coming from the house, from its people, as if they had locked me out and themselves away, never again to invite me into the warm, happy, noisy circle of their lively family — never again to taste Mrs. Ostermann's waffles, her fish balls, her chopped liver that I liked so much. Never again to stand up straight with my back against the wall in that hall inside and have Dr. Ostermann tell me I grew two inches since the last time. Never to listen to Cousin Lina again, playing the piano, trying hard not to laugh, watching Franz acting the monkey behind her back.

My lips had begun to chatter.

Suddenly it seemed very dark on the street.

I turned away to run all the way home. What was wrong? Why did they not like me anymore?

I walked back into the house as if I had been but in the garden, covering up the wooden stall that housed my white Angora rabbit, Putzy. Shortly after, my mother locked the door against the coming night, against whatever was stirring out there. I said good night and went up to my room, glad that I didn't have to say another word, think another thought.

I was in bed with the light out when my father came up

the stairs and looked into my room. "Are you still awake, Lissy?"

I pinched my eyes closed and didn't answer. He waited a moment longer. Then he left, his step on the stairs sounding tired. All seemed so very sad, so confusing. Even Black Peter couldn't cheer me when he came to lie down beside me on the bed, pushing his nose into the palm of my hand, obviously wanting to know what was the matter tonight.

I remember very distinctly being sick the next day. With the measles, I think. For two weeks or so I had to stay at home, could not leave the house. When I came to see Dr. Ostermann, I found the front door locked, the green shutters over the downstairs windows closed tightly. On the door someone had painted a Star of David, and on the wall was written one word. Juden!

Out on the street again I asked a kindly looking woman walking by if she could tell me please whether the Ostermanns were at home.

"The Jews?" she asked, instantly suspicious, looking me over for signs of an invisible disease, not looking kind any longer.

Bewildered, I said, "The Jews?" I felt strange having said that, seeing her staring at me. "He is a doctor, Dr. Ostermann. For eyes and throat, I think."

She interrupted me. "I don't know where they are now, really. Some say they have left for good. Seems strange, though, with all that furniture still in the house. Who knows — ?"

I never found anyone since who could tell me where the Ostermanns had disappeared to, nor what became of Ilse and Franz. I never heard from them again. For a while the house stood empty. Then the Red Cross took it over, making it into a way station for traveling soldiers of the Wehrmacht. A sign now hung over the spot where the Star of David had been, a sign reading: *Pst! Der feind hört mit!* And against the wall: *Räder müssen rollen für den Sieg!*

Then one night, our house burned down along with most of the other houses on the street, the whole city. And I began to live another part of my life. Until after the war I believed Dr. and Frau Ostermann had gone to their children in Vienna, had left because of what had been done to their house of worship.

Sometimes I wished — abruptly I came to a stop.

In the street the rain was now falling heavily, running down the windshield of the jeep, its top, its sides, running over the shining sidewalk and into the gutter, into the river — all the way to the North Sea.

Two strong arms reached for me. Held me. Two lips began to speak gentle words, words shaped in the heart of one who understood.

And I heard.

And I listened.

Oh, how I listened to those lips gently saying healing words. Like the parched soil, I drank. Drank.

Chapter 8

In the nearby city, in The Village, in most every town big and small, astonishing feats were being accomplished.

The huge mountains of rubble began to shrink. Many of the smaller ruins vanished entirely, making room for new beginnings, for the buildings and homes of a tomorrow I could only imagine. Ah, it was indeed inspiring to be able to look at such pictures and drawings dreamed onto paper by courageous men and women, showing how life would be again one day in the future.

Out in the fields bending with Mother Nature's bounty, assigned men were out nightly hunting with shotguns the poor devils who could not deny their rumbling stomachs and dared being shot for a few heads of not yet fully grown cabbages, for a few sugar beets, a small bag of early potatoes — anything growing out there so promisingly if so exasperatingly slow.

Yes, the stomach was still tyrant king.

In The Village a small score of babies had announced their imminent arrival to their smug-looking mothers and to their not-so-long-returned-home fathers.

Uncle Max, too, had been busy in that field of procreation. The Village expected to see before the coming of fall a small army of apricot-colored kittens beside the usual black, grey, and whites. As a matter of fact, Uncle Max had definitely overdone it when he appointed himself right hand to whoever-made-baby-cats. I was plain worried with one particular cat pregnancy, soon to show up for all to see — a sure case of paternal proof involving none other than Uncle Max.

It all had to do with Frau Waldhauser's cat, Anastasia Sophia, and, of course, Uncle Max. I was dragged in because Uncle Max was part of the Forster family. Not that I could be held responsible, morally or otherwise, for his smooching with every feline beauty, tirelessly, efficiently all over The Village.

This is what it was all about.

Frau Waldhauser's pure-bred, high born, Blue Russian Anastasia Sophia was suspected of being in the family way, having been put into this condition by Uncle Max — having forced his way into the house where she was kept night and day, under guard, carefully reserved for that day when she would be mated with the only other Russian Blue in this whole dog-loving countryside, this certain one residing in Heidelberg in a pink villa overlooking the Neckar River. A true prince among cats, according to Frau Waldhauser. And now it was too late!

The milk was spilled, I felt like saying to her. But it would only have added to her grief, her fury, which made her try a well-planted kick at the sly fiend — the vulgar alley-cat, peacefully asleep under the table, not caring a whit with whom he had done monkey business weeks earlier.

It was "Sehr schlimn" indeed and a bad situation all around.

And this was not even the end of it! More was to come! In a couple of months . . . all of them on four, silky little paws!

All this happened in The Village.

Outside The Village, and daily now, streams of ragged, wild-eyed, half-starved men, women, and children kept arriving from the Russian Zone into the British and the American Zone. Each one of these unfortunates told almost unbelievable stories of brutality, of murder and rape, raging unchecked by the Russian Occupation army.

One day a neighbor gave me a letter to read, one smuggled out from the Russian sector of Berlin, written by an eighty-year-old grandmother shortly after the fall of Berlin to the Russians. She wrote:

I am now beyond shame, terror, and belief in human dignity and mercy. What more can there be? The Russians, Mongols, and Tartars broke into the cellar where we had been hiding since the siege began. They raped Lotte. Your mother Maria. My sweet, innocent, little angel Karin. It meant nothing to them, I being an old woman of eighty. They broke two of my ribs because I made a mistake and cried out when they took their turn with me. Little Karin. She died that same night. There were six of them, and she was only a child of twelve. As for Lotte, they took my beautiful Lotte with them. We haven't heard from her since. I tried to take care of Lotte's other young daughter, Linda. She was there, seeing it all. Seeing her mother dragged away from her — all, all. She is now but a small pale ghost, a frightened little bird of a child who had forgotten how to sing, to smile, how to be happy.

Give her a chance! For the love of God, give her a chance. Please understand and forgive this old woman for acting before asking you: little Linda is on her way to Mannheim and her to you with the Frank family. God bless them.

I will stay here, waiting for Lotte to come home, hoping and praying she is still alive. Praying to Our Father in Heaven not to forsake us completely, to have mercy on the children and the innocent!

"Where are you! Here with me or in a place where I can't follow?" Andy had wanted to know, jokingly waving a hand before my eyes, standing there beside me in the kitchen, just having returned from guard duty, the sun red and enormous behind him, sinking to make room for the night.

"You might as well give, unload to your Andrew. He always knows when something is bothering you!"

I turned to him in a sudden uprush of tenderness. I held him tightly, to be clasped in his arms, instantly safe.

"Of all the Americans, you are the sweetest, kindest, the best! What would I do without you?" I mumbled, burying my face in his chest.

"Then something did happen today?"

I began telling him about the letter, what the Berliner grandmother had written onto paper spotted with tears. His eyes filled with pity, but it wasn't news to him. He had heard similar stories. He knew them as facts.

"I am so glad your army and not the Russians came to us!" I said.

"It seems," he replied slowly, his eyes thoughtful, concerned, "our Allies are doing their best to plant a new crop of seeds for another war. It seems this one is not over yet . . ."

There was one other, who shared with me my admiration for the Americans: my father. He followed closely all that happened — with the French, the English, the Russians — but he and I wished the U.S. would be our friend someday, as many in Germany wished.

And then, one day, came what we had known would have to come. Andy was told he and the rest of the soldiers still in The Village were to be moved to Mannheim and into the American Zone, to join their old company, in the next few days.

Surprisingly, we both felt rather relieved with the news. We had long feared he would be stationed just about any-where in Germany, or even France, far from The Village.

The French Occupation army was taking over the part of the country known now as the French Zone. All of Ger-many had been divided into four parts: the French, the American, the British, and the Russian Zones. At times it seemed strange and bewildering to think of the familiar countryside, the city on the other side of the river, as an-other place almost as a foreign country one could enter only with a passport. And such precious papers could be ob-tained only by those who held a job across the river or for special occasions. There were many who would not see friends or family on that other side for a time to come.

I had my own thoughts about it all. I was worried. I could not take it lightly, as Andy did.

Andy had made friends with old Police Sergeant Krauss, whose daily duty was down by the ferry, checking passports by the side of a French sergeant. Having worked with him once in a while, Andy had come to know the elderly man as a kind, decent soul.

Now he assured me, "Old Krauss will let you cross any time without a pass. Don't worry about passes and papers," he said.

Red, who had crossed several times without papers, just handing casually a package of cigarettes to the French ser-geant on duty, agreed with Andy on this. He swore ciga-rettes worked every time.

I knew well, of course, that American cigarettes were highly valued by soldiers and civilians alike and had long become the magic medium on the merrily thriving black market. Still, I insisted I must have a pass and legal papers.

In this I was truly German, taught early, heaven knows, the importance of legal papers.

I knew better than to trust blind chance or the fickle Lady Luck in this country, at this time, in this Europa! I was aware my way of thinking was European, was part of my heredity, a way of life. But I knew better than to make unnecessary waves with the authorities. So, stubbornly, I insisted I needed a pass.

How different Andy was.

Had I not known him so well, loved him, at times I would have thought him unbelievably unaware, naively innocent in such things. Instead I had come to look with admiration on his unafraid ways of thinking, feeling wistfully sure in such instances that he came from a place I did not know, from a country still young, not yet traumatized by the decay one could find everywhere in Europe, in her burial grounds made by too many wars, in her petty squabbles and jealousies along her borders and fences, in her many people, in their real and imagined differences.

At times I wished myself to where Andy came from.

But I was too aware of borders.

And so, small wonder, I was much concerned to find a legal way to cross the river — one such border now.

I know my friend Inge had been working as a secretary to the manager of a large spinning factory in Mannheim. To her I turned now with my problem. And with a plan: to help me find work across the river and so the right to a pass.

I had worked once before in an office for a while. I was sure I could do so again. Eager to start as soon as possible, I was convinced that this was the way to a passport for me, to the other side of the river where Andy would be soon.

Too impatient to wait for Inge to come home that following day, I walked down to the ferry to wait for her there. Before she had a chance to put her feet on dry ground, I began calling to her. Before I could touch her hand, I began asking her my important questions.

Sadly she shook her head. "There is nothing at all open just now at my office."

My heart slowed for an instant in bitter disappointment. Hesitating Inge went on, "They might hire you to work on one of the spinning machines down in the factory. The hours are the same, only — well — it means standing on your feet all day long, changing full spools for empty ones, oiling parts, getting dirty, and being dog-tired come evening." She tried to warn me, her eyebrows raised.

I did not care what I would have to do all day long if it would get me a passport to Andy. That was all that mattered to me.

I thought evening would never come, when I would see Andy, tell him my wonderful news: that now we could be together no matter where in Germany's American Zone he would be stationed!

At first Andy was as glad as I was. Then he began to worry, thinking the job would be too much for me. I laughed, telling him I would tame wild horses, dig ditches if I had to if it meant being with him. And I meant every bit of it, convinced of my own strength.

"How do I tell you how much I love you? So very much," he whispered, and tenderly he touched my face.

"Working will not kill anyone, not even working on a machine." My father had spoken up almost roughly, an undercurrent of deep emotion in his voice. I knew he had seen and heard us, was touched by our happiness.

It took weeks to get my passport — weeks and all my patience and energy to wade through a tangled mess of red tape and paper shuffling. But I did not worry. Not even when Andy left The Village. No border was to keep us apart! No border could!

A few days later Andy returned, with the evening bells and the setting sun behind him, proudly wearing the stripes of a first sergeant. Ah! He looked so very handsome, I could only think how wonderful it was to see him standing there, filling the doorway with his tall frame, lighting up the kitchen with his warm, happy smile.

"We missed you," my father told Andy.

My mother wore a smile as wide as her face, urging him to sit down in his chair and have some of her Dampf Nudles she had made just for him, knowing they were his favorite. Uncle Max gave a cry of sheer delight when he discovered his friend had come back, he returning from a visit to The Village with his pussycat friends. Immediately he tried to climb up Andy's pant leg and he purred his heart out in ecstasy when he found himself lifted up to be held in his friend's arms.

"It's kind of nice knowing one was missed," Andy grinned, taking a deep breath. "Heck, I missed all of you, too. And did I ever miss you, hon! Real bad!" His familiar grin lighting his face, shifting Uncle Max around a bit, he reached into the front of his jacket, handing me a small package. "A bathing suit, honey! The latest model, straight from Paris. The slinkiest bikini this Village has ever seen. That I guarantee!"

I was delighted.

My mother was shocked, looking at it critically, thinking of how much of me would show should I wear the wicked thing. She didn't waste a minute to tell me her thoughts, saying darkly, "You wouldn't dare show yourself in that!"

Ever the optimist, my father told her not to worry. He wasn't disturbed himself, being sure it would not fit me anyhow, that it was much too small even for a doll. *"Viel zu klein sogar für eine puppe!"*

Andy and I knew better!

But this we kept wisely to ourselves, saving us all an argument. Later, when we were by ourselves, Andy told me with a twinkle in his eye that he had bought the suit from a Frenchman while on duty near the bridge. Eager for peaceful international relations — or was it American cigarettes? — the industrious Frenchman had offered anything in his ladies' wear shop in Paris — for American cigarettes.

From then on, in months to come, I found this French connection humming with business, my darling forever out of cigarettes, insisting he had given up smoking on account of his health. Grinning sheepishly, he would mumble, "I can't believe how much better cigarettes look changed into a dress, a smart suit, a sassy little hat. And ooh — how about those exciting little underthings the French put together so cleverly? And I do love to rub my nose into a certain girl's neck, thinking, this doll wears Chanel No. 5!"

I would laugh with him, thinking how it tickles having his nose rubbed into my neck, while Andy held out his arms to me, having me come into them eagerly, to hug him to myself, to kiss him tenderly, then wildly and in shameless abandonment, making him groan, "Wow! I must be dreaming!"

The woods and the swamp stood painted in color; our tree was even more beautiful now, decked out in blazing reds, browns, and yellow, its autumn dress.

Already the air was brisk as glass in the daytime. In the early hours of morning one could find a white curtain of fog hanging over the river and the swamp — winter's calling card — which the sun, still strong enough, would burn off almost as soon as she showed her deep-red face over the woods of the Odenwald. The swallows were getting ready to fly south to their winter quarters. The stork family living over the Metzes' barn all summer was discussing the flight capabilities of their young, looking philosophically down their pointed beaks at one another, making up their mind that the time had come for their long flight down the Rhein and over the snow-covered Alps to the Nile delta in Egypt.

Resolute to wear at least one time before the coming cold weather my infamous, zebra-striped, puppet-sized, bikini, I smuggled it out of the house, wearing it under my dress. And we did find the weather still warm enough to take just one more splash in the glassy, bottle-green river — only to run out again quickly before our breath could freeze to our teeth. For already the water was as cold as ice, reminding us with a shock of the coming of winter.

Of winter, when we could not come here any longer to swim. To swim?

We certainly had more exciting, more interesting things in mind when we came here to our tree, to Erl König's Kingdom!

We would cuddle up in the warm sun, sharing a blanket hidden from the world, playing Adam and Eve, Hansel and Gretel, Romeo and Juliet. Playing a game of "fraternizing" as we mischievously called it.

"Do you know, that when you kiss me you are fraternizing with an alien?" I asked Andy, looking prim and stern as a schoolmarm.

"Heavens! Who told you that?" He looked at me as if truly horrified.

"That's what I heard it called, in Mannheim, across the

river. Who cares, though? I adore fraternizing! With my alien!" I giggled, tousling his hair until he began to look like an overgrown Bushman with a pair of uncommonly blue eyes. "Or would you rather have me stop, break off our friendly relations?"

"You go right ahead with your fraternizing! This here alien has gotten such a hankering for it, it would rightly kill him should he be forced to change his ways!"

Something quite devilish had come into his voice and eyes.

He caught me just as I was getting ready to flee the blanket, seeing him developing ideas all his own. He began tickling me in places only known to him and myself, taking little nips of what I could barely manage to hide under my skimpy excuse of a bathing suit, to have me thrash about, just able to squeal with my own awakening eagerness, "Soldier boy, you are the devil! You will go to —"

He stopped tickling me. Bending down, looking into my eyes, looking actually remorseful he said, "May I have one last wish before I go there?"

"Well, all right!" I granted him that much, trying hard to look severe. "If only for showing some remorse!"

He said softly, his lips arousing on my ear, "Promise to write on my gravestone: *It was worth it! Every sixty-second-minute of it!*"

I gave up watching the little hollow at the base of his neck, which seemed to pulse with a life of its own. He moaned deep in his throat, while I drew a breath as if drowning, feeling him against me, hard and erect, throbbing with lust for life, with living.

And we had another game . . . a game we could not play often enough.

Andy, much aware of the little dell in my belly just above

the lower part of my bathing suit, could never manage for long only looking at it. And so, one sunny day, we discovered this truly delicious game we named "Mrs. Meggs and Mr. Man," an invention of our love.

It went like this.

Making believe he was pushing a doorbell, Andy would press the tip of his finger into the little hollow. "Ding ding," he would say, "Are you there?"

"I sure am, Mr. Man!" I would giggle.

"Why, it's Mrs. Meggs! How about giving me a dozen diddle-doos — fresh ones, please!" he would say, according to the rules.

"Fresh and hot they are as always. And twenty nuttniggs a dozen. However, to you they are free," came my turn to say.

Andy would bend down to me now to whisper, "I'll take them all! The small ones and the large. I must insist on paying you, my dear Mrs. Meggs. Twenty hot ones!"

And now I had to grasp him by the ears with both my hands, kiss him hard on the mouth, giving him dozen hot ones, for which he paid me in full and on the spot with twenty nuttniggs, which we both counted out faithfully one by one.

How silly we surely would have looked to anyone seeing us just then, to someone not in love and not so lighthearted and playful!

We surely were all of that, there in our hidden corner of paradise on earth. Where we looked at each other as if for the first time. I, seeing Andy forever anew — the sun-browned skin of his face, his muscular arms and legs moving so gracefully, smoothly, how it felt when I ran my fingers through his thick mane of hair, seeing the hair under his arms much lighter and curling. While he reached for me, holding me close with gentle hands, the love in his eyes like two lamps glowing from within.

While we forgot once more time and space, soaring away with the autumn wind, dancing with the brown and yellow leaves between heaven and earth, shaping them into a fine bed to love in . . . coming back to earth together enfolded in each other, filled with our singing, soaring love.

It was Andy who felt responsible for both of us in such moments.

"We must be careful. Your mother worries about us."

"I know," I answered him, still drowsy with his love.

"One day soon it will be all right. Then we'll make us a beautiful little baby — a houseful of babies!"

"The first one will be a boy," I said dreamily. "He will have your blue eyes and your handsome face."

"He will have your happy spirit and your dreams." He smiled tenderly.

"Vom Mütterchen die froh Nature, die lust zu fabulieren."

"What are you saying, love?" Andy murmured, curious.

"It's from a poem by Göethe." Softly I kissed him. Softly, softly he kissed me back.

While Father Time and his Brother Destiny watched us, jealous with having been told by two mere humans to wait with their decisions, already written in stone and not to be tampered with.

Chapter 9

Then fall, too, slipped away.

One day I woke up, looking out my window, and it was snowing. And now it was winter.

I had not missed a single day of work; faithfully I had walked daily the two miles through fog to the factory, thankful for the pass it gave me, glad to have found a way to cross the river to Andy. The work was neither difficult nor strenuous, only dull most times in its sameness. I did not mind. I was much too happy. I knew how to fill each minute with my dreams, with my splendid dreams. When the day's work was done, I was free to leave through the tall iron gate, where I found most every evening with a rush of gladness Andy waiting for me at the entrance to the factory. Then Andy would come home with me to spend a quiet evening in the old house with "his" family or to see a movie with me in the tiny theater of The Village, or to play chess, or a game called "Mench ärger Dich nicht" with my father and Inge's father, Herr Keller, who would join us eagerly. And we would leave again, together, in the half-darkness of the following morning, I for my job in the factory, and Andy to his, once more a military policeman.

By now Andy had become a well-known, accepted figure in The Village. There were many who greeted him and a few who would go out of their way to strike up a conversation with us, inviting us to come in and visit for a while. Even our old enemy, Mrs. Moll, had given up on us. We seldom heard from her now. The Village urchins followed Andy about, walking him all the way to our house, jostling each other for who would carry his green bag, his raincoat, his newspaper, anything — sure of a generous reward of chewing gum and rolls of Life Savers, which Andy carried in his pockets just for them whenever he came to The Village.

At first all had called him mister and sergeant, Mr. Andy, then just plain Andy.

I was proud hearing Andy speak now my own language so well. I was amazed that he had learned it so easily, having no troubles with different dialects.

My room had become also Andy's room; whenever he came to stay in The Village, it was his. Then I would happily climb onto the creaky couch in my parents' bedroom for the night, content that my love was safe and with me in this very house, under the same roof. It also made my mother happy, she who had her own rules and what I thought of as old-fashioned morals. At times I tried to convince her with my quick, "Times have changed!" still, every so often she thought it necessary to lecture me on what it meant to be "a nice girl." I would listen to her, only to forget it all, the minute I found myself in Andy's arms; in love and alive as never before, jealous of every minute passing when I could not be with him. Everywhere for me was Andy, Andy, Andy — in the house, in the garden, in my room, even when he was not in The Village at all.

He certainly was much present in my room.

Next to my comb and hairbrush atop the dresser snuggled his shaving lotion, sea-green and showing a sailing ship. His toothbrush loved keeping company with mine — I could tell by the way they leaned toward each other, hugging in between them a giant tube of American-brand toothpaste I adored using after all that salt and wood ash I

122

had to use during the war years. Uncle Max loved it, too, licking it every chance he got, enchanted by its delicious peppermint flavor, I guess, and because it held the scent of Andy, his tall friend.

The top drawer in the tall walnut dresser belonged now exclusively to Andy, holding his underthings, his socks, all his whatnots. His civilian clothes — a blue and white shirt, a blue and a yellow pair of pajamas. But my little bookshelf was bending over with the honor and weight of Andy's books. My Heine, Flaubert, Göethe, Zola, and my Russians, found it interesting indeed to rub jackets with such giants from the other side of the world — Hemingway, Mark Twain, and many more.

Till Eulenspiegel and Pan with his band of pink-bellied nymphs still hung on my wall over the bed; the girl with the crippled legs, however, was gone. One day, in a great thunderstorm with my windows open and no one at home, the wind had torn it off the wall and blown it out the window and into the rain, ruining it before I could find it. I never missed it. I was much too busy. I was always busy now.

Weeks passed. With much enthusiasm Andy had introduced me to the literature and history of his country, bringing me books by writers famous in his country and in the rest of the world. Several of them I had never heard of until now. I gobbled up all of them, begging him to bring more. Andy gladly obliged me, becoming a well-known face in the American Red Cross Mobile Library. To my own amazement I began to discover that there was a world of treasures waiting out there! And Andy was delighted with my increasing understanding. Gladly feeding my hunger.

The day came when he threw up his hands, crying, "Honey, you've sponged me dry!" Looking at me comically and as if he suffered a toothache, he said, "How do you like that? The Herr Professor Know-Much will have to come to his student Miss Know-all instead."

Sometimes Red would come across the river with us. "To visit with Ma and Pa," he would say. On such occasions I had the distinct impression Red was making sure Andy and I could see he truly came along to see my father and mother, and not because I, too, was there. He had changed toward me lately. In the beginning he had been affectionate, easygoing, and many times full of tender mischief. Now he was strangely careful not to find himself alone with me. He had become overly polite and sometimes deliberately distant with me, especially when Andy was present. Now he never pulled open the bow of my apron strings, and he never asked me to tie for him his necktie, as he used to do before. Sadly Red seemed to have lost all his carefree ways around me, and at times I found myself wondering if maybe it all had to do with a certain evening at the ferry, when Andy had shown, to my surprise, that he could be jealous. When he had sharply spoken to Red, who had come with us as many times before, escorting us to the ferry after an evening in the club.

"For heaven's sake," Andy had hissed at the hapless-looking Red, thinking me out of hearing range, "find yourself a girl of your own, and stop traipsing after mine!" I couldn't hear Red's reply. But I remember his face, in the lights of the ferry, calling good night to us.

In all this time I had never seen Andy show any concern when I talked to or danced with any of his other friends. He seemed disturbed only by Red, his best friend.

I clearly recall another such an evening, a moment when I had looked up and across the room filled with the laughter of happy people, to see Red, unaware, gazing at us, very intently, so very . . . poignantly, it seemed.

Could it be that Andy had reason to feel uncomfortable with his friend's affection for me?

For a moment I felt sad.

But I was so very much in love with Andy that even in my dreams I could not see another. Only him.

I could not help liking, though, the tall, soft-spoken red head, valuing his friendship. And so innocently enough, I accepted Red's love, naming it to us and the world friendship. Including him in my singing happiness, he snatching at every crumb of affectionate overflow of a love belonging so completely to the other, to Andy alone.

Then it was almost Christmas.

Andy had come to The Village the night before, to stay for three splendid days and nights, for the best Christmas of our lives, we both agreed.

It had snowed the night before, and the fields and the garden, the roofs and the chimneys wore a graceful touch of white. Quite early in the morning Andy and I had brought up from the cellar a sled, and like The Village children, we had soon been out in the white wonderland, heading toward the Martins' farm, where we picked out a dark-green spruce tree. However, not before we had tried out — just like the children — a couple of hills and spills down into the meadow. Only then had we returned to the house, red-cheeked, tousled. *Tannenbaum*-carrying.

In the afternoon we decorated our tree, whispering and tussling behind the dark-green branches, there in the softly-lit room. When twilight faded into the blue mist of a snowy night, covering The Village with Christmas magic, we felt at last satisfied with our creation, with playing Mr. Santa and Mrs. Chris Kringle.

Our tree stood transformed into a fairy tree. Under its silver-shimmering branches waited small and large packages of all shapes, each carefully wrapped and beribboned. There was even a present for Uncle Max — a silver-wrapped hotdog, which thoughtful Andy had brought all the way across the river for his little feline friend.

The room, the whole house, had filled with that special air of Christmas: with *Lebkuchen* and polished, red-cheeked apples, with pine needles, crackling cedar logs inside the big *kachel* oven, with love and tenderness, with heartfelt wishes for peace on earth.

It was time for me to fling wide open the door to the kitchen, where my parents were so patiently waiting, nearly shouting with joy, "Merry Christmas! Merry Christmas!" But Andy had simply taken my mother's hand, guiding my father by the shoulder into the room and to the tree, their eyes lit with happiness.

"Merry Christmas, my darling," Andy said to me in a curiously mellow voice, giving me a tiny gold-wrapped box out of his shirt pocket, where he had kept it hidden from me all day.

His dark head towering above me, his eyes assuring my father and mother, I tore off the gold foil, and opened the black velvet box that held within it a ring sparkling up at me, shimmering with lights, with a single clear diamond. . . .

It was the most beautiful ring I had ever seen in my life.

As in a dream I felt Andy slipping the ring over my finger. As if from far off I heard him say, "By next Christmas, long before, we will be married. I've never wanted anything more." And suddenly I was in his arms.

My mother was crying, and my father's eyes were suspiciously shiny, feeling so keenly their child's happiness.

For some time we all seemed to have forgotten time, the room, and all the presents still unopened and waiting under the tree, many from Andy to my father and mother. Several were from his family, from his home. The largest box imaginable was filled with home-made preserves, cookies, fruit cake, slivered nuts, mixed nuts, and chocolate-covered nuts, delicacies sent by Andy's mother and Goldy, the Morrell's housekeeper, and according to Andy, his ma number two.

There was also a letter to Andy and me from his father, which Andy read to me later, under the softly flickering lights of the tree's waxen candles.

"It seems," he wrote in it, "getting married will be a problem while you are still a soldier and in uniform, I reckon. No matter. Soon you'll have finished with your time in the army and be free to choose for yourself. We all look eagerly forward to the day when we can meet Lisa at least, wishing and hoping it won't be much longer before we can welcome home both of you into the fold of our family."

There was also a letter from Andy's sister, Ann, the happiest, longest letter she had ever written to us, in which she congratulated us, wishing us happiness in the future, easily relating to us the latest happenings at home.

"Two mares are in foal. Bluebell is ripening fast. Grey Nell will be throwing a foal any day now," Ann wrote in her easy, flowing style.

The birth announcement of Sally's son, Snicker, who was also the offspring of one particular devil called Cinder, left Andy's eyes moist for a while. To me, however, this was all very mystifying until Andy explained to me that Sally was his father's most valuable mare and that Cinder was a neighbor's thoroughbred stallion, both of them belonging very much to the family of horse.

"I knew Sally from the day she was born," Andy

laughed. "I remember her growing into the most beautiful horse on the ranch. Smart as a whip! She is hard to breed, though, refusing outright the first time we tried her." For a moment Andy paused. "She danced and clowned, switching her tail — a teaser if I every saw one. The stallion tried to mount her. He wanted her all right. But she had decided to snap at him, to scorn him with loud, horse snickers."

What did he do? I wanted to know.

Andy grinned at me. "What could he do? For a while it looked as if he wanted to kill her for sure — he was furious, disappointed. It was my father who saved his pride by giving him another, more companionable mare."

His thoughts far away, Andy's face gentled. "Yup, Sally is quite a dame — for a horse! We would never sell her. Just keep her for breeding. And she has done rather well — after she gave up flirting and arguing with every choice male we brought her."

"Poor Sally!" I said with exaggerated sympathy. "She was never allowed to choose her own true love."

"Don't you feel sorry for her, hon! Poor Sally's life isn't dull after all!" Andy had laughed, amused. "Indeed, she managed to become the lady-love of several handsome stallions and the dame of three beautiful, promising little racers."

"You sold all her little ones?"

"Sure. Except the last one. On a ranch like ours you breed horses to sell as fast as possible, not to keep around. Besides, a horse eats a lot — more than you can imagine. You understand?"

Having listened to Andy reading Ann's letter, I realized how very little I knew about horses and life on a ranch. I promised myself to read and to learn as much as I possibly could. And I did. It became a labor of love to me, having long admired horses, since the days of my school vacations, which I spent with my mother's relatives on their farm.

Later, that evening, having listened to Andy reminiscing about his boyhood years, aware already of horses and saddles and whatever else came with it all, I, too, felt memories awakening, bittersweet and matchless as childhood itself. Under the tree and in the friendly light of its candles, I shared them with Andy.

How he enjoyed it all.

The very walls of the old house seemed to ring with his laughter, quickly being joined by my father and mother, and by my own happy peals of mirth.

All that talk about riding horses had reminded me of one such an experience of my own. Only my horse was not a horse but a devilish old goat named, ever so properly, Stinker. Challenged by my three yellow-haired cousins, Fritz, Hans, and Heini, I had actually dared to venture into a certain hut at the farthest end of the garden to mount fierce old Stinker, my Aunt's he-goat, the raven-eyed, Vandyke-bearded sire of all the little goats on the farm and in The Village, riding him in a crazy, wild flight through the garden and over the fence into the farmyard, where he finally dumped me onto the compost heap in an arc of knobby knees and skinny arms. Ah! The wild shouts of my dear cousins and the shrieks of my aunt crying out *"Ach du Lieber Himmel!* And she is supposed to be a girl!"

Old Stinker, however, could never forgive or forget the insult of having been ridden, like an ordinary horse or fool donkey, by a girl — a city girl! I gave up on him, it was enough to look at him respectfully from a safe distance, doing myself a favor, for who with a human nose could stand up close to this goat who smelled worse than a skunk?

How I suffered all through the rest of that summer the

jibes of my three cousins, who called me, "Oh, tamer of wild and dangerous beasts, brave explorer of compost heaps!"

That summer, after having graduated from riding goats, I was trusted to ride home from the fields old Hans, weary and eager to go back to his stall and to a full crib, not taking one erring step, just plodding along in the hot sun. These were my total riding experiences, highly amusing to Andy.

It was late when we finally went to bed. But even so I could not fall asleep for the longest time with my head spinning so, restless with happiness and with exciting thoughts of the future. With this precious ring on my finger, which made me Andy's for all the world to see and to know.

Christmas day, after a wonderful dinner, my parents dressed to leave in the afternoon bus for their annual visit with my Aunt Ernestine, living in the next small town just off the highway right outside the big city.

Aunt Ernestine was my father's oldest brother's widow. She was my favorite aunt. I heartily agreed with my father when he said, "Ernestine is one in a million. God threw away her mold right after she came into this world."

My mother would say in her own simple way, "She is a good woman!"

Ah, yes, I, too, loved her dearly, my Aunt Ernestine. How many times had I stayed overnight in her small, neat house, slept in her blue lavender-scented bedroom with its deep, soft carpet in which one's toes vanished, in her four-posted bed right beside her, falling asleep listening to her reading to me a story out of that leather-bound Märchen Buch's time-yellowed pages, all beginning with, *"Es was einmal . . ."*

My parents wanted us to come along, to have Andy meet the one and only Aunt Ernestine, to have her meet their tall, handsome future son-in-law, of whom they were very proud.

But I had looked at Andy, standing there with his hands in the pockets of his grey flannel trousers, wearing scuffed black leather loafers, an open-collared blue and white civilian shirt — an outfit surely against all regulations. We looked at each other, at the tree so bright with its colored balls, with its silver-haired angels, with its red and gold birds and deer chasing one another all the way up to the glittering top.

I saw the friendly room warm with the crackling fire from the pea-green *Kachel-Ofen,* the worn leather couch, the handwoven oval wine-red rug on the wooden floor.

For one incredible second I thought of Andy's firm, warm mouth on mine, how it felt when we made love, seeing the tiny hollow at the base of his throat alive with the beat of his heart, hearing him call my name, making it sound like a poem coming from deep inside him.

Suddenly we couldn't bear thinking of leaving the house.

We made love to the murmur of snowflakes on the window, the wind whooshing over the rooftop, there on the floor by the fire.

Andy whispered, "I am you, and you are me."

And I replied, "Together we are one."

New Year's Eve we spent differently.

In Ludwigshafen with Andy's French connection, with Marcel and his friends — two handsome Frenchmen in uniform, one dreamy-eyed French artist, a German ski instructor and his wife, a giant Swede named Gustav with the biggest thirst and the gentlest manners, never seeming to get drunk no matter how much he poured down his throat. And Andy and I, neither of us drinking much at all, or so we thought.

Just the same, in the early hours of morning I discovered to my great amazement and to the merriment of the others, that each one resembled characters from the animal kingdom, monkeys in the greater share of attendance. This I found irresistibly funny. When I couldn't stop laughing, Andy decided that I was tipsy.

I agreed.

Marcel insisted on driving us home when the party finally broke up, and soon after we stumbled arm in arm into my kitchen, I unable to find the mysteriously disappeared light switch, having Andy fall over his own feet onto the floor. I tried to find him in the dark to help him up. It was my father who had switched on the light, blinking and gazing out from the doorway of the bedroom, finding both of us spilled like Raggedy Andy and Raggedy Ann on the floor, laughing our heads off for no apparent reason. Uncle Max went into hiding, having been the first witness to our unusual entry into the house and wanting nothing to do with us for once.

Morning greeted us with throbbing melons for heads and poison-green frogs for stomachs, which refused to accept even as much as a swallow of black coffee, and most of the day, Andy looked sallow and droopy-eyed — almost like the Kellers' bloodhound, I thought, a short-lived spark of my usual mischief poking me in the ribs.

I did manage to ask him, "How do you feel, companion in misery?"

He could barely groan back. "Awful. Gosh-dog-darn awful," he croaked. "I think I'm going to die!"

By nightfall my mother had run out of remedies guaranteed to help sad cases such as ours, remedies, handed down from a time when an inspired someone had first discovered how to squeeze grape juice and ferment it.

Chapter 10

WALDHEIM

Whenever Andy received a letter from his family, I found myself included. Several times he received packages. Andy insisted on my opening them while he looked on, telling me he had more fun watching me. Listening to my cries of pleasure at everything I found.

"It's more fun than watching a dozen monkeys wearing wigs and high-buttoned shoes," he would say.

I had not yet forgotten the nothingness, the poverty of the war years. Everything seemed brand-new and wonderful to me. And so, I guess, I could not help showing my pleasure over every little item.

For the first time I tasted popcorn!

I liked it so much, Andy walked all the way to the snack bar to buy more. That evening Andy also insisted on my coming with him into the snack bar to have dinner together. I didn't want to go at first because of the sign out front spelling out in great red letters *Americans only*.

"But you are going to be an American soon!" Andy had argued with me. "You're my girl and soon to be my wife. You look as American as — as that female." He pointed with his chin at a slim, well-dressed young woman just leaving.

I looked down at my coat and dress. At my shoes. My dress had been tailored after a model I had cut out from a page in an American magazine after hearing Andy admiring

133

it, bringing me the almost identical material as that in the picture. I winked at Andy, and we stepped through the doorway, just another couple out for dinner. The chicken tasted great. The banana split Andy bought me for dessert I could not finish, it was so enormous.

With the end of January Andy's company was once again moving on — fortunately for us, just thirty miles out of Mannheim to a town on the Berg Strasse.

Andy had been made first sergeant of supply to the company kitchen and dining room, to his own surprise. This job made him quite independent of the rest of the company. It also came with a jeep for his own use.

"The heavens smile on us, baby doll!" Andy had smiled broadly when he told me the good news. "Someone up there likes us, sugar!" he nearly shouted, hugging me.

At first Andy and I were jubilant, finding he was not too far from The Village. But too soon we discovered it was, after all, farther away than we had thought — and not in miles only. We had gotten used to being together. It seemed unthinkable now to wait for the weekend to see each other for just a few short hours.

It was Andy who found a solution to our troubles. He wasted no time persuading Capt. Miller to hire three girls as help in the kitchen and dining room. Surprised, Capt. Miller admitted this was not a bad idea and meant no added work for him, since Andy had the help picked out already and waiting to start.

There was Karin, a pretty little blonde from Mannheim, soon known to all as Jacky's girl, one of the soldiers who had been with Andy in The Village. The other girl was Sonia, a Polish girl with a serious face and the most beautiful warm brown eyes — a discovery of Red's. The third girl was I.

There were also three cooks in that kitchen, by their own admission, each one a genius of culinary delights.

Sam was the quietest of the three, tall and skinny with the sad eyes of a hound dog, nearly bald, with careful manners and few words.

Bill was just as skinny as Sam, surprisingly so, what with having such a fattening position, but he did carry a slight pot belly underneath his starched white apron. Bill's eyes were almost always reddish with sparse eyelashes so fair they were almost invisible. He was allergic to most anything, sounding like a trumpet whenever he blew his nose, daring anyone in hearing distance to laugh. He also had ulcers, in which no one seemed interested, not even the doctors in Heidelberg at the army hospital, though every few months he tried to convince them of their existence.

Bill's tongue was sharp as a sword matching his fierce temper when goaded. However, like the sky on an April morning, Bill, too, could change his moods in a matter of minutes. When he told us with a sour demeanor the first day we started work that he had finished long ago with the human race, with his wife, with all females in general, I believed him. Until I discovered that under the grouchy shell lived a character truly wise to the ways of the world, aware and honest with his own unpredictable self, with quite a touch of saturnine humor and crackling wit — when he felt it worthwhile to let it show. And I must certainly speak of Bill's admirable passion for reading anything and everything he could lay his hands on. That alone kept my interest in him, since I shared with him the same passion, having little time for it now.

Andy called Bill "the man who knows all." I nicknamed him, to myself only, "the old billy goat," on account of his looking and acting, well, like a billy goat.

Best of all, however, I came to like Jonny, the third of the "cookies," happy, always smiling, easygoing Jonny. Jonny, whose real name was Pedro Salvatore Angelo Ramon Puerta, a long and difficult name someone had shortened to Jonny.

Jonny was short and round, like a butterball, and he was forever ready to boil over with his own kind of infectious humor and often delicious nonsense, to which I took ever so naturally. Jonny was part Indian, part Spanish, but mostly a born clown by his own say so. He had the patience of a saint; however, every once in a while he would become excited or angry with the ways of the world, and he was known to erupt like Vesuvius, forgetting his English, mixing it with his native Spanish in an exotic mish mash of words and expressions. And sometimes Jonny would go on a drinking binge and come back plastered like a coot, cooing like a lovesick pigeon suffering a monster of a headache. Only sometimes, though, usually when someone or something had upset him enough to throw him off course. As one day, after we knew each other better, when he returned to our fold after just such a binge.

A bit tottery, he had passed by me, stopping by the door into the mess hall, then turning back to face me.

"Want to know what I know? I drink too much! I talk too much! And I swear too much!" He pointed a finger at himself. "I am also a bastard!" With that he had walked into his room. Slamming the door before I could say anything. This, too, was Jonny!

Soon the three had become to us girls "the three cookies." The kitchen and the dining room we called "the cooking academy." And Andy was known as "The boss up there." His office was in a glassed-in balcony overlooking the mess hall and part of the kitchen.

There was also a small cozy room behind Andy's office.

It became Andy's room, and soon the two of us found it delightfully perfect in many ways. On the first floor of the building lived and slept the three cookies, near kings in this brownstone castle, serenely removed from the drills and most of the discipline of the soldier's life.

Around feeding time we all had to work hard. At each meal we fed two hundred hungry guys, some easily satisfied, others rather difficult at times, many filled with nonsense, since we were all young and alive and at an age when laughter counted more than tears. When mealtime was over, we often had time for a few such laughs. However, Bill had us all well organized, and he insisted that in his domain all worked, ate, breathed, and lived by clockwork. He had a knack for figuring out anything to the minute. He always knew exactly when it was time to start cooking, when to get the ball rolling, the place jumping!

I soon learned how two hundred hungry soldiers were fed in one hour three times a day; I learned to set the places in no time. I became a whiz at peeling potatoes, unsurpassed by anyone. I had more to eat than in all the years during the war. Now it seemed almost unbelievable that I had ever been hungry, and not so long ago. Almost every day we had two or three soldiers helping with the work in the kitchen. This was called doing K.P. duty. Duty, I was much surprised when I learned these cheerful helpers were but sinners paying off some misdeed by doing this K.P. duty. They didn't seem to complain!

By now I knew many of the men in Andy's company, and they knew I was the big Texan's girl.

But best of all was the sense of belonging I came to know, working with these soldiers, getting to know them with each passing day, soon not thinking of them as strangers at all. I was happy doing my job, and I realized I felt more at home there than I had ever felt in The Village. There I had often felt an outsider, not really belonging. But now the lonely war years in The Village had become unreal to me, as if I had experienced it all in another lifetime.

Ah, it was great to be so awake now, to feel myself growing, almost as if I had sprouted wings.

To our delight Andy and I soon discovered that Red and Sonia had become good friends, often going out together.

Sonia was a quiet, gentle young woman. She, too, had been hurt much by the war. She had lost all her family in the beginning, when Poland was bombed by the German Luftwaffe. Alone and very much afraid, she had accepted the kindly-offered protection and home of a courageous elderly German couple living in Poland at the time. Returning to their birthplace in Bavaria, they took her with them as their alleged relative and nurse risking their own safety, perhaps their lives, giving Sonia a chance to survive the war, hiding her Jewish background.

With the end of the war and after the death of her motherly friend, and the retirement of the old gentleman, fate brought Sonia to Waldheim, and the quiet town had become her home. So very many at the end of the war did not know any longer where on Earth was home: Europe was now a buzzing beehive of displaced human beings. In Germany alone one could find people of every race and color, trying to find a place, trying to find an identity once more.

Sonia was nearly ten years older than I, but I liked her right off, from the moment Red introduced us, when she took my outstretched hand, saying warmly, "So you are Lisa! I've heard so much about you. Red seems to have adopted you somehow!"

With that she had given a quick little grin to Red and a

big smile to me, a smile that suddenly made her face radiant.

How mistakenly I had at first thought Sonia plain. Seeing her smile, she seemed suddenly beautiful, transformed. And one day I found Andy smiling at me slyly, saying, "At least from now on I don't have to share you with our shadow, Red."

Soon every Saturday and Sunday night I became Sonia's star boarder on account of Andy and me finding it impossible to separate when the evening had not yet begun when I had to rush off for home in order to catch the last ferry across the Rhein by eleven sharp. It was not easy to get up again in the early morning at four to be at work in time to prepare breakfast for a whole hungry company. And it was plain torture to be apart nearly every evening throughout the week. Small wonder that I soon began to scheme and plan my campaign to leave The Village. I began to haunt my parents with angry tears and clever talks to let me stay in Waldheim, where Sonia was glad to share with me her small, neat apartment for as long as I wanted to stay.

However, it took the four of us — Andy, Red, Sonia, and myself — to convince my father and mother to let me stay in Waldheim and come home on weekends instead. But, oh, how much easier this was said than done. Truly, I had nothing but disappointment and trouble at first, trying to become a resident of the American Zone. They had already too many people, and daily more arriving — from the Russian Zone, most of them. At times I felt like a fugitive from another country. I was finally granted a stay.

"But only because you have a job and a place to live," I was told. I was convinced I had simply driven the authorities crazy with my insistence and never-ending protests.

Sonia was glad to see me moving in with her at last. She

had never liked living alone, and we both felt certain that we would get along fine.

And we did.

We became friends. But we became truly close friends after one memorable evening when we discovered that we had more to share with each other than just these three rooms in an old house.

We had gone to bed early that night, Sonia in her room and I on the quite comfortable couch in the living room.

As usual, we had left the door open between, and lying there in the dark, we had begun to talk. I remember it was I who began with talking about my family, of the years I had lived in The Village, the years before the war in the city, where I was born.

Slowly Sonia began to talk of her childhood in Poland, of her family, of her memories — so very precious to her, I could tell, just listening to her. She began to speak excitedly, close to tears, when she recalled holidays celebrated in her home. Passover, Pesach, she had called them, realizing that very soon Jewish people were to celebrate once again the Passover Holy Week. She explained what this Passover meant to Jews the world over, talking about the special foods her mother had prepared in honor of the holidays, recalling each dish by its name. And when she spoke of one delicacy — Gefilte fish — it was with a catch in her voice, and I knew this had been her favorite, and I carefully listened to her explaining the preparation of these fish balls, listing all that was needed in my memory.

The following noon, by coincidence, we had fish for supper. Being reminded of Sonia's Gefilte fish, I got the idea of making some myself. I asked Jonny if I could have some raw fish to take home to the apartment. Generous Jonny had filled a brown paper bag, asking no questions.

That evening, with Andy away in Frankfurt with Capt. Miller on a short trip to refuel the giant refrigerators and the storage room, and knowing that Sonia had gone to Mannheim and would not be home 'til much later, I took the opportunity to have my first try at a batch of Gefilte fish.

I cut up and chopped finely the raw fish, bones removed, then I chopped into the fish a peeled raw onion, mixing it all with pepper, salt, paprika, two raw eggs, and some Matzo meal. This last Sonia had but a week earlier rediscovered in a Durchzug Heime für Jüdishe refugees. Glowing with memories, she had brought back a small amount. Like Sonia's mother, I hoped, I formed the dough into small balls, which I dropped into boiling, salted water with the fish head and the skin, a carrot and more onion, letting it all simmer for a couple of hours until the balls were firm and ivory yellow, filling the small apartment with a mouth-watering aroma. I set them to cool, letting them jelly in their own savory juice.

I began waiting for Sonia's step on the stairs, for her key to turn in the lock.

When she came home at last, seeing a big glass jar filled with the small ivory balls standing on the table, and me explaining to her that I had made them for her, that they were Gefilte fish, I hoped like her mother's she had begun to sob, sitting there with her hands wrapped around the jar, almost making me cry along with her. Finally I found a fork and saucer for her so she could taste my creation. Having eaten one ball, she smiled at me with her whole face, praising my success until I felt almost ashamed. Then she suddenly began to giggle. "Only one thing wrong with them," she said, her eyes twinkling at me roguishly. "They're not kosher! However, just this once, I'll overlook

it. On account of the chef having but one pot to cook with."
Deep emotion charging her voice, she said: "Shalom, my
dear friend. Shalom to you and to me." She raised her fork
as if saluting at least a one-star general. "May you live to be
a hundred and twenty!" Her eyes had filled with tears again.
"My mother used to say that. . . ."

Ah, these were certainly the best unkosher Gefilte fish I
ever made in my life. For I did make them again afterward,
many times, and I liked them if just for the memory they
brought back to me of a certain hour's warmth and happiness shared together in Waldheim.

Yes, Sonia and I were good friends now. There was trust
and understanding between us that let us share each other's
emotions, hurt, and pain. I felt I had grown inches, and not
in height alone.

All was well in the small apartment on the second floor
on Göethe Strasse in Waldheim.

Soon enough, though, it was the small room behind
Andy's office over the mess hall, up the stairs by the kitchen
that became heaven and earth.

There I came fully alive. Soon Sonia was not to see me
in the evenings at the apartment, not even at night.

Andy and I together furnished the room with several
items we had found in the back room behind the kitchen
and in the basement. From several bed sheets, which we
dyed a pretty blue, I put together drapes for the one tall
window, finding a passable bedspread for the bed, making it
all look quite cozy and not at all like a soldier's temporary
stay. Andy had helped, especially with the dyeing. The two
of us had made such a mess in the kitchen it took us half the
night to clean up. Even so Bill was looking suspiciously at
the sink, faintly blue, the next morning, saying, "What the
hell? Who in all hell did that and how?"

One morning Capt. Miller together with Lt. Kuhn had come to inspect the kitchens and mess hall. I was in the kitchen at the time, helping Jonny, when they opened the door to Andy's room.

"Why, Sgt. Morrell, you have more domestic talents than a dozen females! Curtains over the window, clean sheets on the bed — flowers even, in a real vase. No dust anywhere!" The captain pushed open the door into the small bathroom. "Why, there isn't even a ring around the tub or a dirty sock in sight." Clucking his tongue, he asked, "Are you hiding a *hausfrau* up here by any chance?" Turning back into the room, he gave a wink to Andy, whose face turned red.

Then he had discovered a pair of my precious nylons hanging over the back of a chair. My bottle of Chanel Number Five, a blue ribbon, and a pair of earrings.

Capt. Miller had picked up my stockings, letting them dangle from his fingers.

"Hm! You're not wearing these are you?"

"No, sir," said Andy. "They are a souvenir, sir."

"And this?" The captain pointed to the flask of perfume.

"A souvenir, sir!"

"Hmm," he grunted, seemingly not convinced with Andy's answers.

A short while later the good captain stood sniffing behind me in the dining room, where I was setting tables.

"Do you smell perfume? Chanel Number Five, perhaps?" he asked Jonny, who stood closest to him.

"No, sir, I don't. It's probably the fish frying in the kitchen," my rascally friend had replied, his innocent face hiding his own thoughts as he looked into my suddenly hot face.

"Must be my sinuses acting up again," mumbled the

captain, stepping around the table and right in front of me. "Must be that time of year again." Suddenly he had looked straight into my eyes. "Well, now which of the girls are you?" His sharp grey eyes scrutinized me most unnervingly.

But I held his probing gaze.

"I am Lisa Forster, sir," I said quietly, though my heart was going faster than a windmill in a storm.

"The girl from The Village across the Rhein?" he asked.

"Yes, sir." Now I did nearly stammer, seeing his eyes light up while he muttered strangely, "Well, well, I'll be darned!"

Most evenings we would go up early to the room.

When others came to call on us, we often did not answer, making them think we were not in.

There was nothing better than being alone together.

We would lie on the bed and talk quietly, read magazines and newspapers out loud to one another, or play such delicious games as Mr. Man and Mrs. Meggs, only now without my striped bikini between us.

We made love. We never tired of each other's body, exploring all our secret places, hungry with love, thirsty for one another's mouth and breath and every part.

Afterward we were hungry, and then we ate giant German pretzels topped with slabs of sweet butter, drank pineapple juice from a big can, a hole punched through the top with a screwdriver. We sat by the window watching the branches of the elm tree switching in the wind. Two young trees entwined at their roots, we laughed at the old giant. Tapping on our window with ghostly fingers.

We heard the three cookies coming back later in the night, but we never envied them their fun. We would just say once more good night to each other, huddling together deliciously close on the single bed with the creaky white iron frame.

Sometimes I would sit up, watching Andy with his eyes closed, his hands folded under his head.

"You like making love to me?"

"Mm."

"Am I good for you?"

"The very best."

"My mother — she believes a girl only does this when married, with her husband. Do you know that this evening alone we've made love twice?" I snuggled up to him.

"You say that again, and I'll make love to you all through the night!"

"You can do that?"

"Shameless, shameless girl!"

"Shall I go away?"

"Don't even move! Mmm. Don't you even move."

"I like making love with you."

For a while we were quiet. Then he murmured, "I wish we could be married already. I want it to be right with us."

"I think of you as my husband. Whenever we make love, *you* are my husband."

He took my hand, the one that wore his ring, and he raised it to his face to look at it for a long moment. His eyes touched the uneven scar running across my fingertip. In great tenderness he pressed it to his lips. "I am your husband, body and soul."

For a while I lay quietly. Then I asked, "Can it be possible? Two people loving each other too much?"

He was smiling now. In the soft light of the moon throwing a path from the window to our bed, I saw his face clearly, his smile both tender and just a bit mischievous. "Maybe too often," he answered me, his voice mellow and with a catch in it, "but never too much."

"What do you think is too often?" I asked, the same catch in my voice.

He did not laugh at my naïve question; he simply answered me directly as he always did. "We two are in a special class, honey."

"What happens if we make love all night long?"

Andy gave one of my ears a little tweak, then whispered into it. "I get skinny as a beanstalk. And you round as a barrel. And one day we are three."

I closed my eyes, sinking back into the pillow. But Andy turned to me, and, opening my eyes again, I found him gazing deeply into mine, searchingly for a long moment. His lips found mine, moving over them sensually. Suddenly I wanted him with a wildness I had never known myself capable of. As he wanted me; I felt him hard and full against me. And we came together, rising on eagle's wings, crying out, soaring over a rainbow spanning paradise. Touching down, slowly, so as not to part.

"I wish this night would never end," I spoke aloud into the quiet of the room afterward, when I could talk again, knowing a peace like no other on earth or in heaven.

"We will have a lifetime together," Andy sighed, his voice a murmur in my ear, his heart beating as loud as mine.

Not always did I ask silly questions up there in our room. Nor was it Andy only who I pestered with questions. Curious about people and places in the world, I would grasp on to anybody I found willing to satisfy my curiosity. Jonny was such a one who seemed not to mind being squeezed dry by me.

"Have you ever seen bananas grow on trees?" I started off innocently enough one afternoon, Jonny and I sitting in the kitchen, in the quiet before the storm—before supper-time.

"At home in Puerto Rico I could reach out the window and practically touch bananas without straining. They are so common there, I never even saw them when I looked at them. After I left home, I never felt like eating bananas, I had too many as a child, I suppose."

"Why did you leave Puerto Rico? It must be a lovely place," I said, fired with interest. "Where did you go after you left home?"

"Well, I wanted to see the world. At least my part of it," Jonny had laughed, self-consciously. "I just left one day. Away from all the banana suppers and banana breakfasts, from the din of my ten brothers and sisters all living crowded together in a two-room shack like sardines in a can." He shook his head, scratching his curly black hair as if he remembered now worse things than bananas. "Whenever my money ran out, I would take a job for a while, any kind of a job. Always taking off again for another place, another part of America."

"Did you ever get to Texas, where Andy lives?"

"No, I never made it to Texas. I did see, though, the southern and western states."

"Will you tell me about the United States of America? Anything!" I begged, my eyes glued to his face.

And Jonny began to talk. I, sitting across from him, leaning toward him, silent, afraid he would stop talking if I moved. It was nearly time to start preparing supper when he stopped.

"How I would like to travel, see places, like you did," I told him, wistfully. "Ah, I know already I'll be happy there, in the United States of America. Andy and I will have a great big family of little Americans, all our own!"

147

He looked pleased, then thoughtful. He cleared his throat.

"It wasn't always fun. . . . I remember times when I wished I'd never left home, was back in the noisy, crowded cabin. Especially that year in Mississippi. . . ."

"What happened in Miss-is-sippy?" I urged him on, for he had stopped himself abruptly, looking out the window, then back at me again, his eyes black and bottomless. When he spoke again it was in a tone strangely emotionless. "I was thrown into jail there — for bloodying a man's nose."

"He must've had it coming, you doing that," I said, remembering Jonny's good nature, his patience, his great sense of humor, which certainly overshadowed any other character traits, as far as I knew.

"I gave him a bloody nose for calling me a goddamn yellow nigger when I sat down behind him on a bus. Too far up front, he called it, after he and his buddies had thrown me off the bus and beaten me so I couldn't spit straight for a month, my mouth was so swollen."

"But why should you not have sat down behind him? Or anywhere in that bus?" I wanted to know, much perturbed by Jonny's story.

"Why, you want to know? Because I'm dark. A black. That's why!"

"I don't understand. Many people are dark! Not white —"

"That's what I mean," he spat out. "And that wasn't the only time I was shown I wasn't white enough or black enough, depending on who looked at me." He gave a laugh that was far from merry.

For a long moment we sat in silence; then I spoke once more, greatly disturbed by Jonny's answer.

"But you are an American! You were an American citizen, were you not, and living in the United States of America? What are you saying? Are not all Americans living in the United States Americans?"

"I can't explain that to you. . . ."

"Why not? Why ever not? I want to know!"

"I cannot —"

"Please, Jonny!"

"I better not."

But then he began after all. "Because . . ." And it came out of him like a spring flood. Like a tidal wave, all dams down. I sat and listened. I heard but when he had finished, I still wasn't sure why this was so in the country I admired so.

Jonny did not say another word. He clasped and unclasped his hands, lost in his own kind of pain. I asked no more, and we sat there in this loud silence until the big old-fashioned clock in the dining room proclaimed it was time for us to get up and go about fixing supper. Reminding Jonny that it was time for him to get busy lighting the stoves, time for me to set the tables, slice bread, help with vegetables, and wash the lettuce — seeing Sam and Bill coming in from the yard.

Soon things began cooking again, as every day around this time. For a while my hands were busy indeed. My hands. My mind was free to roam.

Chapter 11

And so the days passed, and the nights. Each much too fast, each different and wonderful, revealing, teaching me lessons.

There was one lesson that began so seemingly funny, so harmlessly silly, at first.

That morning I could have sworn with my first step into the kitchen that Sam, our second-in-command cook, had mysteriously acquired overnight two left hands, while he looked as if he had never felt lower. Then his trouble really started when he dropped a dozen eggs onto the tiles of the kitchen floor, his big feet slipping and sliding in the mess until he ended up on his bottom and in it.

That very moment Jonny happened to enter the kitchen. Forgetting Sam's bad humor of the morning, seeing him sitting there in that oversized omelet like a bewildered cockroach, he cried out in simulated horror, "No! No! No! That is not how it's done! Only the yolks go into the hair — to achieve any result. Then you rub it in well, rinse, and — voila — you have given yourself an egg shampoo!"

"Why don't you shut your mouth, you screwball!" The usually soft-spoken Sam had crawled back up from the floor, picking himself out of the raw egg puddle, marching through the open door to his room, dripping yellow goo, leaving us girls standing there, surprised. This was the first time we had heard him swear.

It was Karin who cleaned up after him. Sonia went to make ready the dining room, and I began slicing bread for our breakfast guests, soon to come storming or tripping into the building. But our thoughts were still on Sam.

"Why is Sam so grumpy?" Karin asking Jonny, taking the question out of my mouth.

"Well, it's rather complicated and kind of silly, come to think about it," Jonny began, scratching his cheek and raising his eyebrows up to his hairline, a trick only he could do. "It's stupid, kind of," he snickered, letting down his eyebrows again. "He's been like that since last night. Because of a girl we met at the club. She looked like real wow-wow stuff — know what I mean? Sam was sure he had it made with her, all the way." Jonny gave another snicker. "But then wavy-haired Mezano came through the door, flashing all his teeth, rolling his eyes at her. She left balding Sam standing there and took off with Mezano, just like that!" Jonny snapped his fingers. "She took off with that sidewinder show-off! Sam was furious. He kept saying he knew why she left, he swears he heard Mezano telling her she couldn't be serious about taking up with a Yid, a Kike!

"I argued with him half the night to forget it. The hell with the two of them. They found each other. But he got angry with me when I asked him if he enjoyed suffering every bum's urge and quirk. Then he started to drink like a fish, getting into an uglier mood. I thought I could get him away from his down feelings, make him laugh. I guess I said the wrong thing when I told him, 'It's all because Mezano has a headful of hair.' You know how he feels about his dome!" Jonny shrugged in comic exasperation.

Yes, we all knew of Sam's touchiness when it came to his prematurely balding head. For a moment I could not help giggling with the others. We all knew Sam's secret, his efforts to restore his hair to its former, rippling glory. Someday. Surely one day. His sudden trips to the PX, the local shops, where he would buy anything, everything available showing promise to hold his receding hairline. He had left but a ringlet of dark fuzz, plus about three or four very long strands of hair carefully arranged over his shiny billiard ball pate. Yes, indeed. We all had our problems.

I went back to my job, cutting up loaves of beautiful white American bread, by the wide-open window in the kitchen, watching two small children and a raggedy old woman picking the barrels in the yard for scraps of food.

Just then, of all the guys hungry at this time of the morning, I saw Crawinsky coming around the corner, carrying his cap in his hand, letting the wind blow through his long, thinning hair. He saw the old woman and the two children hanging over the barrels filled with the scraps of last night's supper. Instantly he stopped, his face taking on a livid color. His arm lifted, and with his cap, he gave a mighty whack to the hollow iron gaslight lantern standing there from another age, making it ring as if struck by metal. Then he began shouting as if a demon had taken possession of him. "That is for our pigs! The ones that go 'oink oink'! Not for goddamn kraut pigs. Eat your own garbage. Eat shit, for all I care!"

The old woman and the two children ran from the yard, terrified. Crawinsky, as if suddenly snapping out of a trance, put on his cap, stuffing his hands into his trouser pockets, and walked into the building as if nothing had happened.

For a blinding moment I felt hot under my skin. I felt like shouting, "Go to hell yourself, you bastard!" But a second later Crawinsky walked by the open door, sticking his head through it, shouting cheerfully, "Hi, you kids! Whatever smells so good in this here joint? Whatever it's called, I'll have a lot of it. I'm starved!"

I never turned around. I just slashed away at the defenseless loaves of bread, piling up more than was needed, in my anger slicing twice as fast as usual.

Goddamn krauts, he had called them. The poor woman and her little hungry children.

I, too, am a kraut, I thought bitterly, I am a kraut. Sam is a kike. There are lymies. And greasers. And wops. And, and —

No. No! I won't give in. Then, instead of anger, I felt a profound sense of sadness. I became aware of a little voice of reason within me. Persisting. I heard and I listened.

I thought of what Bill had told me about the hard-faced, feverish-eyed Sgt. Crawinsky. He had lost his family in a ghetto near Warsaw, killed by Hitler's efficient monsters. He saw his younger brother ripped to shreds by German grenades in the Battle of the Bulge. That should be enough to explain him.

I thought of Sonia, of my friends from my childhood, of Dr. Ostermann, of Crawinsky. So much suffering, so much pain. I had seen pictures of concentration camps, after the war was over. How does it feel to carry a mountain? To live under a mountain for the rest of one's life? How did this happen? How could this have happened in this country I called Heimatland? Where I was born. Where generation after generation of my family had lived and died and loved and hoped.

I remember discussing with Bill what made me feel ashamed for my country, ashamed deep into my soul.

Wistfully Bill had looked at me. "You did not know. You were too young. Too young to understand, to have had a part in it."

Tears burned in my eyes, sudden terror leaping into my soul. "My father and my mother. They did not know until it was over. Too late." Filled with anguish, I looked straight into Bill's eyes.

But Bill had chosen not to answer me, he had shrugged and looked out the window instead, blowing his nose. Hiding his face behind his olive-green army-issued handkerchief as if he was embarrassed. And I had known, like a dark omen, that this was what the world must think, now and in all the time to come. A time as long as eternity.

It was still morning when the sun had broken victoriously through a bank of clouds trying to hold back the light of day, when I swept up the bread crumbs fallen to the floor with my slicing and philosophizing, when I saw the tiny Star of David winking at me from a dark corner of the floor. I knew right off it belonged to Sam. I had seen it many times dangling from his watch bracelet.

In a quiet moment I returned it to him.

Sam took it quickly, mumbling a short, rough, "Thanks."

Hours later, the kitchen quiet once more and the dining room empty, I found him standing beside me in front of the deep window in the dining room, talking fast in his shyness. "My mother gave it to me — the Star, I mean — when I left, going into the army. I wore it through the invasion, through Normandy, my good-luck piece."

He paused for a moment. "My mother — God rest her soul — died last year. I would have felt very bad, losing it."

"I am so glad I found it for you." I turned to him, touching his arm. "You never talk about yourself."

For a moment he looked at me vaguely. Then his eyes became distant, veiled. "What is there to tell?" he said. "Not much."

"You were born in New York City. You have no family. I know you are thirty-six years old. You collect stamps and coins, and you like dogs. You read the newspaper printed in New York City." I looked at him kind of sheepishly. "You bite your nails when you are nervous."

"There isn't much more, I'm afraid." He smiled back at me. Then he looked serious once again. "Anyway, I never got away much, just around New York State, before I entered the army, that is." He shrugged, not sure he should go on. Then his eyes filled with memories and he began to speak, gradually forgetting his shyness. "I went to work. I worked hard long hours after my father died unexpectedly. My mother was not well afterwards, convinced that now she had only me left. From that time on, I recall, she lived in constant fear of losing me, too. She invented all kinds of pains and aches for herself, to keep me at home. In the hospital the doctors could not find anything wrong with her; they thought her in good shape for her age. I grew angry inwardly. You know what I'm saying? I wanted to do things, go out, like other guys my age. Have a life of my own. I wanted to go to California, where I knew this girl I liked. She had moved there with her family."

He looked at me as if he expected an answer. I had none.

"The war came. I enlisted. One day I went and enlisted."

"As many others did, I'm sure," I said.

He gave a sigh. "You know, I never told all this to anyone." He turned to me once more. "The girl, her name is Ruth — she gave me the gold chain. My mother gave me the star."

"I am so glad it didn't get lost," I said softly, moved by the trust in his voice.

"Thanks again for finding it," Sam said, smiling, and for the first time his eyes looked fully into mine.

Most of that afternoon I was filled with thoughts. With

the memory of another such Star of David. One I remembered from years ago around the neck of a slim, dark-haired boy. . . .

I thought of Ilse and Franz, my childhood friends, and I wished I could know if they were alive, where they were now. . . .

It was on the evening of my eighteenth birthday when I was reminded once more of the small gold star twinkling again from Sam's wrist.

Thoughtful, dear Sonia had planned for us a party, inviting our friends from the kitchen and others to come to our apartment to celebrate my and Andy's birthday. Andy was twenty-five now.

In our tiny kitchen, away from all the others, Sam put into my hand a thin gold chain attached to a small cross. "Happy Birthday Lisa." I looked at the small cross in my hand, feeling dampness welling up into my eyes, aware this was a very carefully selected gift. I still have the small cross. I'll keep it to remind me how wonderful it feels when understanding, awareness of another's happiness finds room in our hearts.

Our birthday party!

Jonny had baked for us a great big white and red and blue birthday cake the evening before, after he had so shrewdly convinced us to go and see this terrific movie playing in Mannheim, which turned out to be a silly flop.

Before we left for our party Andy — with a warm, wonderful smile — had given me a great bunch of wildflowers he'd gathered behind the building in the field. I loved the uneven stalks of flowers — almost as much as the stunningly beautiful dress he had tucked into a large box topped with a giant bow. The bow, I could tell, his own labor of love.

The dress — pale tea-rose yellow it was with the barest touch of lace around its deep square collar and tiny puffed-up sleeves. Elegant in every way, it fit perfectly, made after my exact measurements, which Andy knew to an inch.

I had to try it on immediately, up there in our room. Leaning against the closed door with his arms folded across his chest, Andy stood watching me with shining eyes, listening to my happy squeals of excitement before the tall mirror.

"You darling, you," I cried out to him more than once, dancing around the room, making the skirt of my dress stand out around me like a bell. "How did you know my size, my best color, and every little thing?"

He didn't answer me right away. Then, when he did, he mumbled, "Pinch me. Go ahead and pinch me."

"Pinch you?" I had stopped abruptly my spinning around the room. I went and kissed him instead; tenderly and lovingly and full on the mouth. To have him grasp me. Squeezing me to his tall frame, pressing his face into my flying hair, mumbling, "I love you, love you, love you." Lifting me up with his hands around my waist, looking straight into my eyes. "If I had one wish, I would be holding you like this wishing us home with my family." He gave a sigh. "I can't seem to wait." He put me down, not letting go. "I want to take you home, to my home in Texas, to my father and mother, to Goldy, to everyone I know. Then I would show you Dallas, New York City, take you shopping there, buying you anything you like just to hear you laugh. We'd walk down Fifth Avenue, buying more pretty things. Then we go on to Boston, to Philadelphia, to Washington, back to Dallas."

He was taking me on an imaginary tour through his country, all the way to the Mexican border, where we wore giant straw hats and ate hot tortillas. It was a breathtaking trip.

We almost forgot to go to our own party, just down good old Göethe Strasse. We finally did go, and it was a great party, all agreed.

But best of all was our sneaking out of the apartment when the party was still in full swing. Our walk through the empty night-time streets, through the park, where we danced a waltz around the fountain to music only we could hear.

How quiet it seemed in the red stone building, so noisy and bustling in the daytime, when we pushed open the door.

The room still held the faint fragrance of my flowers, which I could just make out in the stout round vase on the table in the path of a trickle of moonlight, the rest of the room veiled in night.

We did not switch on the light, not just yet. Andy turned to me instead, reaching for me. Putting his face close to mine. "Happy birthday, my darling."

I said back, "Happy birthday." But then I could only go on whispering, for my heart was beating in my throat. "Thank you for loving me . . ."

He uttered a broken-off sound. For a moment I felt his cheekbone roughly against my face. "Lisa, Lisa, you cannot know how much I want to take care of you. Always."

Now he reached for the switch to the lamp, filling the room with soft ivory light, giving shape to us and our surroundings. In front of the mirror he helped me open the long zipper at the back of my dress. Gently, gently he lifted it over my head, to drop it on a chair near by.

I looked up. To see him standing behind me in the glass so tall and so very handsome, looking over my head into the mirror. I watched him, fascinated, his long, elegant fingers playing with the straps of my brassiere, sliding them off my shoulders, taking away at last the piece of satin. Taking away all the rest hiding me. Dropping all to crumple around my feet, holding me against him, his chin on my shoulder.

"When I first set eyes on you, that day, coming through The Village, I saw a very pretty girl. Now you are lovely. So very lovely." His voice came low and smoky, his lips brushing my throat alive and warm. "I never again want to be without you."

We both stood looking into the mirror, seeing a picture so right inside it. I looked up into his dark blue eyes, looking, too, at the girl in the glass — different indeed now from the thin adolescent of only one short year ago. His eyes were dark with emotion, then with passion, sudden and uncontrollable, touching me, possessing me, consuming me.

Chapter 12

Then once again it was spring; for me a spring like no other in its splendor. Each day we fell anew in love, each time as deeply and completely as the first time.

I was so unbearably happy, I laughed and giggled aloud even in my sleep. Then I would open my eyes to find Andy bending over me, curious to know what I was dreaming about.

"I dream of you!" I would tell him. "I dream you're making love to me." I wrapped my arms around his neck, pulling him down to me.

"Dreamer," he whispered back, his mouth finding mine in the dark, letting himself fall into the pillow again with a groan, both of us going back to sleep with smiles on our faces.

Then one day, we discovered we were not the only ones in love.

Jonny, dear Jonny, had fallen in love — madly — it seemed.

Every evening he vanished into the flower shop at the corner down the street, to talk, to stand and gaze at the slim, brown-eyed girl behind the counter.

She did not understand a word he was saying. He had given up on language after one infamous attempt when he tried out his astonishing kind of German on the wrong girl, who had promptly slapped his face when he said to her sweetly something quite improper.

Jonny and the flower shop girl had at least one thing in

common: a passion for flowers, which she sold to him eagerly, he buying just as eagerly.

Through these flowers they evidently spoke to each other in a delightful language, or so it seemed to us.

Every night he came back with a new armload of flora. "I'm just wild about roses and tulips and what-do-you-call-them-all." Every evening he went — until that one night he returned without his usual armful of scented beauties and much earlier than usual.

"She is married and has two children," he answered our questioning looks and raised eyebrows, throwing himself into a chair, looking disgusted and just a little helpless.

"Her enormous husband came into the shop tonight, trailed by their two kids and this horse of a dog. I took one look at the husband and his dog, and I thought it smart not to wait around for my change for the roses I had picked out already and paid for. *Madre de Dios!*"

Jonny was holding his head, and we could only look at each other until he burst out laughing at himself, slapping his knees with both hands. Then, we all hollered with him. Good natured Jonny invited us to come along with him to the club to help him drown with the rest of his money all thoughts of flowers and flower girls, husbands and giant dogs.

Jonny went to the club by himself, his nose pointed downtown toward forgetfulness, away from the cruel world and all her disappointments.

When he returned some hours later, he had a hard time finding the keyhole — after he had finally found the door. Only then the whole darn building decided to evade him, not letting him enter even though he had a key. It was so frustrating, Andy had to go down and show him in, guiding him like a big brother to his room and to his bed, to oblivion.

It was but one week later, when Jonny was in love once again, for a while, and even more dramatically than the first time.

She stood nearly two heads taller than Jonny and was even rounder than he, with a flowing abundance of finger-curls of honey-blond hair. She also had a pair of mildly bulbous blue eyes and a double chin in an eternally smiling face. Her name was appropriately Brunhilde, and soon enough she became simply Jonny's "Walcúre" to all of us. We were deeply interested in following the astonishing conquest of our little friend, especially Bill, who wanted to know if Jonny had a hard time embracing the enormous "Walcüre" with only one pair of short arms.

Jonny looked at him owlishly, then said, with great dignity, "We only play Ping-Pong! She is a great Ping-Pong player."

"Yah! I bet!" Bill grunted back. "Son, I would give a lot to watch your kind of Ping-Pong game! I might even learn a thing or two from you!"

I played deaf, trying hard to keep my eyes blank, making believe soldier slang was incomprehensible to me.

It was a fact, though, that Jonny and Brunhilde did play many a game of Ping-Pong in the Red Cross station and in the club in downtown Waldheim. For nearly a month they could be seen bouncing merrily around the felt-covered table.

Then, one day, Brunhilde found another playmate, giving no explanation to Jonny. It took him a while to get over it, to recover his old spirit, his so-what attitude. He made it, though, and that's what counted, his heart tucked away inside his sturdy chest, concentrating once more on his cooking pots, much to the relief of the company. His meals tasted normal again, now that he had given up on love. Even Bill's ulcers had a chance to quiet down.

Yes, indeed, it was once again spring!

Along the Bergstrasse the fruit trees seemed to explode with blossoms. The air was soft and scented with a million flowers. There were days when I felt like rolling in the green, green grass like a young colt, or flying away with the clouds over the gently rolling hills on magic wings.

Early one morning we wandered up to a sun-dappled, buttercup-sprinkled meadow, to sit close together under a flowering apple tree, our eyes roaming the valley below. The doll-sized sleepy town. The river, like liquid, flowing silver in the shimmering distance.

"Ah, it's great to be alive, to be in love!" Andy had cried out, giving voice to my own emotions, folding me into his arms, hugging me as close as possible. I took his hand in mine, holding it against my cheek.

Caught in a kind of wonder, I whispered, "It's as if all is brand-new. Just created. The sky, the earth. Even the wind. Can you feel it? And you and I . . ."

He kissed my cheek in silent agreement. As if in a dream I went on, "As a child I believed I could see the face of God in the wandering clouds, did I look long enough. I saw him as a kindly old man with flowing white hair and beard. How very innocent and uncomplicated everything is to a child."

Andy was playing with a strand of my hair, twisting it around one finger, releasing it again. Quietly he answered, "I would have liked to know you then. I would have loved you even then."

I leaned back into his arm, feeling his cheek warm against mine, aware of the sun covering us in a veil of spun gold.

"Do you believe in God?" I whispered.

"He is watching over us right now. He is smiling, because we love one another so much," he whispered back.

For a while I kept quiet.

Then, thinking out loud, I began recalling to Andy the summers, the school vacations, I had spent in the Bavarian Alps with my father's brother, his sister, and her family, all devoted Catholics. On Sunday mornings, the mist still hiding the valley below, making invisible the mountains, we all went to the church in the valley some miles from their Hof, a half-hour by horse and wagon.

My aunt tried her best to teach me enough religion to last through the rest of the year until I came back again. "To save you from the heathenish thinking of your father," she called it, mouthing words after her brother, my righteous Uncle Johannes.

However, the following summer — the one after my stay in the Bavarian Alps — I would spend with my mother's relatives in the Black Forest. And there I was Protestant.

I was a happy child in those years. I loved being on the farm, the mountains, the fields, and the forest, all the many animals to touch and to love. And so I was one summer Catholic and the next summer Protestant, then Catholic, then Protestant. But in the winter and fall, in the spring when I was at home, I wondered about it all. I would listen to my mother say a little prayer at night before she went to bed, and in the morning when she got up. And I would listen to my father, who went to church only for weddings and funerals, and then only out of respect for someone or to make my mother happy, and so, at one time, it occurred to me that it did not matter much if I was one or the other. The gentle old man up there in the clouds did not seem to mind.

Yes, I rather listened more to my father, I suppose.

My father. He who seemingly had no quarrel with either church or science. To him I listened with my heart and mind. We tramped together through fields and woods, climbed mountains, he talking and teaching, I listening, learning, recognizing in each seed a flower, silver in a raindrop. Becoming aware, because of him, learning to reason for myself.

One day, putting his hand on my shoulder, halting my eager proclamation to him, "Now I know it all!" he answered me with a sigh and "We never know it all."

My father. My wonderful, wise father.

Andy listened closely to my every word, his eyes never leaving my face until I had finished recalling.

On our way down from the meadow I discovered in a grove of trees a small group of Gypsy wagons.

Delighted and instantly curious, I persuaded Andy to go a bit closer, to have a look at the wagons. I had not seen gypsies since before the war, when their women used to come to our house selling shoelaces and ribbons, doing a bit of fortune-telling to the housewives in the neighborhood.

We found an old woman sitting on the stoop of one of the three wagons. Several uncombed, tattered-looking children were playing catch farther down in the road. Four mildew-hided, almost deplorable-looking horses were tethered near the shabby wagons. The war had visibly followed these Gypsies. I almost jumped back when the old crone unexpectedly took hold of my sleeve, rasping that she would read our fortunes, if we would let her.

Wondering, I looked at Andy's face. He grinned at me, encouraging me with a little push. "Why not? Go ahead!"

A bit uncertain, I stepped forward and put my hand into hers. For a long while she said nothing, not a word. Then she looked up right into my eyes and said, "Your lifeline is long and strong. You have many years. Many children. From here your road begins. Leads on to far away. Across much water. Deep water. Your line of happiness is broad, from within, strong. There are sorrow and tears, too. Deep sadness. Deep loss." She gave back my hand. "Be strong. You can be."

"I could have told you that! Except for that last bit about tears and sadness. That she made up to make it all more mysterious, to worry you a little," Andy said into my ear, his voice filled with laughter.

"Now you, tall one!" The old Gypsy woman reached without asking for Andy's hand.

Smiling, shrugging like an impertinent little boy who did not really believe in such silly stuff, he let her take his hand. "Go ahead and have a look, old woman!" He laughed, winking at me while he said it.

She didn't answer him. She never looked up. She just kept gazing intently at his palm, her bony finger tracing a line there. After what seemed a long while, she croaked, "Love. So much love, given and taken. I see —" Suddenly she closed his fingers over his palm and dropped his hand. Her eyes looked straight ahead. "The end is but the beginning." She stopped her mumbling, sitting there now with her eyes closed, as if she was very tired, too weary to go on.

"What does that mean, old one?" Andy wanted to know, a bit uneasy-sounding. "Explain to me. I was never good at understanding hokus-pokus!"

She wouldn't answer him.

"Is there more, then?" he insisted, needing to know now. He sounded like a large, puzzled child, one who did believe just a little after all.

Andy gave her all his cigarettes from his shirt pocket, a roll of Life Savers from another. All quite satisfactory with her, evidently, for she quickly grasped it all from him, making it vanish into the front of her dress. She got up, amazingly agile for her apparent great age, leaving us standing there by ourselves.

It was almost noon when Andy and I came back into the busy kitchen, I with my arms full of white and yellow daisies, Andy with his eyes sparkling like a lake on a lazy summer afternoon.

First off I came across Jonny, singing loudly from inside a cloud of smoke, unperturbed, happy, off-key, swinging a greasy ladle. When I asked him if he liked my flowers, he gave me a wide, impish grin, flicking his eyes comically up to the ceiling, "Nina, Nina," — the pet name he had given me — "I do not only like your flowers, I downright envy them!" He put his hand over his heart. "Ah! To be plucked and carried off by those hands!"

Ah, today he was in a truly romantic mood. I grinned back. Looking at him as if astonished, I said, "What poetry hides behind this man's greasy apron! One would never know by looking at him!" I threw him with one hand a kiss and with my other a flower. My eyes were dancing, and all because of my good friend Jonny. "My brother in spirit," Andy called him, ever since we had first shown our outstanding ability to create mischief of all kinds around the kitchen.

Another incident occurred that same day.

Late that afternoon, Andy had found a nest of tiny newborn mice behind a pile of discarded boxes in the storeroom. Bill and I heard him calling. Running, we came to aid him for whatever was wrong, finding him kneeling over the tiny nest, charmed by the small mouse-mother sitting inside it, surrounded by her still-blind, nearly nude mouse-children, looking up at him with her mustaches quivering.

She was all white, the first white mouse I had ever seen. With the courage befitting a lioness, she never left her young. Brave to the heart, she stayed, protecting them with her own trembling body. I admired the gallant little mother. Thoughtful Andy opened a box of K-rations for a piece of cheese to give to her with our respect. But Bill, who called us all crazy as hoot owls, was all for drowning the mother and her offspring immediately, putting an end to this silly comedy.

Jonny came into the storeroom, just when Andy was proclaiming, with a twinkle in his eyes, "Never yet have I drowned a mother and her helpless children, mice or otherwise. I vote to let them live."

Immediately Jonny, who was superstitious and an expert on folklore, came to the rescue. "A white mouse means good luck. You can't drown your good luck, bring down upon your head the revenge of every mouse dead or alive. Listen," he went on, "I know what we can do. I'll give them to the boy who shines my shoes when he comes tomorrow. He's a kind sort of kid. Anyhow, he already has a pair of hamsters and a trained woodchuck at home. I've seen them myself. He won't mind taking the mice, I'm sure."

However, our plan never worked out. When we came to look for the little family, the mouse-mother had carried off her children to a safer place, and the nest was empty.

Chapter 13

"I open her up all the way, the bitch," Jonny said, "but only a squirt of cold water comes a pissen into the tub, coughing and farting away as if her last hour was here. It makes me so doggone mad, I want to spit, I swear!" Angry, he yanked open the top button of his shirt, a perplexed frown creasing his forehead, unaware of my being there in the corner of the dining room, folding towels.

Sam, having listened thoughtfully, suggested that maybe the hot water was used up around this time of the day, and he advised the bewildered Jonny to take his bath later on in the evening, when the water had heated up again. But Bill had shrugged at Jonny in apparent impatience, mumbling something that sounded like "Aw, hell, I always find hot water. Who knows what you're doing wrong!"

The two had left poor Jonny before he could tell them that the hot water did come on all right and very soon after, when he tried a second time and kicked the pipes good and hard with his bare feet until his toes hurt, all the while swearing, begging the rusty bitch to give already.

Dear bedeviled Jonny. How could he know that I was the culprit, the one who had caused him all the trouble? Ever since I had discovered by chance the key to shut off the hot water to the bathroom with one twist of my wrist.

Seeing my friend Jonny strutting down the hall for his well-deserved bath, I turned the key, shutting off the hot water, running the cold only.

I confess this was wicked indeed, as bad as the tricks

169

Jonny had played on me thus far. But, oh, how he tempted me into being wicked just one more time, while I promised myself, "Just one more time, then I'll stop." Seeing Jonny come by wrapped in his beach coat, looking fetching, were I a turtle.

"This is truly the last time I do this thing to him. Cross my heart," I told my little Lucifer inside me, unaware that this truly was to be the last time.

Holding back a hiccough and a laugh, hard at work turning the key, I waited for Jonny's shout. However, as happens in so many well-planned schemes of mice and men, the greasy key slipped from my hand and rolled away to crash into the wall, giving me away.

I was on all fours, the corpus delicti in my hand, when Jonny charged into the kitchen, wearing his beach coat, his hair straight up, stiff, and wiry.

"Ay de mi!"

He had caught me, the evidence of my crime in my hands, the devil of mischief in my eyes. Quickly he put two and two together. Then, looking a bit like old Bacchus, he began jumping up and down, shouting to the ceiling, "Why, oh why did I get saddled with this evil one? *Madre de Dios!* She is driving me crazy. Loco!"

Jonny slid into his native Spanish. I listened, speechless. Then I, too, became carried away by the sight of him, lamenting, wailing in Spanish, then in English.

I laughed, and I couldn't stop.

Jonny ogled me as if I were a Martian ready to sprout wings and a tail, mumbling, *"Caramba, caramba, caramba!"*

Come evening, I thought I would never live down the ribbing I got when our work was over and we all sat down together — Sam, Bill, Jonny, Andy, Red, Sonia, and I —

around our table in the dining room, playing cards and cracking jokes.

"You fixed the pipes in a certain bathroom, I heard," Red greeted me before I could sit down. He grinned widely, as all the rest. Jonny made me believe he was not over his anger yet, ominously saying to the ceiling, "Revenge will be sweet! Just wait and see!"

They clucked their tongues at Jonny. "You never smelled better!" And so it went, even the next day. Then Andy came up with a new kind of entertainment — one that had to do with my American education.

This is how it started.

"Don't tell me you're interested in that!" Bill had said, taking out of my hand a book on American history Andy had brought back for me from the American Red Cross mobile library.

"You bet she's interested! She started out reading children's books, and already she's reading American History books," Andy answered for me. Our comfortable corner in the dining room had become a classroom for one, I the single pupil and a bunch of assorted qualified and unqualified teachers after Andy had bragged, in a true Texan fashion, that "now I could answer anything on American history."

I tried to deny this on the spot, but without success. They had decided to grill me, and grill me they did!

"Who was Washington?" Jonny began before I could disappear off my chair, worried about just how much or how little I could answer correctly.

"He was the first president of the United States of America." I said. Surrounded by a ring of approving faces, I went on, encouraged, "He never smiled because of his wooden teeth. He never lied. And he liked more than anything to have himself rowed across the Potomac River, kneeling up front in the boat." As I explained about President Washington, I was drowned out by a round of full-throated laughter.

"Who was Thomas Jefferson?" another voice asked, not giving me time to wonder about what I had just said.

Suddenly my little inner devil took hold of me, overpowering my good intentions effortlessly. And so it was he who answered for me.

"Thomas Jefferson? Let's see. He was the one who thought four cents an acre was enough to pay Napoleon for everything between the Mis-sis-si-pi — how is that pronounced? — and the Rocky Mountains!" Approving grunts came from Bill and Red, and "Is that so?" from Jonny, followed instantly by thunderous laughter — upon Jonny's head! My devil meanwhile was sharpening his tongue. He loved laughter.

"Sam Houston. Let's see. Who was Sam Houston?" I began, trusting my devil. "Oh, yes! He was the adopted son of a Cherokee Indian chief who gave him the name Raven. Houston fought at the Alamo. By the time of his death he was known as the noblest Texan of all!"

"Well, it's a bit short, with a few facts missing here and there," Andy said from my right. "Tell us about the Alamo now, remember? Davy Crockett, Santa Ana, Jim Bowie, and all the others," he hinted anxiously wanting to prove to them all that I truly remembered our lessons.

I opened my mouth to tell them all I knew about the Alamo, wanting to please Andy, only to find that my little devil didn't let me give a straight answer, making me look into Andy's face and say, "The Alamo is also known as the Plymouth Rock, a tiny fort built upon a small island on the coast of New England, where Columbus landed for the first time with his merry band of Pilgrims. Where Drake —"

"Stop it! Stop it right there — before Columbus sails right by, never discovering a new continent!" Andy had to shout to make himself heard above all the laughter and cat calls. I stopped immediately, having a heck of a time trying to look innocent. Anyhow, my testing in American history was over and done with, at least for now.

Smiling outright, a rare phenomenon indeed, Bill handed me back my book saying, "Here. Take it and study some more. It might prove worthwhile one day. There's nothing like history!" And then he surprised me by putting his hand on my shoulder and squeezing it lightly. I know that Bill seldom touched anyone, that he shunned most all physical contact. He said, "I wouldn't be surprised if you came across several of your German landsmen who became good Americans in the course of history."

From then on I liked Bill immensely.

Jonny had been my friend from the beginning, my partner in mischief, my brother in spirit. He was the most uncomplicated soul. Easy to get along with. He did have his moments, though, as on that fine morning when he felt it was time to repay me for the cold shower he'd had to suffer when I shut of his hot water.

One morning he asked me sweetly if I would please climb the ladder in the storeroom to the cupboards where the napkins and paper towels were kept. Glad to be of help, I climbed the ladder up to the oversized cupboards under the ceiling. All was neatly stocked way in the back. I had to climb inside the cupboard to get the items Jonny wanted. Quick as a weasel, Jonny rolled away the ladder, cackling like a hen laying an oversized egg. I looked down at him, wondering what it was all about.

"For past crimes committed!" he called up to me, his

round face gloating. "I promised to pay you back. This is it. Pay day!"

I was speechless but not for long. "It's nice up here. I think I'll just stretch out and get some sleep. Of course, now you'll have to make do without towels and napkins, my clever friend!"

"I'll look in on you by evening — if I remember," Jonny said ominously.

A short while later Bill came into the room, looking for napkins and paper towels.

He pushed the ladder back to my cupboard, preparing to climb up, when he saw me looking down at him.

"What are you doing up there?" he asked, surprised.

"Looking for napkins and towels," I answered him.

He looked at the ladder and back at me. "How did you get up there without a ladder?"

"I flew. It's easier on my legs."

Jonny bustled in just then. "I always thought there was something strange about her!" Jonny shook his head, making believe he, too, was much perplexed by my wingless flight.

Bill looked at Jonny deviously. "What's this all about?"

I climbed down, passing by Jonny. "Practice your ladder climbing — you'll have to do a lot of it from now on!" We both were grinning, good friends as always.

"Clowns!" I heard Bill say while I closed the door behind me.

Chapter 14

I have forgotten when, but it must have been soon after my botched examination in American history, when Bill started his long conversations with me, arguing with me about all sorts of current and past events of interest to him, as I soon discovered. To my own surprise, I, too, liked our discussions, even those that left either Bill or me angry and excited at times, about the problems of our world and time.

One day he asked me to explain to him the supposed difference between a German Heimatland and The Fatherland, while a hundred chickens were slowly browning and while Jonny kept pointing at the clock, muttering threats and trying to interrupt our serious conversation.

At another time Bill challenged me into taking apart that which seemed to make him furious — "the Superman complex of Das Deutsche Fatherland." He had become deeply involved in Hitler's convenient translation of Nietzsche's thoughts and philosophy, I finding myself face to face with a born politician, a clever, red-hot juggler of words. I experienced a nostalgic longing for my father's bookshelves and all those wonderful pages they had held, realizing how little I knew and how much there was to know. Surprisingly, though, in spite of my shortcomings, Bill seemed to think afterward that he had spent a worthwhile hour, for he told me, "We must talk again soon, you and I." We had quite a few such enlightening conversations together. However, not always would we part so peacefully.

One day we ended up arguing quite ridiculously, and of

all things about the meaning of *"Deutschland über Alles, über Alles in der Welt,"* the German national anthem which Bill translated into, "the Germans openly advertising their desire to conquer the world."

"These words but express a German's idealistic feelings for his country," I insisted firmly to Bill, only to have him blow up at me. Indeed, this particular argument I left in frustrated tears, with Bill calling after me, "Why in hell are you getting so all fired up? Come back! Or don't come back. See if I care, you infant, you!"

Hot and angry, I kept on walking. An insulted infant politician indeed. When Andy wanted to know what the fireworks had been about, I told him how I felt about Bill at that moment. "He is an old goat! A bleating goat with horns and hooves. I think he enjoys needling me, quarreling with me, poking his horns into me! He makes me so angry I could scream!"

Andy had looked at me, surprised, then began smiling from behind his hand so I wouldn't see. "Nonsense! I happen to know the old boy thinks well of you. That's more than he does of the rest of us. Heck, he likes you, all right. It's just his way of talking at times, of not wanting anyone to come too close to him, to find him out. You should feel honored, hon, being the one person Bill enjoys locking horns with!"

He gave me a reassuring grin. "Heck, sugar, you know yourself, that old Bill is brighter than a new penny underneath his grouchy hide. And the old so-and-so wouldn't waste a single minute away from his precious books were it not worth his time!"

Andy kept looking at me inquiringly. "Want to know what else I think? You rather like him, too. You seem to share many interests, and you both worry the same bone —

he the old War Horse and you mein Katzenjammer Kind, my *Weltschmerz* thinker!" He gave my ear a little tweak, playfully.

How well he knew me!

I did like, after all, the temperamental Bill the cook who had been a chef of distinction in one of Philadelphia's finest hotels, as Jonny had told me more than once, proud to stir the great one's soups, salting his fish, paprikaing to death his steaks. For Bill, who had forsaken fame and fortune to be a cook in Uncle Sam's army.

Sure enough, the following afternoon we were at it again, the two of us having forgotten already my childish tantrum of the day before, our sharp exchange of words. And I, the naïve infant. Ah! I could see I was growing on him.

This time we discussed the possibility of a world government, which I believed, could well be the answer to providing peace for the whole of mankind. Bill thought this was an idealistic dream and not possible yet. We went on to talk about the war. Unfortunately, at one point in our earnest discussion Bill became angry once more.

"How outrageous can you be, to mention what happened here in Germany, the bombing, the burning? Why, I feel like clobbering you when I think back to what I saw in London, in France, in Belgium, and in Holland! Whole cities blotted off the map!" Bill had turned beet-red and had to rip open the top button of his shirt to breathe, he was so angry.

It took some effort to go on in the face of his fury, to make clearer to him what I had been saying.

"I was speaking against war," I began with a trembling voice. "I was talking about man's inhumanity to his brother man, especially in times of war, when you suddenly decided that because I am German born, we were on opposite sides of the war. You spoke about sides. I spoke of human beings the world over. Individuals who suffer most in times of war and unleashed hate. I wanted to tell you about a man I knew. I saw him crying one day when he heard a neighbor's child had lost both legs in a bombing attack. The very next day he went quietly mad, digging out from under the rubble of what used to be his home, limb by torn limb, his own family of six."

I couldn't stop myself. "I wanted to tell you of a mother whimpering in despair until she mercifully fainted away out there on the sidewalk in front of her burning home, her four children trapped inside in an inferno set by incendiary bombs."

I went on. "There was this small boy I knew, dying long before his time, screaming in agony. But do you want to know how he screamed? Not in any language. Not in German. He screamed in the universal language of pain — horrible, unbearable pain. He was human — not German, not English, not Russian — just human, of flesh and blood and bones as all of us are."

I had to stop for a moment, unable to go on. But then I did. "I heard that little boy scream. It has been years now since that day, yet every time I think about war, I remember his screams!"

I looked at Bill. He sat there quiet. I finally said, "I did hear what you said before, when you spoke of London, of Rotterdam, of all these other cities. One day on a train out of Mannheim, northward bound, I listened to a group of English soldiers talking about the raids on London during the war. The Blitz, they called it. Oh, Bill! I heard every word, though they spoke quietly, unaware of my listening, understanding. I think it was then that it occurred to me how exactly like mine their stories were. How in the end our stories are all the same. Bill, how I wish there would never again be war."

He looked up, as if coming out from deep thoughts of his own, as if he, too, could remember screams.

"Bill," I began again, my throat hurting. "Bill, if you still want to clobber me . . ."

He looked at me, then shook his head. "Last night — many times," he answered at last, looking at me as if seeing me for the first time, "I watched you dancing at the club, whirling like a pretty little butterfly without a thought in her head. Today . . . you seem older than Methuselah's daughters." He shook his head again.

"No. I don't want to clobber you," he said, getting up and rather heavily walking away toward his room.

One afternoon just before suppertime, I was heading upstairs where Andy was waiting with a batch of newly developed pictures he wanted to look over with me, deciding which of them to send home. Bill was holding open a newspaper when I walked by.

"What's new today?" I asked casually, stopping to say a few friendly words.

"Those damned Germans," he began just as casually. "Now one can't find a single one guilty of the war, of all the monstrous atrocities committed. They're all suddenly clean. Not one ever lifted a hand and shouted 'Sieg Heil!' Bah, the bloody wolves have turned into sheep. A bunch of innocent sheep without a master now."

With his first words I let myself down onto a chair, my stomach knotting. I noticed breadcrumbs from this noon's meal still lying on top of one of the tables, forgotten. I always knew when Charlie was doing a round of K.P. He had left the darn back door open again to the strip of tar where the garbage barrels stood full to overflowing, inviting the flies to come in for free lunches. I thought of getting up to close the door, but I never moved.

"What makes you so quiet today? Yesterday you had all the answers," Bill said, putting the paper down on the table before him, looking at me as if he was getting ready to put me on hot coals once more. Had he not been Bill, I would have been worried, for surely he was after me again with something bothering him. But this was Bill, and so I had to find the words to answer him once more. For answer him I must. It did concern me — very much.

"I can only speak for myself," I began. "After all, you cannot expect just one voice to be the conscience of a whole nation. And you are convinced already — I can tell, just hearing you now."

"Go on. Go right on," he prompted me, looking at me as if he were drilling holes into my forehead to get at my thoughts.

"You'll be disappointed with me," I warned him. "I do feel great shame, but not guilt. And guilt is what you are after, is it not?"

"Since you are but a lamb, shame will do," he said.

I looked at him sharply. Not a muscle in his face moved. I felt I had to defend myself. "I was eleven years old when the war started."

"Perhaps you knew already then that you were going to marry an American and leave this 'Deutschlantd über Alles'!" he snorted.

I bit my lip to go on, not to be overwhelmed before I started.

"You want me to be truthful, fair, when you are certainly not. I was still but a youth when the war ended."

Bill's lower lip did a fast twitch. "All right. I was not

fair," his mouth said, but his eyes were cold and hard.

I sat up a little straighter. Something was wrong with Bill today, and I better watch out. Still, one must say what one had to say.

"Yes, I am German, if that is what you are referring to. I am quite aware of my ancestry, of my ancestors who failed to leave me the choice to choose my own nationality at birth," I said sarcastically. "Just think. I could have been an Eskimo, perhaps, a Bushman, an Australian aboriginal." I couldn't help winking at Bill, then I shrugged, becoming serious again. "And so I was born German. One of seventy million or so, if there are that many left now. Fewer than one million were registered Nazis. Some were patriots, idealists, socialists, Communist soldiers too, and soldiers who had no choice, being drafted to become cannon fodder. There were many who cared a lot and those who cared not a wink. There were many who were afraid of the goose-steppers, the torch-lighters, the *Sieg Heil* screamers, and God, help us, the gas oven lighters, fanatics without a conscience."

I couldn't go on for a moment because I wanted to cry. But I swallowed hard.

"There were children, old people. And, whether you count them or not, there were also a large number of Germans who fought and died for their beliefs in the concentration camps. More than you think possible for such a shameful nation. I found out long ago that in the eyes of the world all of us are one. There are no exceptions. All make the whole. *Einz, zuei, drei!* Does that not make us all guilty, too? Why not dig a giant hole, or, better yet, why not drop an especially potent atom bomb on us all? Doomsday for all the big and little Germans. The bad and the good. Och! There are no good ones, as we all know!"

181

I stopped abruptly, having gotten a glimpse at Bill's face, muscles stiffened, fingers sniffing out the cigarette he had just lit. But I was too angry to keep quiet. I had to go on.

"Come to think of it, would you dare to be the conscience of *your* nation?" I asked him. "Would God Himself come down and ask you about Hiroshima, and —"

For a moment Bill's face paled ghastly, then the blood came rushing back into his cheeks, making it seem unnaturally flushed. "We had to end this war. And we did. What do you know, to come up with this?" His lips were trembling with a kind of muted intensity, his voice heavy and strange. I would have preferred it to be loud and angry. I had expected him to burst out in scalding anger. Not this.

To cover up my bewilderment, my sudden unsureness, I spat back at him, "As much and as little as you! Remember, I am but myself. One small voice among millions."

He only sat there, looking at me. Not answering me. Just sitting there, his eyes two dark pools of otherness, looking straight at me, forcing me to be honest once more — with myself first of all.

But who was he? What right had he to torment whatever it was there inside me that wanted to be left alone?

To be honest with myself!

All too soon the fire in my eyes became but a sad little flicker. We were gazing at each other. I saw him. And he saw me. So naked my soul.

Honest with myself?

"I am sorry, Bill. Ever so sorry."

"Why must we dig at each other?" he answered me at last. "I only wanted your opinion about something. Before I knew how, I was ready to hate you and fight you. Is that how wars start? Is that how it begins?"

His voice was that of a stranger, of another Bill I had yet

to know. Suddenly I had to look away. Down to the floor. To stammer, "I . . . Before, I, too, felt unreasonable hate. I resented you asking me all these questions. You stirred me up. I got angry, and I've never felt like that before. You seemed so, so smug, so righteous. I wanted to puncture your righteousness. I wanted to hit you for not leaving a shred of anything good or decent on my people. Not on one single individual, even." I stopped with a sense of defeat, my eyes shut tight, shutting the world away, not wanting to see Bill sneering at me, condemning me.

But then, gently, his voice came to me. "Don't hide your eyes. You don't have to hide yourself."

I opened my eyes to look at him. He was not sneering at me. He looked only very tired.

As I felt tired. Aching for relief from having to carry a share of that mountain of accusations so very steep, so unforgiving.

And the mountain threatened to bury me under its weight, its ashes, while I told my foolish little voice to be patient, to be brave.

"Bill, I do want to answer you. Perhaps there is more than one answer."

"There is?" he said, and he sounded encouraging.

I nodded. Then I began carefully, slowly, "I believe there are many answers, given by many voices, not all of them German."

I waited. He was lighting a cigarette. He took a puff and sat back.

I went on, my confidence growing. "Let us find a man, one wise and just, exceptional among men. One not constrained by nationality or personal grief, not by good or bad memories or by misleading emotions. Let us find a prudent man from among the crying and the babbling, the begging and the demanding." I looked up. "Find such a rare one among the many."

There was something more I wanted to say, needed to say. But would it make Bill angry, bring on his scalding sarcasm?

I would tell him anyhow.

With the mountain of ashes towering above me, my eyes begging for understanding, I did. "There is one more thing I would say." And now that I had plunged in, I had to go on, whether Bill wanted to hear it or not. "If I could, I would say to the world: Forgive us the past. Yes, so I would say." I had to take a deep breath, my voice trembling. "I would say: Let us try once more, if but for the sake of those white sheep among us." My voice stopped trembling, was clear now. "For the sake of the children. Those not yet born. The innocent. For the sake of those who remember. Forgive. One day, forgive. So would I say!"

"And so are you saying." Bill's voice came as if from far off. He sat there looking at his long fingers, studying them intently, not seeing me.

"Bill?"

"What?"

"When one feels genuinely ashamed about having done something very bad, very foul, unforgivable, what does that show?"

He looked up sharply, alert, speculative. For a moment he wetted his upper lip. "Hmm. Well. Hmm. I think, I believe, one can experience shame for several reasons."

"Recognizing one's mistakes, one's misdeeds, wanting to correct wrongs done, to make good again shameful acts committed. Would you accept such remorse?"

"Your conscience is big enough for . . . for . . ." He was evading my question.

I persisted. "To have a conscience one can feel shame."

"There is more to that," he replied thoughtfully. "It seems to me such a one needs . . . many graces. Have the necessary guts, belief, patience, and strength to await the world's forgiveness. It must first of all make good again what it did wrong. Prove itself."

"It isn't easy to face a suspicious world with a battered, bloody face, you know," I said, suddenly shy again before Bill's cold briskness.

"It's much worse to have bloody hands and not care," he answered sharply, ignoring my flushing face.

"I think," I mumbled back nevertheless, "the country I'm talking about has what it takes . . . given time." I wanted to believe it very much.

From Bill came a grunt. I looked at him, gathering my boldness. Suddenly it had become very important to make him see, have him understand. And this uprush of strong feelings swept away the last dregs of my timidity. I lifted my eyes and challenged that very mountain of ashes once more.

"Some time ago," I began bravely, "you asked me what I felt was the difference between a German Heimatland and The Fatherland. I recall answering you, 'The Fatherland stands for the male, the warrior, for the warlike, for the wrong-or-right, my country!' The Heimatland stands for the peaceful, so I said to you then. The Heimatland, which gives birth, creates. The mother who proudly watches her children build bridges and cathedrals, create music and poetry, follow science for the good of all mankind. For the mother it stands, who leaves her children free to reach for the stars. So did I tell you then. How you laughed at me! I wasn't sure for quite a while if you thought I had told you a ridiculous joke. You may very well laugh again now. For I still say the same. You see, I really do believe there exists such a Heimatland, one conscious of today and tomorrow. A Heimatland even The Fatherland gone insane has not been able to destroy, do away with. It's still around. Shyer maybe, but so much wiser. Braver and better, better, and . . . and . . . more capable of teaching her young to live in reality, to be more skeptical, to never again accept the madness of a Hitler.

"Why do you smile so, Bill, as if you are listening to the wishful chatter of a child, while I am pleading with my very soul?

"When I was a young child my father took me wandering, showing me this Heimatland: its mighty rivers, singing and talking to those who love them, its mountains and dark-green forest he showed me, making me aware 'til I wanted to shout, looking upon their heady beauty, sensing their foreverness. Bill. Bill, look at me and tell me that you have never felt that way about your own country! Remember that day when you told me about your trip through the Rocky Mountains? The sunrise you saw, one morning? You had tears in your eyes just recalling it. You said you wanted to kneel and pray, but you couldn't find the words. You could only mumble, God, Oh, God! You felt then how I felt, seeing my lovely Heimatland. Growing older, I peopled my Heimatland with men and women I admired, with its poets and writers and great thinkers, with splendid characters. I was proud to link them with this Heimatland. And I was young and foolish enough to ignore for a time that other part — The Fatherland. The war came. No, it was before the war, when I began to look about through my father's wiser, more experienced eyes, discovering rot and cancer. Worms, spoiling my too perfect apple.

"Do not interrupt me just now, Bill. Listen, for just a while. Anyhow, the part with the worms you know as well as I do, I think. It is about the Heimatland, I need to talk. The Heimatland in which I need to believe, to look forward to in the future. For peace, for all the world. For her I need to speak up, for her do I beg forgiveness. For this Heimatland, which belongs with the rest of the world. Go ahead and call me a dreamer. Only tell me first that you understand. . . ."

"How very convincing you are," Bill said finally after I had begun to think he never would answer me. He picked up the newspaper from the table. He put it down again. He pushed it this way and that, drumming his fingers on it for a moment. "Son of a gun!" he mumbled, uneasiness leaping into his eyes, into his voice. "Too profoundly convincing!" He was once more impatient with me, with himself, for having to answer me, aware of my eyes patiently waiting on his.

"If your Heimatland is as hot as you think, then time will show. A *long* time from now. It depends on how much there is to be forgiven. On how much The Fatherland can be forgiven that is!"

He began pulling at a tiny thread on his trouser leg just above the knee. It was pulling longer. He broke it off, glowering at it as he held it before his eyes, releasing it to the floor. He looked uncomfortable. Then he added, "A very long time from now! Your Fatherland has sown a tidy crop of hate while your Heimatland kept her innocent, beautiful and — according to you — peace-loving eyes closed. Kept still and slept. Hate isn't an easy growth to lose; it sticks. Ask Crawinsky — he'll tell you. He can tell you better than I or any of us."

"Crawinsky. He, too, must live in the future, no matter how much he remembers the past hates." I clamped my teeth together in defiance, unwilling to show my unsureness. I was never sure when it came to Crawinsky. I mumbled, "Anyhow, how long can hate last? Can you tell me how long? Surely not forever." I was being the naïve young creature once again, needing to believe in something kinder, in the power of forgiveness.

"Crawinsky's kind of hate?" Bill asked. "With him it's 'til death sets him free," he answered me, deliberately flippant, his face averted. "You certainly are in a rush to get things over with. Almost indecently so, I think." He did not look at me.

"You speak as if he is a prisoner."

"A prisoner of himself. A waste!"

"After so much *waste!* How I wish the past could be changed!"

"One cannot change the past. What has been done is done."

This time I did not fear to go on.

"But one can learn from it, from the past, can one not?" I asked. Convinced by this growing hope, sitting up straight in my chair, I said, "Perhaps the Heimatland, too, can learn. To stand up against The Fatherland."

At first Bill seemed unsure what to say to that. Then, being but once more his grouchy self, an expression of rather violent satisfaction coming into his eyes, he began throwing at me my own earlier words.

"Only a short while ago you said that all make one whole. It seems to me, your Heimatland and The Fatherland are two such halves, together making one whole: Germany. You agree? Of course you do, my clever little one. One Deutschland they make. One complex Deutschland. One apple — just like the one in Snow White's story. One bad apple. It poisoned her, too, did it not? All her dwarfs, all her twelve little men couldn't help her. That makes me wonder now, how many prudent men do you need in your fairy tale? Can you tell offhand? At least a century of thinkers, I'd say. It's all such a big mess. Such a stinking mess to sort out. Even prudent thinkers have only human brains to do the sorting with!" Taking out his handkerchief, he gave a frightful snorted blast as final as that of the last trumpet at Judgment Day, or so it sounded to me.

Everything seemed blurred, as if I was looking out into the rain, into a thickening grey dusk.

"How hopeless you make it all seem! So utterly hopeless!"

Holding on desperately to my shaky self-control, my heart fluttering away under its cage of ribs like a little sparrow, I said, "What a fool I am, blubbering about what I feel. Feel and cannot help feeling." I had to take a deep breath to go on. "But if I am a silly fool, you are a cold, unfeeling one!"

Now I had said it all.

Not one word more need I say.

I put my face into my hands, wishing to be left alone, be still. Bill was sitting there speechless, giving up on me at last.

A fly crawled up my arm. I had to let drop my hands, chase away the fly. Because of a fly, a small insect, I had to look up and face Bill.

He was still sitting there as if speechless, only now his face held something else. The mocking expressions had left it, left it looking strangely helpless, naked. Then he said, "I am sorry. It wasn't necessary, I know, to say all that. You were but truthful, saying what you felt, braver than most." He gave a funny little sigh. "How profoundly innocent you can be. How touchingly — forgive me — naïve, too. I had to hide from myself, get nasty, while I wanted to smile once in a while, listening to you." Again he shook his head.

"How young you are. Just eighteen. No, don't say anything. I know myself. You are right, though, about one thing. I am a mean, disenchanted sourpuss at times. A . . . goat! That is what you call me, do you not?" He was looking at me as if he wanted me to answer him.

A sound — strangled and relieved at once — escaped my throat. I bobbed my head up and down. So emphatically did I shake my head, one of my hairpins went flying, sailing off into the room. Embarrassed, I looked at Bill and quickly away again. I had said so much with my soul showing.

Then Bill suddenly got off his chair and moved backward, out of my sight. His voice had changed. I could feel his hand on my shoulder, pressing down lightly. And I could hear and understand what he was saying.

"I am not what I must seem to you, to the others, most times — a block of granite without emotions or feelings." He held up his hand against whatever I wanted to say. "It's all right. I have it coming to me. I do know about . . . all kinds of love. The one you spoke of before — you called it Heimatland. And I do know loving someone . . . how that feels."

A soft smile hovered around his mouth, his eyes. "And I remember being eighteen — so marvelously young and alive!"

Bill moved forward to gaze at me intensely. I felt the blood rush into my face.

"At certain times you remind me of her, though her hair was fair and her eyes blue." He nodded to himself. He looked out the window, up into the blue sky where, I was ever so sure, he was for one fleeting moment seeing a pair of blue eyes smiling back at him. His voice took on a deliberate lightness. "It was all such a long time ago. I married another eventually." He shrugged. "Would you believe it?"

He laughed, but I could hear how his heart still hurt. "Not too long ago I spent a whole month's pay buying a painting of your lovely Rhein Valley. I always wanted a cuckoo clock from the Schwarzwald, a Leica camera, a pair of those sharp Jena fieldglasses. And I most certainly will leave here owning a pair of genuine Bavarian lederhosen and a green hat with a stiff Gemsbart and an Edelweis. How do you like that?"

"You sure would look funny in Lederhosen," I babbled, odd tears coloring my laughter. "You will look like Franz Josef himself!"

"Whoever he is," he grinned back.

All the while I was thinking of our discussion.

There must be a better half. There is.

Bill, however, had looked up, had seen the clock and how late it was, how time had run away with us once again. Instantly he became Bill the cook and once more his abrupt, untouchable self, hollering at Jonny, busy out in the kitchen all by himself. "Jesus Christ Almighty! Will you cut out your paprikaing and peppering already! Achoo!" He was sneezing just watching Jonny.

"Gesundheit," I said, reminding him of my presence, promptly having him turn on me. His eyes still glaring with having witnessed one of Jonny's peppering jobs, he began to commandeer me now.

"You. Start setting the tables. And hop to it! I've had enough monkey business for one day!" But he couldn't entirely hide a certain something in his eyes.

And I, heaven knows, could snap back as fast as he if necessary. I sprang to attention, giving him a stiff salute. "Yes, sir!" I turned smartly and marched to the kitchen to give a hand to Jonny the peppershaker.

Four hands are supposed to be better than two. Well, I

must confess, the beef stew that night was out of this world. Where it belonged. And as most everyone tasting a spoonful agreed on.

"Go to the U.S.A., kid! Get away from here, and forget the whole frigging mess. Marry your big guy — he wants you badly enough. Do a little looking around at the rest of the world. You'll be all right! Some stretching, some growing is all you need. Never fear!"

As suddenly as he had appeared, Bill disappeared again, leaving me by the sink in the kitchen, stacking used dishes. I wanted to run after him, tell him that I really couldn't say what made me so all fired up at times. That it was indeed disturbing to feel the way I had earlier. When I but wanted to be with Andy, married to him, have his children. Be home where he was home.

I never did go after Bill to tell him all that, but I think he knew just the same.

Only one thing I brought up again, one day much later. It made him laugh and me laugh with him, though in my heart I felt sad.

"You were wrong, Bill, naming Germany two halves of one apple. Remember? It is four slices now. One of them behind a wall."

Chapter 15

At last I could say in all honesty that now I had been to a baseball game. My first!

It nearly turned into a disaster, however.

I was the reason for the disaster. A disgrace to the pride of the guys from the mess hall. A pox on every self-respecting baseball fan in the company, I was. And after the men had shined their shoes, polished their buttons, pinned their medals onto their brand-new constabulary uniforms, all in honor of their team.

You see, I cheered for the wrong team!

"For those buzzards from the Air Force," quoting Bill. Not knowing a thing about baseball and having forgotten the rules Andy, Bill, and Jonny had explained to me on our way to the field, I had actually stood up, and shouted, overcome by enthusiasm when one of the buzzards struck a home run. Thunder and lightning should have struck me down!

Poor Andy. He pulled me down onto the bench. He couldn't even speak.

I looked at Bill, with the eyes of a puppy dog. "I goofed, huh?"

"You goofed all right!" he said, giving me his most disgusted look.

I turned my hangdog face to Jonny, the easy, always forgiving Jonny, who would surely understand.

Jonny looked straight ahead gulping popcorn, not offering me a single kernel, though he knew how much I like popcorn. I dared not look at the rest of the guys.

In the jeep on our way back, I really got what I had coming, and from all directions, Bill wielding the scalpel, snorting like a racehorse before the run. "After all we've done to Americanize her! All of us, from myself down —"

"— to Charlie," Jonny assisted Bill, finishing his sentence.

That was really scratching bottom! Considering the only thing that Charlie — a soldier doing more K.P. than any other duty — could have taught anyone was how to gas-up a room until everyone in it fainted away.

"To learn his specialty," I dared to say, "one surely doesn't need to become Americanized first."

Bill opened his mouth, but Jonny, throwing a fast look at Andy at the wheel, was just a little faster. "I didn't mean that!" he assured me.

"Charlie plays a pretty good mouth organ, yes?" Jonny tried hard. "He can wiggle his ears, no? He can pick his nose with the tip of his tongue. Yes! He can —"

"He is a natural born fart!" Bill briskly cut off Jonny.

Andy burst out laughing. "Honey, you sure learn more doing a stretch in this here army than in any finishing school!" On that we all agreed.

Spring had come and gone.

Andy and Red were given a ten-day furlough plus a choice to go to either Switzerland or Paris.

Red decided on Switzerland. Andy, however, did not even consider going anywhere. He just wanted to stay with me, though I thought it a shame, his being in Europe and missing a beautiful spot like Switzerland, and I told him to go.

"We both go. On our honeymoon we both go together," he said, lazily. In the end it took a heap of convincing from both Red and me to change his mind. Up to the last minute he looked as if he was considering staying behind after all. It was a long lonely week at the apartment, but I did catch up for once on my ironing and cleaning.

On Sunday afternoon Andy and Red returned, Andy with the cutest carved weather house under his arm to be hung outside our window. And a precious gold Swiss watch — my very first gold watch. I thought it indeed the most precious of all the many gifts Andy showered me with.

Red came back with a cinnamon-colored windburn on his face and arms, a little deeper than the color of his hair, with two flasks of perfume and two identical boxes of lovely lace handkerchiefs, one for Sonia, one for me.

Then, shortly afterward, the company was moved to another part of Germany, this time quite far from The Village, to a small town near the city of Wetzlar in the midst of the romantic woods of the Westerwald.

I felt uneasy about this move, even though Andy laughed at my worries and called me a very dear but foolish little woman.

I knew Wetzlar was close to the Russian Zone. I had discovered on the map that the town where Andy would be stationed was right by the border. And there were many so-called incidents just then between the Russian and the American sectors in Berlin and all along the Zones. It did look as if ugly new clouds were piling up once more on the political horizon, ready to let loose another deluge of war.

"I shiver just thinking of another war!" I told Andy.

"There won't be another war. Not just now," he replied. Then he gave me a convincing grin. "They just move us about a bit to show us the rest of the country. That's all, hon!"

But I wasn't diverted so easily. The all-too-fresh memories of the war were still with me, though Andy's comforting presence assured me not to worry too long about it. I would snuggle a little closer in to his arms, to be held by him, holding him. Yes, we were much too happy to let anything bother us for any length of time.

Drowsy, soul and body fulfilled with having made love, I whispered, "What if I become pregnant?"

He laid his cheek against mine. "You are my baby for just a little while longer. You're my baby."

There was not much time left to persuade my parents to let me go so far away. I could tell Andy was much concerned with what my parents would say.

"If only I could marry you already," he worried aloud one day.

"So long as I can be with you, anyplace, anywhere, I'm happy," I assured him.

Sunday came, and with it our last chance to talk with my father and mother before Andy had to leave the next morning. I was supposed to be working, but Sonia and Karin assured me they would each do a little more so I would not be missed.

Since I belonged now officially in the American Zone, I had not been able to get a pass to enter the French Zone where my parents lived in The Village. To get a pass took lots of time, and a maze of paperwork and red tape. I had long felt discouraged by it all and so had never bothered. It was so much easier to sneak across the Rhein, when old Sgt. Krauss would look at my last year's pass, suddenly turning blind at its overdue date. But he would turn red every time Andy pushed a pack of cigarettes into his hand, protesting weakly that it was certainly not because of them that he let us pass.

Then, I had found a much better way to show him our

appreciation, a way less embarrassing and with all those eyes looking on.

I knew Sgt. Krauss kept his lunchbox inside the hut on the ferry. It was easy to walk inside and deposit a couple of fried chicken legs, a meat sandwich, or a few bars of chocolate into his lunchbox.

Andy found this amusing, and sometimes he would teasingly remind me, "Honey, did you bring your ferry fare?"

I would smile, holding up a small package.

The day we were to visit my parents, Bill offered to drive us down to the ferry on his way to Mannheim. Just before we came to the river, Andy asked me his usual question, at which I held up, as usual, a small package. Hearing us kid around so, Bill looked disgusted. Then he was growling, reminding me that he was since that morning in one of his crabby moods, brought on by Jonny perhaps or by his ulcers.

"What gluttons most Germans are! They would rather eat before anything else, I swear. Take that old policeman for instance, that good friend of yours. Letting himself be bribed with a chicken leg! A chicken leg, of all things!" Bill blustered away at Andy and myself.

"He never asks for anything. But I know he is hungry — he has no wife, no family. So —"

"Oh, bull! He can't be that hungry," Bill interrupted me, his voice grating. "He can fill up with beer if it comes to that!"

"He is a kind old man. Whenever I need to cross the river to The Village, not having a pass, he lets me go. With or without a little package!" I insisted just as stubbornly.

"He is a crook, mark my words," Bill insisted.

"Crook? I've never seen you rejecting a well-turned leg either, chicken and otherwise. Or a stein of beer, come to think of it!" Andy told Bill, faintly annoyed, impatient with wanting to be gone. But Bill, to my amazement, though heaven knows I had often enough seen him change his moods, suddenly turned from plain grouchy to happy, breaking into a puckish grin. Ignoring what Andy had just said, letting his sense of humor take over, he pointed a long finger at me while looking at Andy.

"And guess whose chicken she is giving away? Guess, my friend. *My* chicken, which I fried and watched over, my brow dripping sweat over a hot stove! That's what she is handing out so generously. What do you say to that!"

"*Your* chicken leg. Ha! The guys in the dining room asked if it was beets they were being fed or paprika chicken. I told them it's called Bill's Own!"

"Did you hear that?" Bill was looking at Andy, his eyes sparkling. "Do you believe me now, hearing the fresh little thing talking back to me? That's European gratitude for you." He was in his element now, winking his nearly white eyelashes like a belly dancer her fan. He was giving me the go ahead for a battle of words.

"European gratitude my foot!" I cried.

"Oh, no you two don't!" Andy jumped from the jeep, lifting me up and out like a rag doll, grasping his bag from the seat in one smooth move. "I don't want to listen just now to one of your bullfights. Thanks a lot for chauffeuring us. That I appreciate!"

"Be here at seven tonight. I'll drive by and pick you up on my way back," Bill said, looking actually a little disappointed at having lost a chance to argue with me.

"Thanks, Buddy. We'll be right here waiting!" Andy accepted for both of us, turning away, missing Bill's silly grimace meant for me alone.

He had to have one more word, being Bill. "Tell her father," he called to Andy, "he should be glad we are willing to take her away with us, the insolent little brat!" He laughed, much pleased with himself, roaring the jeep off toward Mannheim, vanishing in a tremendous cloud of dust.

"Lay an egg, will you!" I called after him.

"Make it square with speckles!" Andy joined in, laughing, taking my hand.

Our happy mood accompanied us onto the ferry and stayed with us all the way across the river and into The Village. A tinkling, quick silvery kind of happiness it was. Andy squeezed my hand and whispered into my ear, "Have you got your loot?"

"Yes, master, I do!" I giggled back, pointing toward the hut. "It's in there already!"

A young man by the name of Willi Holzer, recently returned from a prisoner of war camp in France, was watching us with a dark look on his face, abruptly walking to the other end of the ferry.

A short while later we were pushing open the heavy iron gate into the narrow run of the courtyard, calling out hello, instantly answered by my father and mother, both having waited for us since morning, happy now to see us coming up the stairs, happy to have with them their children even if it was for a few hours only.

There had been weekends when we had time enough to visit with Aunt Ernestine for a little while, when we stayed overnight, leaving again Sunday by late evening. The sweet, elf-like little woman had tried hard every time to hide her oversized heart and her open joy at seeing us coming, hand in hand, up her ruler-straight garden path and into her small white house, concealing under much talk and many trips into her pantry her joy at having us with her for a little while, bringing us delicate sweet things she had especially baked for Andy.

That first time when we came to visit her, she had been a bit apprehensive, much impressed with the tall Texan. She had stood beside him as if measuring her own tiny size by his, claiming in genuine awe, "*Himmel!* Wherever you come from, they sure make them tall!"

Andy had smiled down at her and said, "I come from Texas, Ma'am!" And, winking at me, he added, "From the United States of Texas," having me roll my eyes at him, for this was our own private joke, and Aunt Ernestine did not understand much English.

This Sunday, however, we had barely enough time to discuss with my parents what was uppermost in our minds, what had brought us home.

It was my mother, who seemed to know from the start that there was something troubling us today, for right off she had many questions. When I finally sprang our news, sitting beside Andy on the brown sofa, both my father and my mother were openly uncomfortable, my mother clearly upset. My father said nothing at first, thinking it over, as he would with matters of importance.

"Well," my mother finally said, looking at my father, "what do you say, to our eighteen-year-old daughter wanting to go even farther away, now?"

I turned to face my mother, suddenly gripped by anger. But I didn't get to utter a single word. Andy pulled me back before I could say anything rash, regrettable. Holding my hand tightly, he answered for me.

"I am sorry. We never meant to cause you pain or suffering or worry you. Right now it's not up to me to do as I want. Under different circumstances Lisa and I would have been married months ago. Please, won't you understand? Believe me, I could not feel more responsible were Lisa my wife. God knows how much I love her."

Andy's hands had come up, palms open. He wanted to say more, but the words failed to leave his lips. He put his arm around me instead, in such a meaningful gesture that a stranger would have known what he felt while he looked at my mother pleadingly.

She looked back at him, and she clearly couldn't resist his begging eyes. She had to look down at her hands in her lap. Saying almost inaudibly, "What I said before — I did not mean to speak so harshly."

My father sucked on his pipe, blew out the smoke, then pointed the pipestem at me. "Would you go anyhow, if we said you cannot go?" There was the slightest tremor in his voice, making me look up even though I did not want to, feeling uncomfortable.

"Yes, I would go. I have to go. Please don't ask me to stay. Please don't. I do not want to hurt you. Don't make me hurt you. I would die in this village without him! Have you forgotten? We are engaged. He is almost my husband! I love him. I love him!"

Like shots from a rifle I fired words at my father, unthinking, unaware at the moment how much I was hurting him. I was desperate to go with Andy, to be near him, no matter where. Nothing else seemed to matter.

"Then," my father said after a pause, so quietly it was hard to hear, "you must go. How could we hold you?"

I turned to him, now aware of the tremor in his voice, seeing suddenly new lines in his dear face, his eyes bright and searching mine. Seeing a slow, sad smile touch the corners of his mouth. Touching my own anger, fading it away.

Then I was happy and sad in one, knowing I would go with Andy, and sad seeing my parents' eyes blurred with tears.

But my happiness won out, making me get off the sofa to flit like a bright-eyed bird from Andy to my father, to my mother hugging one and kissing the other. Even my mother could not hold out long against my intense happiness. Looking into Andy's eyes, into my animated face, she finally threw up her hands in defeat.

"What can I say now? Perhaps it is all meant to be. May God be with you always!" She tried hard to smile saying this.

But oh, how desperately she had tried not to show her tears, when Andy and I left the house that evening. It made me wish I would not have to remember how she had stood by the window, looking out, crying after all, standing there long after we had walked away into the setting sun.

Andy would be gone by early morning. We had said our good-byes.

That night I was lying on the narrow sofa bed in Sonia's apartment with lots of time to think. Wondering if it would be long before Andy could call for me. If it would be difficult for him to find a place for me to stay. And I was also uneasy about Sonia. She was staying behind in Waldheim, by herself, alone again, as she had been before.

Lately Sonia had grown even quieter than usual, almost as if she was doing a lot of thinking about something. About Red?

I knew that it all had somehow to do with Red. It had been weeks now since she had gone out with him, that he had been up to the apartment. When I had asked her, outright and concerned, she had looked at me probingly, her eyes unfathomable black. She had walked to the window, and, looking out into the rain-soaked street below, she said, "Were I not so utterly convinced of your love for Andy, of your friendship for me, I could dislike you and so get over it all. These past weeks I often wanted to cry, telling myself I was glad you would all go away and leave me once more to myself."

I looked up at her sharply, surprised, feeling hurt slicing through me.

Sonia saw it. Her eyes softened instantly. "Oh, don't look at me like that," she went on quickly. "I realize my self-indulgence, my self-pity, or whatever I call it is not your fault. You did nothing to hurt me." She came to a stop, then went on again. "It's Red. He never loved me. He loves you. Hopeless as it is, he loves you, and you never even seem to know it!"

For an instant she looked at me as if surprised by what she was saying. "He would never speak of it, though. He is proud. But I . . . I knew all about it since first I met him. Call it a woman's intuition. I knew . . . when I let him make love to me . . . or more truthfully . . . when I went to bed with him. I knew it all along. And I was not proud. Because I was lonely, perhaps. Because I knew both of us were lonely and hurting, and sometimes just because we were left here to ourselves, two lonely people together in a cold world after you and Andy left. Staying away all night. Oh, Lisa! The way you two looked at each other when you walked out that door! As if you needed no one. Only each other."

She once more began pacing the room, folding and unfolding her kerchief. She gave a sigh. "Red is very much a man, and I am only a woman. Anyhow, we both knew, every time and when it was over, that this was not love. Only a need of the moment, and so not enough — not for him anyway. After a time I was ashamed. Disgusted and angry with myself. I told Red to leave me be. He respected my wish."

In front of me Sonia came to a halt. She laid one hand

on my shoulder, the other on my cheek, making me look into her eyes. "Don't look so sad. I said I don't blame you. I'm not that unhappy, nor am I heartbroken. Just a little wiser. And I am almost ten years older than you. How goes the saying? There's no fool like an old fool. Perhaps I am such a one. At least sometimes."

In the last days of our being together, Sonia had many serious talks with me.

One day, both of us in the kitchen, I ironing and she knitting a blue and yellow sweater, she said to me, "Your mother worries about you a lot, you know. She is worried with your being so young, so unconcerned with what could happen, seeing so much of Andy and he not able to marry you so long as he is a soldier." She looked up from her knitting. "For her sake, for your sake — be careful."

So far I had been listening to her attentively. Now she reminded me suddenly of our abandoned lovemaking, what Andy had whispered to me that last time when we made love. "When we are married we will make a baby. A beautiful little boy or girl."

"Should it happen now, I would not mind," I had said with my heart suddenly pounding, forgetting for a sweet, breathless moment all the rules binding us to the rest of the world. "At times I want it to happen!"

"Hush, sugar. Don't tempt me. It's difficult enough remembering and reminding myself not to —" He had groaned, his heart racing mine.

From far away I heard Sonia repeating her well-meant advice. "Don't get pregnant. Listen." And now her eyes looked straight into mine, filled with grave intensity. Quickly I came up and out of my daydreaming.

"We are careful. We are taking precautions. We try to be very careful."

Chapter 16

GRÜNFELD

Three days later I received a telegram from Andy. With flying fingers I opened it.

> *Be ready to leave with Red Friday. Early morning.*
> *Sorry, not able to come myself. Love Andy*

I spent all Thursday packing, Sonia sitting most of the day with me, talking of all kinds of things, though not another word about Red. At one time she said, swallowing, "I'll miss you very much. I've kind of gotten used to having you around." She tried to smile, but it didn't come off too well. "You've been a good friend, a sister, to me. My little sister."

I was glad knowing she had already a job waiting for her the coming week, a job so right for her: taking care of small children in a day nursery. She readily promised to go and see my father and mother once in a while. They had come to like Sonia the few times she had visited them with us.

"I'll write to you as often as I can," I promised her in return.

"I expect you to," she answered. And she smiled warmly, her eyes bright.

At last Friday morning was here. I believe I unknowingly hurt Sonia with my impatience to be off, to depart at last. Then, several hours before Red could arrive, Sonia left,

Erika M. Feiner

claiming an emergency visit to the dentist. I knew she was pretending, and I knew that she would stay away until we had gone.

And then at last, had come the tooting of Red's horn from in front of the house.

I flew to the door, ripping it open, seeing Red taking the flight of stairs in giant steps, three at a time. "Hey, stranger!" he called.

And I replied, "Hey, stranger yourself!"

At the open door he came to a sudden halt and before I knew what he was doing, he had picked me up as if I was a bundle of feathers, whooping, "Are you ready, babe?"

"I sure am," I shouted back, overcome as he. "Since yesterday morning!"

Red broke into peals of happy laughter. I took his hand to pull him into the apartment.

"Tell me quickly about everything," I begged him, pushing him into a chair.

"Well. Let's see now. Hmm!" He scratched his chin, making a face, trying to make me believe he was thinking hard. "Oh, yah! I'm to tell you first off, Andy still loves you, some."

"I am ever so relieved to hear this!" I said. "But this is not news." I laughed. "Not what I am waiting to hear!" With that I sat across from him on the couch.

"All right, all right. I'll tell you about Grünfeld and where we are. Grünfeld. Grünfeld is a quiet town in the valley of the Lahn, in the romantic woods of the Westerwald — the Harz Mountains. Its surrounding woods and dark-green and emerald-covered mountains give it the setting of fairy tales. Brothers Grimm fairy tales! For here indeed, in these very deep woods and rolling hills, the two fabulous brothers created for children the world over their

206

wonderful, imaginative stories. But let us return to Grünfeld once more. The fair one, whose lovely eyes look upon the very impressive cathedral town of Wetzlar — a quite ancient city close by — where Göethe once lived and wrote his Werther. Where Germany's famous Leica camera is at home. Where —"

I interrupted Red with my impatient laughter. For Red's little speech had seemingly come straight from a travel catalogue, his gestures copied to an inch after a certain accomplished orator.

"Well," Red admitted with a sheepish grin, having listened to my accusations, "most of it *is* out of a catalogue. The rest I saw with my own two eyes."

"But where do I stay in this idyllic town?" I wanted to know as excited as a child on Christmas day. "In the woods with Hansel and Gretel? With the seven dwarfs and Snow White?"

"Oops! I nearly forgot the best news! Andy has found a room for you with this nice old couple. Hoffmann is their name. He can't seem to wait for you to see for yourself. After six tonight Andy will be off duty and at the Hoffmanns' house, waiting. He has them waiting, too, filling their ears with all about Lisa for these past three days. They are nice people, a dear, elderly couple. I'm sure you will like them and their house. You will see for yourself soon."

Now I was more than eager to be off. I gave Red just enough time to swallow a bun and gulp down a cup of coffee.

The day was beautiful and clear, not too hot, with a soft breeze playing over the fields and green hills. The road was smooth and open. Shortly out of Waldheim we could simply follow the Autobahn in a straight line to Frankfurt, to

Wetzlar, and on into Grünfeld. Red was a wonderful travel companion. When we were not talking of the many things I had missed, we would sing together, loud and clear and undisturbed by our fellow travelers passing us on the road, tooting their horns at us.

"Jonny misses you. He wants me to tell you to hurry up and start working in the kitchen again." Red grinned telling me that. I knew he was thinking of all the nutty things Jonny and I had cooked up together back in Waldheim.

Seeing his grin, I grinned back. I didn't need to say anything.

For a while we drove on in silence. Then I told Red how good it was of him to come so far to drive me all the way to Grünfeld, and on his day off.

"It's fun, driving and all. Besides, Andy couldn't get away for a whole day."

"You have always been a good friend to me, ever since I first met you. Remember? On the road to Ludwigshafen, I riding my bicycle with my finger all bandaged up, and Andy and you rescuing me from two road bandits. I thought you were two angels sent down by heaven."

To this Red answered in a strange-sounding voice, unsmiling, looking straight ahead, "That's all I can be. A good friend." He gave a laugh more like a bark. "Imagine. If I instead of Andy had walked on your side of the street, that day when we came into The Village." Impulsively his hand reached out to me. Slowly, he forced it back to the wheel.

I could not think of one word, one kind little word, though I wanted to.

Red saved me from giving an answer.

"Forget what I said just now, will you? I don't know why I had to shoot off my mouth. Andy is my friend, the best one can have. You love him. He loves you, as I know well."

His voice became harsh, as if he was angry with himself. Into my silence he said, "I . . . I . . ." never finishing what he had wanted to say.

Deliberately I hardened my heart. Red's words were better forgotten. They had been spoken by an unguarded tongue. I felt sad. I liked Red very much. For a long time we did not say anything, just drove on, each nursing our thoughts.

Until I broke the uncomfortable silence by reading out loud the signs by the road, the names of towns and villages coming and going swiftly. I could tell Red was glad for it. Slowly he, too, began to relax again and join my easy-flowing chatter.

Now the countryside had become indeed beautiful, romantic, as Red had called it earlier, with its hills and forests of pine. Sometimes we could see the remains of a castle atop a mountain, and sometimes we saw heaps of ruins, ancient ones and very new ones.

Then we were driving into Grünfeld at last, I falling immediately in love with her steeple-roofed houses, with the clean-swept cobblestone streets, with the whole enchanted-seeming little town.

It seemed but a short way past the town itself, where the street climbed a pine-crested hill overlooked by a darker-green mountain, when Red suddenly stopped the jeep in front of a small, timbered Black Forest house.

It seemed indeed to be hiding behind four tall fir trees, ringed by a garden ariot with color and every kind of flower I could think of. A constant soft humming, like singing, seemed to drift from the trees, come winging down to the flowering shrubs, from the bees busy over the flowers, all the while the pretty little house dreaming in its garden, serene. All of it belonged together, making one, with no double anywhere, surely.

"Well? How do you like it?" Red asked, looking at me, pleased at my expression, trying to stretch his large frame in the small vehicle.

"Why, it's almost like a house in a fairy tale," I whispered, entranced by the beauty of the place. "It's like — it is real?"

Just then the carved front door flew open, and I was out of the jeep and through the low swinging gate, crying, "Andy!" and running into his outstretched arms to be hugged, hearing his mumble, "My darling, my darling, my own sugar," his voice with a thicker than ever Texas accent.

Breathing in deeply the scent that was his alone, I pressed my face to the open front of his uniform jacket.

"How I missed you! God, did I ever miss you. I was waiting for you since Red left early this morning!" he murmured, his fingers running over my face, my hair, as if he was making sure I was real and truly here.

"I, too, missed you, I was so lonely without you!" I couldn't let go of him.

"And now you're here!" he cried. "And I'm so glad!"

Red came up the garden path, bringing my suitcases, calling out, "All right, all right! That's enough for now!" Making us step aside and let him through. And only now I saw figures of a man and woman standing in the open doorway to the house.

Both were smiling with red-cheeked faces, watching us. Both had hair like fine-spun silver, and both were round and short and so much alike. I could only tell the woman apart from the man for the dress she was wearing.

"This is Lisa." Andy introduced me to the smiling couple. Taking my arm, he said, "Meet Mrs. and Mr. Hoffmann."

"Welcome! Welcome, Fräulein Liesel," Mr. Hoffmann said heartily. I took his outstretched hand and let him wring mine. "I trust you will be happy here."

"I hope you will like your room, Fräulein Liesel," Mrs. Hoffmann warbled in the melodious speech of this part of Germany, taking my other hand. Holding on to it, she began to usher me into the house, talking all the while. "It's upstairs. But it's bright and airy up there. We put in a small bathroom only a few months ago. That way you can feel private, and no one will bother you. It's all yours up there. We live down here. I think we will get along fine!"

How could anyone not be happy here? I wondered, very much moved by it all, looking around. The homey-looking living room and the sparkling clean kitchen seemed proud to show off their beamed ceilings and beautifully carved corner posts. The deep windows, surprisingly wide and generous in the low-ceilinged living room, boasted red and pink geraniums. But the colorful chintz furniture belonged as much as the hand-woven rug in front of the enormous fireplace and the cuckoo clock ticking away on the wall, the ancient grandfather clock sounding the hours in the hall.

But Andy couldn't seem to wait another minute to show me the upstairs, our room. He took me by the hand and swept me up the curved stairway to the second floor, where an open door invited us to come into a large bright room, somewhat removed from all the rest.

With a sense of delight I walked in to be greeted by warmth, by a feeling of welcome, from the blue of its wallpaper, from the checkered blue and white curtains waving to me in the breeze of an open French door. By the handsome furniture, hand-carved and painted in bold peasant style. By the great white and blue checkered feather coverlet on the comfortable bed. By them all, greeting me, and I calling back with a cry of joy!

Curious with what I saw peeking at me, I went down on all fours pulling out from under the magnificent bed the cutest, rose-patterned, blushing-pink chamberpot.

"Look! Look what I found!" I cried out.

"For goodness sake! A genuine antique! A real-life pee-pee pot!"

Andy came to join me on the floor. "How does one ever use this — it's so small! I can't remember ever seeing one. It sure is pretty. All those pink and yellow roses! What a shame to use this pretty thing for such a common purpose!" He was marveling over my find, laughter tickling the corners of his mouth. "The goings-on this pretty little thing must have seen! The nightly abuse it has suffered!" He shook his head, putting the pot back in its place under the bed.

A week later I planted violet pansies in it. It made a splendid conversation piece. Mrs. Hoffmann thought it so funny, she forgave me on the spot for making a flower pot out of "the pride of the upstairs." Especially since the new modern bathroom rendered it obsolete.

I let Andy pull me off the floor, looking around. I had the strangest feeling about this room, as if I had been here before.

Curious, I stepped through the French doors and onto a narrow balcony, to cry out in pleasure at seeing the whole valley rolling all the way to distant green fields and thick forest, at seeing below the small town of Grünfeld, dreaming in the late sunlight and green-dappled shadows.

"How lovely! How utterly lovely!" I felt drunk with beauty when I came back into the room — and straight into the open arms of my darling. I wanted to tell him about the indescribable valley beyond our window, but I never got to a single word.

Andy closed my lips with a kiss.

"Ahm!" Red banged open the door, his arms loaded with my suitcases. Andy let me go reluctantly.

Looking awkward and flushed, Red put down my luggage right in the middle of the room. "I wonder what's in there. They must weigh a ton each," he snorted, not knowing what else to say.

Andy pushed the bags into a corner. He turned toward Red, putting his arm over his shoulders affectionately. "Thanks, buddy. Thanks for everything. I owe you one."

"I guess I'd better shove off." Looking embarrassed, Red took a step toward the door. He shrugged and gave his cap a little push, making it slide forward over his brow. "I'm on duty tonight at the motor pool. A few winks won't hurt, I reckon." He turned and was gone from the room, from the house, before I remembered I had not really said thank you.

I had just started to unpack, shortly after Red left, when a polite knock on the door made me turn away from the wardrobe. "Come in!" I called.

It was Mrs. Hoffmann, her eyes round with surprise at seeing Andy busy in quite an un-European way, putting on hangers my dresses and skirts, wearing jauntily on his head two of my hats, chiffon ribbons streaming down his face and back. She exploded with laughter, and Andy and I laughed along with her, seeing her shiver like jelly, her generous bosom dancing to the most astonishing laughter I had ever heard.

When she found her voice again, she invited us to come downstairs for a snack. Suddenly I felt ravenous, and Andy seldom refused food, so we followed her downstairs.

What Mrs. Hoffmann called a snack, turned out to be

enough for a band of hungry woodchoppers, fit for a king's palate. There was Reibele soup with Leberknödel floating on top, a roasted chicken stuffed with mushrooms, a green salad, a mixed salad, a potato salad crowned with parsley and sliced boiled eggs. But just looking at Mrs. Hoffmann's Zwiebel Kuchen made my mouth water. When I told her this, she promised to teach me her fine art, which Andy accepted heartily.

"I would love a wife who can cook like you!" he told her gallantly. Her face turned red, and her husband gazed proudly at his glowing wife.

She, however, being an honest soul, said to Andy, "If not for your generosity, Andy, all my skills would not have been enough to cook this meal."

Ah, it was a marvelous dinner and a memorable evening!

When Andy left — quite late and unwillingly to be sure — for camp at the foot of the hill, I, too, vanished upstairs and into bed. Despite wanting to recall the happenings of the day, I soon gave in to the softness of the bed, falling asleep before I even came to the road that led through green fields to the town of Grünfeld.

Chapter 17

One day I studied the calendar, trying to find the correct date to head a letter to my parents, when I realized weeks had flown by since I left Waldheim. Unnoted, spring had passed into summer.

I was happy in the cozy little house, and I had become attached to the easygoing Mr. and Mrs. Hoffmann.

From the first day the Hoffmanns had opened to me their big hearts and all the doors in their house. I was as much at home in their kitchen and living room as I was in my upstairs room — Andy's and my mansion in the sky — ever since that evening when the sun had just left the sky, her last light still lingering on in our room and I awakened to a soft knock on our door.

Drowsily I had looked at Andy, deeply asleep beside me, not hearing a thing. Then, before I could comprehend, Mrs. Hoffmann had peeked into the room, then shut the door again, quietly, after herself. Fully awake now, I sat up. Carefully, so as not to wake Andy, I left the bed to cross the room to open the door and call out after her. But Mrs. Hoffmann was gone, her step already faded from the stairs, her voice and that of her husband coming now from the living room directly below the landing. I stood there, undecided, for a moment. Until I heard Andy's and my name. Then I began to listen unashamedly, so as not to miss a word.

"They are asleep. Like two children! Ach! Ever so like two beautiful children," came Mrs. Hoffmann's voice.

"Two such lovely creatures they are!" Mr. Hoffmann's voice followed. "Well, if I were a blind man I could tell the two are in love. Head over heels!" He paused and cleared his throat. "What did you expect? A big strapping young man like him would have to be blind and sapless to keep it bottled up with a pretty girl like her just full of love for him."

Then came Mrs. Hoffmann's voice. "I do hope they change the law soon so the two can marry. Mr. Andy told me about it."

There came a short pause. Then, deep from Mr. Hoffmann's chest came the chuckle of a pleasant memory. "Remember how it was with the two of us, when we were young and itchy for each other? When I came courting you? Remember? I would climb up to your window and right through it. We bundled in that very same room up there, in that same bed! One night your brother Conrad almost caught me, sneaking through the garden after I had left you. By Joseph, my namesake! That night I must have sat for one full hour inside that darn boysenberry bush — the one by the wall — my arm around old Bull, scratching his flea-bitten ears. Your father's hound dog he was. A sly brute, as I recall. Ah! I sat in that bush, feeding him a week's worth of good tobacco bit by bit, just so he would keep his fangs shut until Conrad went back into the house. Wonder what would have happened had I not carried that tobacco on me!" He gave a sigh. "Ach! Such nonsense you and I got up to!"

Mrs. Hoffmann snorted.

In my imagination I could see her looking at her husband sternly, though she, too, liked to remember.

But I, wearing a smile like the Cheshire cat's, sneaked quickly back into our room, locking the door behind me, slipping out of the garment I had shrugged into while following Mrs. Hoffmann to the stairs. Then carefully I crept back into bed and close to my softly snoring love, touching his warm nakedness, snuggling up to him, putting one arm around him, holding him with my face pressed into the black patch of hair curling on his chest. I loved him unbearably.

Abruptly his soft snoring stopped, then went on again. "My big, strapping, handsome hunk-of-a-man!" I whispered, repeating Mr. Hoffmann's fitting description. Growing more amorous, I took one of his earlobes between my teeth, biting it a little. He began to look like a lazy, shamelessly-enjoying-it-all tomcat. I could almost hear him purr, lying there, having a hard time keeping his eyes closed so I would think him still asleep. "Know what you are?" I began once more. "My big, faking hunk-of-a-man! And I love you," I whispered into his ear.

"Who-who said that? Who is waking me up!" he mumbled at last, unable to continue with playing make-believe any longer, reaching for me, putting his arm around me, hugging me to himself. "Ah! It's you, Mrs. Meggs! Ah, you!"

From then on Andy was seldom found in camp at night.

And from then on, whenever Andy was on duty and I would find myself with time on my hands, Mrs. Hoffmann, true to her word, delighted in teaching me the art of cooking. And dressmaking.

She was a strict teacher, never letting as small a thing as a crooked stitch pass by. I made her happy by trying hard. All too often, however, my attention would wander, leaving her behind by the side of her ancient, foot-pedaled Singer sewing machine.

And I did miss the easy companionship and the busy life I had known in the kitchens.

I even missed querulous old Bill! His acid tongue when politicking, his approving grunts and his contemptuous snorts at my attempts at getting through to him what I thought about "Die Welt." I trying to get past Bill's talk so lucid and articulate, so infuriating, too, compared to my own groping and often painful search for words and expressions. And then the day seemed twice as long, waiting for the evening, when Andy would walk up the garden path whistling a tune, halting expectantly halfway for me to fly through the door shouting his name.

Then, one evening, I told Andy of my latest desire: to go back to work in the kitchens. He would not see why I should work now when it was not necessary.

"Whatever for?" he protested, reaching for me. "I don't want you working those awfully long hours in that hot, sticky kitchen. As a matter of fact, I don't want you to do anything but love me. That's work enough!" He grinned at me wickedly, his breath warm over my cheek, his thoughts already wandering in more pleasant pastures. And promptly I tried to hit him with a pillow snatched off the bed, which he caught just as promptly in mid air putting it back in its place. But then, faking a mighty struggle, we both tumbled, too willingly, on to the thick blue and white rug before the blue and white bed. Soon I had forgotten my plans for one more day.

However, in the end I persuaded Andy. "It is the law, that every person newly moved into a city or town has to register at City Hall in that same city or town. I, too, must give a reason for staying here. And I must have a job in order to receive food stamps, don't forget."

He laughed at me. "I didn't know your stomach was rumbling, honey." And quite stubbornly he insisted, "Quit kidding me, Rapunzel. Your Daddy here will take good care of you. Let City Hall keep their stamps! Darn it, I swear I never heard of so much red tape anywhere."

I knew it was time to bring out my strongest point if I wanted to win in this. "The police can give me trouble and send me back home. I am not yet twenty-one, remember."

This hit a mark. Grudgingly he promised to ask Capt. Miller to give me a job.

That same night Andy came in to the house wearing a hangdog grin. He had seen Capt. Miller and spoken to him with satisfactory results.

"What did he say? Tell me!" I begged Andy before he could even close the door behind him.

"Well, I simply walked into his office and said, 'Sir, the guys in the kitchen need more help. I'd like to suggest this girl for the job, should you hire anyone, sir!' Andy showed me how he had swaggered into the good captain's office.

Capt. Miller had taken my papers from Andy's hand, and, reading my name, he had looked up into Andy's face for a long minute. Finally he said, "Isn't it amazing how many girls named Lisa are in this country . . ." He'd paused significantly, expecting an interesting answer.

Andy had not hesitated to give him one. "Sir, I know of only one, sir. I hope to marry her, one day soon, sir!"

Capt. Miller had signed me on without another word.

Jonny gave a loud shriek when I walked into the kitchen the following morning, then he ran to hide his well-nourished, well-rounded self between the door and the wall, showing but a bush of black hair and a pair of impishly smiling black eyes, crying out, "Oh no! Not you!" in simulated terror from behind his protective door. "Not now, just when I have come to realize how uncomplicated my life can be away from you!"

"Yup, I am back! And with a full bag of tricks, none of

them tried out yet," I promptly assured my rascally friend.

Jonny came out from behind the door. And in spite of my promises of coming events, he grasped me, giving me a rib-squashing hug, shouting: "Hello, Lisa! Ah, it's good to see you back. I've sure missed you around here! Like salt for my soup. No kidding."

This was a compliment indeed. He certainly adored salt, together with plenty of pepper and paprika.

But it was an insult to Bill, who had just come into the kitchen.

"More salt? More salt he says, the Dummkopf!" And to me he said, "It's about time you showed up, you loafer! Have you brought all your wits along, too?" His hand went significantly to the pocket where he kept his little blue notebook.

"Of course I have! And they are as sharp as your pencil, having had so much loafing time!"

"Be fresh, kid, and I will fire you right now instead of later!" he barked at me as if he really meant it, exactly as he used to do in Waldheim.

Only now I knew better. I knew him better. And so I laughed and said, "The world is becoming a better place to live in. People are kinder to each other, less selfish. That's new. Or haven't you noticed?"

"No, I haven't. All seems the same, if not worse. Then again, we might differ in our points of view. Go ahead, explain!"

"Well, now, let me think." I sat sideways on the edge of the table, one outstretched foot planted on the floor for support. Bill began to trim a small mountain of chops with a long, sharp knife. "Yes. For instance, I saw only yesterday Sgt. Crawinsky throwing away an extra long cigarette butt, deliberately and right into a fresh batch of horse manure.

Two boys went after it to pick it up. One got it. He looked at it for a moment, smelled it, and finding it soaked and stinky, he gave it to the other boy. That's kindness. The world is getting better!"

"Rubbish!" said Bill.

"All right. How about this one? I watched a farmer in a field eating his lunch — a giant hunk of bread and a lump of cheese. His helper was looking on, his belly rumbling and his mouth watering. The farmer felt uncomfortable after a while, and he quickly stuffed the cheese into his mouth, throwing the bread to his dog, who played with it, then swallowed it. Now everything was well again. The hungry man had nothing to be envious of any longer. The dog rolled over to go to sleep for a while. And the farmer felt good, his stomach full, all peaceful. The world is getting better!"

"Rubbish, rubbish!" Bill mumbled, going on with cutting fat off the chops. "Come up with something better or stop right there!"

"Yes, sir!" I saluted Bill. I began, "A couple of weeks ago I went home to visit my father and my mother in The Village. I had to cross the bridge at Mannheim by foot, and since I had come by train, with a real and honest pass for once, signed by the Bürgermeister himself, stating that I am Lisa Forster, with a scar on my right middle finger. I carried presents with me: some pipe tobacco for my father, some chocolate bars for my mother, a small jar of instant coffee in the pocket of my jacket, plus a giant sandwich made from an entire loaf of French bread baked by Mrs. Hoffmann, spread generously with liverwurst and sliced pickles in a paper sack. I had decided from the onset of my trip not to eat it but to bring it home instead as a welcome gift in these still-hungry times.

"The two American guards on the Mannheim side of the bridge didn't even bother looking at my bag and paper sack. They just mumbled to each other, then waved at my pass, saying nothing.

"The German policeman at the other end of the bridge instantly ogled my bag, discovering my chocolate bars. He took them out. 'Got any cigarettes?'

" 'No.'

" 'You sure as hell have them somewhere!' He looked all around, getting ready to pitch my chocolate into his own pocket. 'You don't want these, I say.'

" 'They are mine. You can't take them.'

" 'Take off! *Schnell.*'

"He had taken on the wrong person. 'Give them back or I start screaming!' I made as if getting ready to scream.

"A handsome French lieutenant standing by the guardhouse came over, asking in bad German what was the matter.

" 'Nothing,' my fine landsman said, handing back the chocolate. The Frenchman saw it and asked, 'American? You make love with American soldier?' He was, after all, a Frenchman. Love sounded almost elegant from his lips.

" 'General Eisenhower is my boyfriend,' (Beg your pardon, Mrs. Eisenhower) I told him in English."

At that Bill snorted like a goat. Jonny rolled his eyes up to the ceiling absent-mindedly throwing another handful of salt into the soup, engrossed by my story.

" 'Come into the guardhouse, *bitte,* to show papers?' the lieutenant said.

"In the guardhouse sat two sergeants playing cards. The three now began to discuss it all in such rapid French, I could not follow it. Then they decided to look into my paper sack. They found my giant sandwich. It did smell good, I saw them sniffing. I thought, maybe they are hungry. I took it out of its wrappings and laid it open on the table. 'For you, please. Liverwurst and pickles!'

"The lieutenant laughed. The two sergeants laughed with him. And each took a piece.

"I pointed to the door. The lieutenant opened it with a smart bow from the waist. 'Bonjour, mademoiselle!'

" 'Bon appétit,' I called back, walking away.

"The German policeman was waiting for me. 'Did they take everything away from you?'

" 'What?' I asked, innocently.

" 'The cigarettes you had, of course! And the food!'

" 'All of it, all!' I looked pitifully sad. 'I would have let you keep some of it, at least.' He shook his head at my clear stupidity.

" 'I'll know better the next time!' I bobbed my head, looking miserable. 'I'll surely remember to come to you when I cross again!'

" 'Gut. Sehr gut. Wir müssen doch zusammen halten, nicht wahr! Widersehen!' He tipped a finger to his cap, all smiles. I wouldn't have been surprised had he clicked his heels to-gether.

"I walked off the bridge fast. You see, the packages of cigarettes under my blouse were itching me, poking at me awfully."

"You are a wicked girl!" Bill grunted. "Impertinent, in-solent, outrageous!"

He liked my story, I could tell. But Jonny tied around my middle one of his big white aprons with the largest of grins lighting his face. "First slice that bread over there. Then set the tables like a good girl. You little smuggler, you!"

"Blockade runner suits her more!" Bill laughed even

when I stuck out my tongue at him.

I was back!

The work was the same as it had been in Waldheim, except the kitchen was smaller and more old-fashioned. The upper floors of the building housed at least thirty soldiers. One of them was supposedly Andy, but he used only the small office next to the dining room, and solely in the daytime.

Soon I felt as if I had never been away at all. I helped Jonny and Sam in the kitchen, I cut bread, set tables, peeled potatoes by the sackful. One day, finding Jonny all done in with a tremendous hangover — acquired on account of a little redhead this time — and Sam with a burned hand, Bill and I fried a hundred eggs in the morning for breakfast, lamb chops at noon, and in the evening, on my suggestion and with my mother's time-proven recipe we whipped up a giant pot of German *Katoffel suppe* with *Knackwurst,* a meal of which Bill had at first not taken to, mumbling "Hmm, the guys won't care for it, I'm sure."

The guys liked it after all, according to their emptied plates and request for seconds, even stiff-necked Bill had to agree grudgingly.

In the evening, forgetting, he remarked to Andy, "It really wasn't so bad after all. As a matter of fact, it tasted darn good. Even I ate it. This was one day I was glad to have Lisa around!"

This last Andy repeated to me twice that evening.

I remember another such day, when Jonny pulled out a sack of potatoes to be peeled for the evening meal. Quickly, Jonny, Sam, two soldiers doing K.P., and I followed with a bucket of cold water and our potato peelers. Sitting in a circle, we started peeling as if it was our only goal in this world, singing in different accents but in harmony. "You

Are My Sunshine" and "Sentimental Journey."

Suddenly Capt. Miller's voice came booming like a fog-horn into the middle of our chorus: "Why, those guys are having fun, a party, instead of feeling punished!"

Before we found our voices Capt. Miller disappeared into the kitchen to see what was cooking there and, as he liked to do every so often, taking samples, munching, sitting on the window sill watching the goings-on.

I had come to know Capt. Miller as a nice, likeable Martian, in spite of his frightfully loud voice and sometimes rough-seeming manners. I had known him now for sixteen months; I had more than enough opportunities to see him as he really was, through the admiring talk of his soldiers, most of them with him since before the invasion. And I was convinced that under his bulky chest he was hiding a heart of kindness and his own brand of humor, an understanding for all kinds of people in different circumstances.

At times I could not help running into him. Then he usually had a smile for me and sometimes a wink, followed by a friendly inquiry. "How are you?" *"Wie gehts?"* I was always "Just fine, sir."

By the end of each day Andy and I left behind the noise and all the bustle of the busy kitchen for the drowsy quiet of our room, our blue and white heaven. And only then did our true day begin.

Some evenings we would enjoy the theater in nearby Wetzlar or take in a movie in downtown Grünfeld. Sometimes we would go to the club, where we would find Red surrounded by the prettiest girls and, for all to see, the life of the party. But more than once, turning unexpectedly, I found him gazing at Andy and me, his face edged in lonely thoughts amid all the happy laughter and admiring glances.

However, many an evening we never made it any farther

than to the swing hanging in the garden behind the house between two gnarled pear trees that had for years now given up bearing fruit. There we would sit, Andy's arm around my shoulders, I with my head resting against him, talking of our innermost thoughts.

I would begin and end with, "Tell me a little something."

He would pull me close and say, "I love you so much, sometimes I don't know if I'm in heaven or still on earth." Then, after a little while, he would begin.

"Eighteen years and five months ago, a good fairy dropped a little girl baby out of a fluffy white cloud. The wind blew strongly that day, and instead of coming down onto a certain side of the Atlantic, the girl baby was blown to the other side instead. Since the good fairy had already promised the little girl to this boy living in this big country across the Atlantic called Texas, U.S.A., the place where she was supposed to have landed, something had to be done about it. It took time. Years went by, and the boy grew into a man. One day Uncle Sam called him and gave him a free ticket to the very place where the girl lived — all grown up and very pretty and waiting for him. The boy wasted not another minute. He took her by the hand, and, looking straight into her eyes, he said, 'For you I would fight the devil himself.' Then he put her into a large bag with holes punched in it, and he carried her on his back, swimming all the way home with her, where they lived happily ever after!"

"That was the best story you've ever made up," I told him, exhaling wistfully.

But he was quick to reply, "Who said I invented it? I only tell true stories!" He sighed. Then he pulled me even closer, giving us with his foot a push, making the bench swing a bit higher. Settling back again, he said, "Now it's your turn to tell me a little something."

I thought for a while. Then I came out with what I had known somehow, being female. "Did you have many girls before you met me?"

Andy looked at me a little sheepishly, shrugging his shoulders. "Some."

"Did you make love to them all?" I wanted to know.

"Why do you ask? It doesn't mean anything now."

"I don't mind. Really," I said. But after a while of silence I began once more. "I don't mind about before. . . ." Then I had to giggle. "After all, I was only eight when I was in love for the first time. He was eleven and my Bavarian cousin."

"You never told me that one, you wicked girl," Andy grinned, interested to hear more. He made a fierce face and said, "I think I'll have to throttle the little so-and-so."

"His name is Erik," I went on, unperturbed. "For a while I thought him cute and strong and brave. He would do all kinds of deeds to impress me. He showed me how to drink milk right from the cow's titty. He combed his hair every day all through the summer just because I told him it was very handsome hair. And one day he put his arm up to his elbow into a red-ant hill just to show me how fearless he was."

"What else did the little rat do besides show off?" Andy wanted to know, sounding threatening even while his mouth twitched with laughter. "Go on, confess. I might forgive you!"

"Well, one morning my cousin, Karl, my girlfriend, Lora, Erik, and I went up into the mountains to my aunt's apple orchard to collect the fallen apples left up there to dry. It began to rain when we got there, so we all went into this lean-to built against the mountain for just such an emergency. After a while we became bored, and Karl — he was twelve and a kind of a wiseguy — suggested, we could show each other our you-know-what, our private parts — pull down our pants and have a good look close up. I didn't want to at first. I really didn't. But then Lora whispered into my ear how we could trick the boys into showing us theirs without us having to show ours. I agreed.

" 'You show us yours first,' we told them coyly, 'then we show you ours.' This they found fair enough, since we were girls and more shy about such things. So down went the lederhosen and up went their shirts. The two of us took one look, then turned and bolted outside with a screech of deliberate horror at what we had seen, leaving the two gullible boys to pull up their lederhosen, disappointed. Lora and I ran all the way down the mountain path, through The Village, and into the house, where my aunt soon got out of us all about her two sons' growing pains. Only that is not what she called it. She readied her paddle, and when Karl and Erik came through the door that evening, she let them have it. Down came her paddle on Erik's bum. And on Karl's. That evening, in the darkest corner of the hayloft, Karl and Erik swore to be women-haters for the rest of their lives. They didn't keep their word — Erik is married to Lora. Karl was killed the last year of the war, in Russia, where he lies buried. I decided from that day on that I didn't love Erik after all and that he was not really all that good-looking."

"But you did take a look at his little dingo just the same. Hmm!" Andy said, trying to look stern. He shook his finger at me. "Imagine! Corrupted at eight!"

I made a face and looked tragically crestfallen. "It was only a teeny weeny dingo." And now *I* had to squirm, feeling his laughter tickling my cheek. His warm breath, his very closeness, while the night came into the garden, filling it with darkness.

In the Hoffmanns' bedroom the lights had long since blinked out. Suddenly the mosquitoes were ravenous, gorging away on these two conveniently warm-blooded rations. Slapping and scratching, Andy sprang to his feet, taking my hand to pull me up and off the swing, marching me away.

"Where are we going?"

"We are going upstairs, my girl. Maybe we'll play Erik's game if you like. Lederhosen droppen!"

I came to a stop in front of the door, suddenly filled with mischief. "If you promise to look only, I might let you have a quick peek!"

"A quick peek only? I can't promise that!" Andy whispered back, a catch in his voice. Then he shut the door behind us.

Later, lying in bed with not one inch between us, I heard him mumbling into my ear, "Sometimes I feel we've known each other since the beginning of time, you being part of me before I could think and reason."

For a while we lay in silence. "I used to be very shy about myself. Never with you!" I whispered. "I know every part of you. Every inch that's you!"

Suddenly we both were laughing, thinking the same thought. Andy moved. All the way down under the sheet.

"Andrew Morrell! You naughty boy!" I managed to giggle. "Where are you?"

He mumbled back, "I am studying rose petals, sampling honey!"

"Come up this instant, you decadent bee." I couldn't hear what he was saying now, for my heart was pounding like a sledgehammer all the way up into my throat.

Then there were evenings when the guys came to visit, Bill, Jonny, Sam, and sometimes a couple of others. And Red, always Red. Andy had conquered his jealousy over Red, and it was now as if Andy and I were married and lived in our own home and our friends had come to visit.

Sometimes we all sat in the garden behind the house, drinking Cokes and Mrs. Hoffmann's homemade apple cider. Some evenings the boys would arrive with beer and pretzels, and they would play cards. Sometimes we just sat around talking for an hour or two.

"What will you be doing when you're home again and civilians?" I asked at one time, looking around into their faces, pale in the fading twilight.

"For Chrissake, why do you have to remind me? I'm married to a woman unable to understand me. Jealous and empty-headed! Why do you think I'm in this here army!" This came from Bill, followed by cheers from the rest.

"Don't complain so much, you grouchy sourpuss. I'm sure you're saying that to make us feel sorry for you." Red chuckled, putting his hand on Bill's shoulder, giving him a friendly push.

"Oh, yah? Well, you just wait until one of them broads gets her claws into you. You'll be twice as glad to light out to that job in Alaska!"

Surprised, I looked at Red. "You are going to Alaska?"

He shrugged as if suddenly uncomfortable. "This morning I received a letter from the company that employed me before I went into the army. They're offering me a job, electronic engineering, somewhere in Alaska, when I get out in a couple of months. I might be tempted, since there's no one waiting for me at home. Anyhow, I haven't really thought it over yet."

"You're almost as lucky as the guy over there." Jonny

pointed at Andy. "He, too, can step right back where he left off. And with a partner to top it!" He grinned, kissing his fingertips.

"What will you be doing?" I asked Sam quickly, feeling myself blush at Jonny's compliment, seeing the others looking at me thoughtfully. I leaned back into Andy, feeling his arms folding around me, his chin on my shoulder in an affectionate, possessive way.

With a fingernail Sam kept scratching away at an ink spot on the wax cloth covering the rough wooden table. Then almost shyly he answered, "I'm not sure. Before the war I worked in a garage, pumping gasoline. It was just a job. My mother, may she rest in peace, was still alive then. I had her to care for. Now I guess it doesn't matter what I do, for a time at least." His face took on a wistful smile. "Who knows? I might even go to California one day."

After a while I asked where Jack was these past several weeks.

"The little rover boy has surprised us all, coming down with a so-called social disease, a burned tail!" answered Bill casually. Sucking on his cigar, letting the smoke gush out from his nostrils as if they were twin chimneys in a boiler factory.

"Oh, no!"

This came from me, for I had thought of Karin, back in Mannheim with her parents, after having given birth to a little boy about a month ago. Jack's child.

"Oh, yes," said Bill, taking another puff. Letting go a cloud of smoke. "Jackie boy peddled his tail once too often!" He puffed, then went on in a much more serious tone. "And I wouldn't be surprised if the fornicating, baby-faced joker did like a few others in this army — make like a lover but not like a father." He took another puff. "It would

231

be interesting to know how many little 'Americans' will grow up idealistic Germans after we leave."

"Enough for a small Wehrmacht, I bet. To give us a helping hand in the next war," threw in Jonny.

I looked up sharply; I had never heard him sound so disgusted.

For a while we sat in silence, each weighing his own thoughts, until Andy picked up once more the conversation. "I wonder how long Crawinsky will be in the guardhouse this time. He and that good-for-nothing horse's ass Krassner got punch drunk the other night and beat up one of the German bartenders — because his name was Adolf! He told the MPs who pulled them off the man."

"Krassner is being sent back to the States, I heard," Red put in. "He's drinking himself to death. Anything he can get his hands on is OK with him. Have you seen him lately? His hair is falling out in patches. His eyes look like a pair of fried eggs."

"The poor sonofabitch," came from a passionless Bill.

No one laughed. For a moment I wondered which of the two Bill meant.

"Crawinsky is in and out of the clink at least once a week," said Sam. "A month ago it was for having told Lieutenant Kuhn what he thought of his having changed his name from Cohen to Kuhn. Of course Kuhn didn't like his remarks. And how about that other time — before he beat up the bartender — when he took off his boots and threw them in a drunken rage at the piano player in the club, while the man was playing 'Lily Marlene,' requested by Sgt. Evans. He broke the man's nose and gave Evans a shiner." Suddenly his eyes went wide and round.

"Holy Moses! Maybe he was the one who put those nasty things into Kuhn's bed, on top of his desk, into his jeep — standing there right outside Kuhn's window in the light of day!"

A week earlier someone had haunted Lt. Kuhn with of all things, prophylactics filled with water, blown up to gargantuan size. Lt. Kuhn had reacted with such demonic rage, even Andy thought it better to go to his seldom used bed over the mess hall for a night or two 'til things had quieted down again.

"Well, whatever drives him sure is powerful," Bill said to no one in particular, taking a puff, looking straight into the flame of the lantern, closing his eyes as if they hurt. Then, almost surprisingly quiet after his intense words, he said, "I've known Crawinsky a long time now. We used to talk — before. Before he started to drink, to hate, to change."

Bill stopped talking, leaning back once more into the darkness, away from the yellow circle of light.

Chapter 18

Summer was now fully blossomed, with laughing sunflower eyes and hair of golden wheat rippling in the wind. The garden surrounding the house seemed aflame with her gracious blessings, the fields pregnant with her bountiful giving. Blissful in our own love, we were alive as never before, aware of every precious moment shared.

It was so good to be alive!

One day Sonia arrived to add her own good news to ours.

We had only to see her glowing face, look into her sparkling eyes, to know that she, too, had found love at last. Just recently married, she and her husband were soon to leave for Palestine, where they would start a new life together in the country she spoke of wistfully. She had come to say good-bye, to see us before she was to leave Europe.

Delighted at seeing her, Andy and I took her upstairs to our room, where the three of us sat on the bed — there were not enough chairs. We laughed a lot, and we talked solemnly. I could tell Andy was as moved as I at seeing Sonia again, seeing her so changed, so determined, so beautiful in her happy excitement, bringing us up to date on her life apart from us.

Impulsively I took from my wrist the watch Andy brought me from Switzerland, and I put it into Sonia's hand. Looking up at Andy, seeing him smiling at both of us, I knew it was all right.

"But this is your most loved present from Andy!" Sonia

stammered. "I can't accept that!"

"That's why I want you to have it," I said.

"To remember two good friends."

Andy nodded his agreement.

I placed the watch around her wrist, aware her eyes were bright with tears. I had to swallow quickly, feeling my own eyes beginning to sting.

The following day she said through the open window of the train, "I'll write from time to time and let you know how we're doing when we get there. I can't say just when."

"Sonia — Sonia how will you get there? You did not tell us." Something in her face, in her voice, was bothering me.

"I am not sure myself. My husband knows."

"Sonia, can we help you?"

"No. But God bless you for the thought. Just remember me, and wish us good luck!"

"I will!" The locomotive gave a shrill whistle, and the train began to move.

"Shalom, Sonia!"

"You haven't forgotten! Oh, Lisa, Shalom! Shalom! Peace be with you, too!" Her face became obscured by distance and by a streaming flag of white smoke which the summer wind had soon scattered into floating wisps for the poppies and daisies by the wayside to catch. I began walking slowly back to the little house inside the shimmering garden, dreaming under the summer sky.

It was the height of summer now, grey-green fields of oats turning golden, waving with the kiss of a willful summer wind.

There was a small mountain path slinking by an ancient ruin overgrown with blackberry bushes, climbing ever up and up to the top of the mountain overlooking the smiling valley.

And there was this enchanted meadow hugging the mountain, blanketed with yellow daisies, honeysuckle, and clover all the way to a ring of tall pine trees, straight and proud guards to incomparable peace and quiet. The only interruption now and then came from a darting dragonfly, a humming bee, a bumbling drowsy insect.

"Is it not as if no one ever came up here?" I whispered to Andy, lying there beside me on the blanket with his eyes closed, stretched out in contentment, his head resting in the curled fingers of his hands. "It's like being in a holy place."

"We *are* the first and only ones," he whispered back, for the majesty of the mountain and the mighty forest had captured him, too.

A little Herrgotts bug landed on his arm and crawled slowly up to his bare shoulder. I took it off and set it on my hand, so as to count the black dots on its stiff red wings.

"Five! It has five dots," I announced with satisfaction. "You and I will have five children one day." I informed Andy of what the small lady bug so clearly told me. Then I blew on it, gently making it fly away into the fairy-tale sky.

"Only five?" Andy wanted to know, sounding somewhat disappointed, creasing his forehead.

"Yup. Five!" I said, lying back once more into his arm, accepting it as a pillow.

For a long while we did not move or speak, just listened to the whispering forest, to the wind in the trees singing and whispering and giving voice to the mountain.

"I could stay up here forever," I murmured.

For answer Andy simply pulled me closer to him, not saying a word.

Until I turned over in his arm to look into his face, his eyes, solemn, narrowing against the bright blue and gold of the sky.

"In another month I have to leave. In one short month," he said, looking away into the thick grass by his side.

I couldn't seem to find words for a while. Then I said, "I can't imagine you not being here with me. Being apart from you. It's — I'll be lost, without you. Afraid . . . and . . . and . . ."

Suddenly his cheek was touching mine, caressing my face, his hands pulling me tightly against him. His voice had never been more serious.

"Don't, sweetheart. Please don't. I can't stand it. I can't even think of having to leave you behind while I must leave. You are my life!"

He was stroking the hair off my face, looking into my eyes. Intensely, earnestly he continued to talk. "If only I could give you my name already. Before I have to go. Oh, God, how much I want you to be mine!" Talking softly, he went on, "We have so little time left. They take so long to change their rules!" He took a deep breath. "I'll be back as soon as I'm out of this army. Then we marry — twice! Here and in the States!" I looked up at him, and now he seemed larger than life. Then I was in his arms, he burying his face in my hair, going on softly, gently, "Do you want me?"

I had to swallow hard before I could answer, seeing his eyes nearly blue-black in their intensity, looking into mine, being touched so profoundly by the tenderness in his voice. "Do I want you? Do I want you? Nothing in this world have I ever wanted more in my whole life!"

For a time, seconds in eternity, there was only he and I, no sky, no earth . . . Then, once more, he stretched out beside me, talking softly, in a reminiscent mood, his eyes wide and thoughtful. "Strange, how I had to come all the way to Europe — to fight in a war, to destroy, to have — to find you and fall in love instead. And one day soon I'll take you home, never to leave you again!"

He considered for a moment. "It all had to happen so. There was a time when I did a lot of nothing, leaving almost everything to my father. All that will be different from now on. I'm eager to change. I want to do many things. I have plans — all kinds! I'm thinking of building a house of our own, not too far from my parents' house." He gave me a quick little squeeze. "They'll love you!" Excited, he went on, "I'm going to enlarge the stables. I have this idea for a brand-new exercise track. I'm thinking of breeding more and better stock."

With this last of his noble plans for the future, Andy suddenly grinned widely. The he laughed out loud, pulling me playfully to himself. "And I don't mean horses only!"

Ever so meaningfully and with just a bit of sweet mischief he kissed me — until we both toppled over, swallowed up by the tall grass, the trees above us openly whispering to each other, shaking their crowns.

The sky, however, smiled brightly, pushing a fluffy cotton cloud over the curious sun's face, and shadows moved across the meadow like a sun dial.

We ran barefoot through the grass on our way down the mountain, shouting with joy at being alive, catching sunbeams before the night could send them home, before the darkness took away their warmth and light.

Chapter 19

Soon, so much too soon, the cooler winds of September made the sun-kissed, heat-shimmering days of August but a memory.

There were moments now when in the midst of happy talk and easy laughter my heart would suddenly miss a beat. When I remembered that soon Andy would be gone, and I would be alone for a while. It always made me feel like burying my face in my hands, wanting to howl like a wild thing.

I knew Andy felt as miserable as I did. I saw it in his face, his eyes, heard it in his voice. All we could do was hold each other 'til we fell asleep, mercifully forgetting for a few short hours our sorrow.

Not always, though.

One night our misery followed us into our restless sleep, giving us both horrible nightmares.

One night I awoke from such a nightmare. Still in a kind of daze, I felt Andy thrashing about, moaning in terror, calling my name over and over. I held him in my arms, feeling his body damp and hot, his face wet on mine, his heart beating rapidly. Afterward we assured each other we both had a scary dream. And I thought, incredulously, *We both had nightmares at the very same time.*

"I dreamed I was locked inside a dark, tight place. I heard you calling me. I shouted your name, over and over, but you could not hear me, could not find me, in this dark place somewhere far away, I felt I had died, was buried.

. . ." Andy looked at me sadly, much troubled.

I held him close. "I, too, had a scary dream. I dreamed I was in a strange city, where all the houses were in rows, all made of marble or stone, all with one small door. I knocked on each one, frantic with fear. I knew I was looking for you. I couldn't find you. I tried and tried, crying all the while. Then I must have felt you thrashing about, calling my name, moaning and calling, waking me up at last. I had to shake you to get you back from wherever you were. You couldn't seem to breathe!"

"It was only a bad dream," Andy murmured, taking a deep breath. "It was only a dream!"

We held each other for a long while, until we fell asleep once again, knowing we were still together.

Morning came as always, and Andy would tell me once more how very quickly he would be back, never again to go away without me. "You'll see. I'll be back before you can count how many letters there are in my name!"

This always made me smile again, and I did count the letters in his name and how long it took. It didn't take long at all. He would be back in no time! I laughed to show myself how silly I was being after all. I told myself, if nothing else, I would at least have time enough to fix myself a new wardrobe out of all the yards and yards of pretty material Andy had bought for me, have a chance to say good-bye to my relatives and friends, spend some time with my parents. Yes, I had man-to-man talks with myself at times, 'til I could sit up straight again, as if my backbone was made of nothing less than steel and I was looking ahead to the future again.

But then, somehow, deep inside myself, I was not so brave. Again and again, in spite of my supposed steel spine, I could not fight off completely this dark, strange, unreasonable fear gripping me whenever I thought of Andy going away . . . soon . . . sooner . . . with each day passing. Now nothing was better to us than lying close to each other in our darkened room, making plans for a life together. Dreaming about the future, the family we would have one day.

Often it was Andy who did the talking; it was enough for me just to hear his voice, know him to be close to me, to turn and see him still there beside me. How he delighted in painting pictures with words, pictures I could see in color with the eyes of love, almost touch in the soft darkness of our room. I came to feel that I knew well and long already Andy's home, his father and mother, his sister, Ann, the big grey and white shepherd dog that adored small children and kittens and disliked cars and all noisy, smelly machines. At times I could almost feel the soft nuzzling of a horse's lips touching me over the rough wooden fence of a corral, hear the neighing of an impatient stallion, the earth thunder under galloping hooves. I was familiar with the rambling house and all its rooms: the first floor, the large kitchen in the rear, where melodious-voiced Goldy, housekeeper and former ear-puller of Andy's younger days, reigned.

In my darling's pictures, painted for me with the brush of his warm voice, I walked up the stairway to the second floor, where heavy drapes kept out the dust drifting with the wind. But most of all I liked being on the top floor, in Andy's room, admiring with him the curios he had collected as a boy, at his desk, into which he had carved his initials years ago, a dark, slim boy doing his homework. In my imagination I would follow Andy to sit with him on the flat roof of the house, where his mother was forever raising all kinds of flowers in large earthen containers. Ah, I could see it all clearly, Andy's home, which I began calling to myself the home of my heart. But secretly, fervently, I would close my eyes and pray, *Please, Father above, take care of my love, and bring him back safely to me. I love him so much.*

In the moonlight's silver I watched him sleeping peacefully beside me. I heard him whisper my name, and softly, softly I would move even deeper into the circle of his arms.

I had stopped working in the mess hall, making sure I would be free to be with Andy at any time, not to miss a single minute of the hours we had left. Hours that began early in the morning, when Mrs. Hoffmann's many-colored, conscientious rooster raised his arrogant voice, waking the harem locked up with him inside the fancy henhouse down by the end of the garden.

Andy never left our room until it was just barely possible for him to make it back to camp on time. I, having much leisure time now, left by myself in the big bed, simply loved watching him: how he got out of bed, how he stretched, and dressed, and shaved and moved around the room.

Resting on one elbow, I would lie there, my eyes never leaving him, seeing him step into what he called jokingly his "Uncle Sam's britches," shrugging into his shirt, stuffing in the tails carefully, and closing swiftly the top button of his Uncle Sam's britches, zippering up the fly and buttoning his shirt. Then he would sit down on the bed, reaching for his socks and shoes, putting them on while I snaked my arms around his middle, pressing my face into the small of his back. Holding him, having him to myself for just a few minutes longer.

Most mornings he had just enough time to grab his jacket, cap, and tie and kiss me, calling from the door, "Be good, Mrs. Meggs. See you tonight!" His hair he would comb on the way down to camp with the small tortoise-shell comb I had given him that first time we crossed the Rhein together on the ferry when the wind had so willfully tousled his hair.

For one last time we drove together to The Village, to my parents.

Afterward I could remember only what was said just before we drove away from the house. Only that seemed of significance.

Taking Andy's hand into both of his, deeply moved, my father had said, *"Behüte Dich God, mein Sohn."* My mother had pulled down to her his finely shaped head, and, pressing her cheek to his, she had cried in speechless emotion.

"Take good care of Lisa while I'm away," Andy had called back once more from the moving jeep.

Like a whisper on the wind had come my mother's words. *"Auf Wiedersehen!"*

Back in Grünfeld I said good-bye to Bill and Sam and Jonny.

Sam pressed my hand warmly and said, "So long, Lisa. Be well and happy wherever you go."

Bill had taken both my hands in his, and, looking straight into my eyes, he said in a voice sincere and just a bit husky, "It was great knowing you, girl. Great indeed." And to my astonishment he added explicitly, "Good-bye, my friend. I'll stay in touch with Andy. See you again — in the States — Mrs. Morrell!"

My dear, fat Jonny had sentimentally held me to his big stomach and mumbled, "I'll never forget you, chiquita. One day I'll come and visit you — when I'm sure where home is for me. Andy invited me to see him about a job. I promise to cook for you the finest dinner!" With that he grinned largely. "With plenty of salt and paprika!"

Jonny, dear, round, funny Jonny! I had to get out of the

kitchen fast, for suddenly I felt I could not bear saying another good-bye.

However, before I could close the heavy door of the building behind me for the last time, I bumped into Capt. Miller. He looked at me with those knowing, steady grey eyes of his. Then he smiled, saying pleasantly, "Why, hello there!" I took his outstretched hand, thinking, how I have wanted it to be like this for so long now. With growing astonishment I listened to him saying, "I wondered where you could be! Indeed, I was beginning to feel disappointed, thinking I would have to leave here without saying farewell to you. You see, I am not entirely unaware that we may be neighbors one day." He winked at me. "My family lives in New Mexico — practically next door. We might just see each other from time to time." He stood straight. "Well, so long until then, Lisa," he said in a low, sincere voice, touching the visor of his hat, then turning away and walking off, while, surprised, I realized he had called me by my name for the first time.

Later, when I spoke to Andy of this, pondering how Capt. Miller could have possibly known so much about us, Andy smiled widely and said, "Why not? He's had more than one long talk with me. He seemed very interested in us from the start. Especially about you." Andy grinned at me. "Now don't let this bother you, sugar, but our captain is not only the captain, he also knows my father, our ranch, from way back I believe. He knows more about my family than I could say about his."

But of all the farewells I had to say, the one to Red was hardest. He had been so very close to us right from the beginning, sharing most of our secrets, to me both friend and guardian angel. I suspected he was feeling sad, for his laughter sounded hollow, his gayness seemed forced, making me think I would not want to know what he really felt.

"Don't say good-bye!" he cried. "Before you can miss me I'll be saying hello to you back home in Texas."

But quietly he had mumbled, "So long, Lisa," hugging me for a moment, kissing me with his eyes closed, tenderly. Swiftly he turned and walked away, my eyes following him 'til he vanished behind the bend in the road past the thick hazelnut bushes.

Andy and I thanked Mr. and Mrs. Hoffmann for all their kindness and understanding, for all the happy hours we had known together in their warm, friendly home. I could tell the big-hearted old man was very moved when he said, "It will be too quiet and lonely around here with both of you leaving tomorrow. It won't feel right!"

Mrs. Hoffmann had a hard time not crying. She had to swallow several times, hiding her face in a big, red-checkered kerchief before she could say in Andy's direction, "If Lisa would like to stay here with us until you call for her or come back for her, we would be pleased to have her. Surely I don't have to tell you she is much more to us than a girl who happened to rent a room in our house."

Unashamed of the tears forming in my eyes, I embraced the round, motherly figure. She was holding on to me as if she never wanted to let go, openly crying now. "We never had children. You are like a daughter to us."

However, I wanted to go home, to spend these last few months with my parents. I know my father and mother were waiting for me, waiting to have me home with them for at least a little while before I would go away so very far.

And then there were suddenly but hours left for us to be together, to walk hand in hand just once more, for the last time, on the dreaming hillside, our feet having found the grassy path leading up to the pines.

Without speaking of it, we knew we had come to say a last good-bye: to the mountains, to the memories they held for us of so many happy hours, to the forest, to the wind singing in the trees, to the earth who had cradled us whenever we came up here to forget the world below.

In silence we returned to the waiting quiet of our room; to lie down together, not touching, for a while afraid to touch, to talk; I thought I would surely start crying, terribly. And I didn't want to cry.

But then I was in Andy's arms, he holding me so achingly close that I felt the stubble of his tomorrow's beard scratching my face, my throat. I was glad for the pain, glad to hurt so as not to feel the much greater pain sitting there in my heart like a stone.

"Tomorrow. Where will you be tomorrow?"

Now I had spoken aloud, leaving my heart in the open.

"Tomorrow I'll be far away . . . yet still here with you, my love."

"I wish I could come with you tomorrow."

"How I wish you could!"

For a while we lay quietly, our thoughts the same. Then I spoke once more into the gloomy darkness. "I'm . . . I'm going to have a baby. It's more than a month now, I think." The darkness and gloom scattered miraculously, making Andy rise from the pillow we shared to lean on one elbow.

"Are you sure? Yes! Of course you are. As sure as I am! Ever since . . ." but then the shadow of another thought sprang into his eyes, darkening for a moment these happy first thoughts. "God! And tomorrow I have to leave you. In only a few hours . . ."

"I thought, at first, I would write you about it. Then all

day long I wanted to tell you. Now I have told you — and you are worried!"

"A baby!" he cried out. "Our baby!" He was excited now, realizing the significance of what I had just told him. "I wanted this to happen! By all that's true! My darling, my sweet darling." Gently his hand sought and found me. To touch me softly.

Oh, God! I thought. He is saying hello and good-bye. For one unbearably sad moment I dug my fingernails into the palms of my hands, and I bit the inside of my cheek 'til I tasted blood. I did not want to cry. But I could not stop.

"You must see a doctor soon. Promise me you will take good care of yourself — and of my son. Oh honey, honey, now I'd better hurry back twice as fast as I intended. I'm going to have a baby!"

"I will have the baby, you big, funny man. You are so silly!" But still I wanted to sob aloud. I groaned, swallowing hard. Then in the bluish darkness of the room, his happiness swept away once more the tears gathering in my eyes. His voice, charged with emotion, soon carried me along, too.

"The pickles!" He audibly slapped his forehead. "The pickles and the awful herring you've been eating for days now! You've been eating almost the entire contents of Mrs. Hoffmann's marinated herring jar, and you never even liked herring before!"

"And you! You've been eating radishes and black bread and drinking beer. You gained weight. Yes, you will certainly have a great big baby! I can tell already you're pregnant!" I teased him all the while feeling my heart must surely break into tiny splinters.

"All right, we shall each have a baby," Andy murmured. "Better yet, I will have two all at once — girls. You'll have just one to start you off — a boy! We need a boy. You can sing to him *'Hänschen klein und Fuchs hast die Gans gestohlen'* — I heard you singing that to the little girl down the road the other day. I'll teach him 'Humpty Dumpty sat on a wall' and such. No, you can teach him all that much better than I. Come to think of it. I'll show him how to sit a horse, how to walk straight and tall, be a man," he said excited. Then he became serious once more, solemn almost: "You have no idea how much I need you, how very much I love you!" He deeply sighed. "Strange, how absolutely sure I feel it was all meant for us to meet, to fall in love. Instantly but for always. Now I am convinced, sure our child was meant to be conceived now, before I had to leave. I am so glad this happened, even though I have to leave tomorrow!"

I felt happiness and unreasonable fear slicing through me, hearing his joy over the child and being reminded of him leaving, listening to him, feeling his forehead damp with perspiration and his lips warm on my face, knowing him closer now than when we made love.

Quickly I put my head down on his chest, on his beating heart. "It will be only for a short while," I whispered bravely.

"For a short while," Andy murmured back. "For a very short while only! I promise. And now you won't have to wait all by yourself! Part of me will be with you all the while, right there inside you, keeping you company." He moved, his arms encircling me, his breath coming warm and even. Suddenly, startlingly, he said, "I know the very instant we conceived our son!"

I had to swallow several times before I could say anything. "You remember?" whispering, trembling with this moment's sweet wonder and surprise. "I, too, knew. The very moment it happened."

"Tell me," he whispered, leaning over me. "Tell me how you knew."

"It happened near morning . . ."

"Yes! Yes! With the sky turning brighter by the minute. We, lying here holding each other."

We had loved each other, and afterward I had fallen asleep in his arms, my legs entwined with his, his arms holding me to him. I woke still sprawled atop him, he holding me to him exactly as we had fallen asleep. I had opened my eyes to look into his, open and filled with great tenderness, gentle thoughts. And strangely — I can't say how, though it was not for the first time — I knew that I had felt his eyes on my face long before I awoke, had felt his thoughts, whispering to me, touching me.

"Good morning, dear heart." He had smiled at me, seeing my eyes greeting him, with hearing his voice nearly singing in my ears, seeing his smile, feeling the touch of his hands and lips. Touching me so, holding me, 'til I felt him wanting me again, needing me, as never before.

I pressed my face into the pulsing spot on his throat, becoming aware of an ever greater need building in my body, too, he kissing me atop my head, on my brow, my nose, my mouth, my throat, rolling over, taking me with him, covering me completely. With his fingertips he began touching me, caressing my stomach, my thighs, making me tremble with wanting him.

Then we were as one, and as one we rode into wildly surging clouds, shouting into the storm overwhelming us, he engorged, brimming over with his fullness, I, pulsing, spilling over at last into eternity itself.

"I couldn't let go of you afterward," Andy suddenly said into our long, silent reveries, bringing me back to the present, making my heart wrench with thinking how it had happened again, us thinking and speaking the same thoughts at the same moment, as it had so often come to happen before.

"You whispered to me, 'Stay. Don't leave me just now.' Do you remember?"

I went on from where he had stopped. "And you didn't let go of me, not for one second. And we held each other, still being one. We shared the same dream, welded together, your life and mine, starting a new tomorrow."

Much excited, Andy raised himself on his elbows until his face was above mine. "Our dream — I, too, felt it! Together, we both felt it so," he murmured, a turmoil of emotions coloring his voice. After a long while he said, "The child. It will be a boy. I know it."

"We will name him Andrew, after you."

"Little Andy!" he said, and I could tell he was pleased.

"I wonder what he will look like. Like you? Or maybe like both of us?" I questioned the darkness, moving deeper into my love's strong arms.

"He will have two eyes, a mouth, a nose, two legs, and two arms. And hair — black or blond. It doesn't matter," Andy mused. "I'll be tickled pink with him — even if *he* turns out to be a long-haired, mischievous *she* like her mother!" He tugged the blanket around us against the night.

Like this we passed the rest of the night — in stretches of whispering softly to one another and in silences almost like thunder, like voiceless praying, holding each other close, not needing to speak at all. Each hoping into the silence that morning was still far away, that somehow it would never come, while in the hall downstairs the antique grandfather clock ticked away the seconds, calling out the hours, unconcerned by the sorrow of our parting, by the sweetness growing between our locked bodies. While the darkness turned into a greyish gloom, while the cold dawn came — oh, all too soon — to take away my love.

And now we could not bear to utter a single word. As with a heavy ball of iron, those last words we had meant to say upon parting were chained now inside us. There were dark circles under Andy's eyes as he stood beside me in the open doorway.

And I saw those dark circles. I wanted to touch them, erase them, but softly, gently, he closed the door behind himself — for the last time.

Only hours later I was on my way west, going home, the train's rattling and creaking beating out words to me, talking to me, singing to me of my Andy, my love.

"It won't be long, not long, until we are together again," Andy had promised.

"Soon, soon, soon," the wheels were singing, carrying me away from the mountains and the forest, from the house and from the room where we had been so very happy. Bringing me close to The Village.

Bringing me farther away from Andy. Putting miles upon miles between Mrs. Meggs and her Andrew Morrell.

Chapter 20

I was back in The Village. Back in the old house.

It was as it had always been. Nothing had changed.

If there were whispers or curious glances following me when I walked into The Village, I did not know or care much. I was but one who had been away, soon to leave again. Soon, I would go away, and those of The Village who voiced their suspicions and their open curiosity in seeing me back did not count.

There were some who set their cruel tongues wagging, more hurtful than before; for now I was alone, and Andy was not here by my side to protect me. However, there were also just as many who were as friendly as they had always been. And there was once again Uncle Max, who tried and nearly succeeded at singing like a nightingale, seeing me home again, talking to him, brushing his fur 'til it shone, treating him as if he was indeed a kind of, well, dear uncle.

My parents were overjoyed at having me back, for at least a little while, and both my father and mother could not do enough to help me span the difficult time of waiting. Again I held long conversations with my father, and I listened — this time willingly — to advice from my mother.

When I revealed my sweet secret, neither could talk for a moment overcome with the intensity of their emotions, hearing they would be grandparents. After their first feeling calmed down, they looked thoughtful and a bit sad, remembering that before long I would be leaving them, before their grandchild was born, and they could not hold in their arms the dear small bundle when first it arrived into the world.

I agreed with my mother, as I had promised Andy that last night in our room, that I would see a doctor; for already my mother was a loving grandmother, a proud mother eagle, making me feel happy and protected under her wings, though her grandchild was not much more than a seed.

With the beginning of the second week I began to watch for the mailman, each morning, for any day now he would call my name to give me a letter. A letter I would take eagerly from his hand, to read, in Andy's firm handwriting and right there on that left corner at the top of the envelope, *Mr. Andrew Morrell, Larchmont, Texas, U.S.A.* Then I would read on: my name, The Village, West Germany.

"Danke schön!" I would say to the mailman proudly. For this letter was from my Andy, from my love who had to leave me for a short while but was very soon now returning to take me away with him.

And *"Danke schön"* I would say every day from then on to the astonished mailman, who would come to us now every day — seldom only every second day — with a letter from my Andy in America, and I would not be able to help smiling with delicious anticipation.

In my delighted thoughts I always took that first letter of Andy's to the back of our garden, to the shack, where I sat back against the brown-stained wood, against the very spot where one year ago, in a playful mood, my love had carved the words A.M. LOVES L.F., and there, away from all eyes, I read this precious, still invisible letter. Over and over and over I would read it, each word.

The second week passed.

And the third week passed, slower than the second, much slower than the first.

Almost daily now I went for long walks along the river. Or through the fields and meadows, passing by that single slim cherry tree where the summer before Andy and I had helped ourselves to its delicious berries, big and shiny as a Gypsy's eyes, as Andy had said. The two of us carried away between us a bandana-full to eat later on while sitting by the river, spitting the stones into the water, betting on who could spit farthest, or hit that mossy old stone out there, giving that lazy eel sunning itself the biggest scare in his wet life. Laughing ourselves silly afterward, after having finished with our fruitful activity, ogling each other's blackish-red teeth and lips, which Andy would try to kiss back to pink, no matter how long it took.

One sunny day I came upon an empty, rain-bleached candy wrapper. I picked it up and put it into my pocket, convinced it was one thrown away by Andy.

On another glorious fall day I walked along the edge of the forest, where giant oak and chestnut trees stood rippling in the soft wind, sun-kissed leaves, finding the ground littered with shiny chestnuts. There I stopped for a little while, sitting down on a fallen tree trunk, my hands filled with the smooth, large seeds of the trees.

Andy and I had sat under these very same trees, taking the seeds with us all the way down to our oak tree, where Andy made them into a round-cheeked chestnut doll, giving it matchstick arms and legs outfitting it with a little cape made from a Kleenex. Inside one of the deep knotholes of the funny twisted willow down by the river, we fastened it down with a lump of chewing gum, naming it, after a playfully staged argument, "Guardian of All Lovers."

Remembering now, I felt suddenly curious, wanting to know if it could possibly still stand there in that oddly shaped tree, in that shoulder-high knothole. I ran to see.

But when I came to the tree and looked into it, it was empty. One of the squirrels inhabiting these woods had found it. Disappointed, I walked out from under the trees and away.

Over by the river I walked, slowly, turning my steps homeward.

I didn't get very far.

A way off yet from The Village, Willi Holzer stopped me. Riding his bicycle from out of the fields, stopping suddenly in front of me, blocking my path, he startled me. I had not heard him approaching, still deep in my thoughts.

"Look what we found here!" he sneered, pushing his rodentlike face nearly into mine, his large front teeth like fangs over his lower lip. "And all alone! Has he gone and left us with a fat belly? With a little bastard, perhaps?" He snickered, pointing a finger at me. And then he stopped snickering. For I with all my might had slapped him in the face, had turned away to walk on toward The Village as if nothing had happened.

Willi hollered after me in impotent rage, "You — you bitch, you!"

I didn't look back. Nor did I look twice toward the steps leading down to the river from the embankment, where much like a vulture Mr. Stein sat, listening, with one hand behind his ear so as not to miss anything, pretending he was fishing. The only thing I was not able to control to hold in was this funny sound, like a hiccough, and my feet, going just a little faster when I thought I heard Willi coming after me, imagining he could very easily run me over in his rage, make me fall. I did not want to hurt my baby, Andy's baby.

Home again, I did not speak of the afternoon's unpleasantness to my father and mother; they had enough worries of their own. They worried because Andy had not yet written, I knew. For one day I had overheard my father talking to my mother and her whispering back and softly crying to him in their room when I returned to the house unexpectedly early one afternoon. No, I could not add any more worries. It was enough seeing at times my father's great efforts to appear untroubled, unworried, with the coming and going of the mailman, seeing his forced cheerful smile. "The mail is slow, you know, and America is far away — over quite a lot of water and land!"

"I know," I would reply, for had not Andy, too, told me that sometimes the mail took longer now than back in the horse-and-buggy days? I would laugh along with my father when he reminded me: "Columbus took months and months just going one way." He ruffled little Karl-Heinz's straw-blond mop of hair. Karl-Heinz Baumgardner, my latest and youngest friend, he was standing by my side, listening to us with wide, interested blue eyes. "Know who Columbus was, young man? Have you learned about him in school yet?"

The boy was just about ten years old, bright and alert, one of The Village children from down the street. A friend of Andy's he was, simply devoted to the memory of him, speaking of him — and that he did often — as of a saint. Now Karl-Heinz had transferred his affection to me.

Karl-Heinz followed me everywhere, talking his head off, but sitting quietly with me in the garden when I needed to be still. He came early in the morning, asking what he could do for me today, shopping with me, helping me take the wash from the clothesline, bringing up wood for the stove by the armful. Telling me all the while, over and over, about how Andy had driven him home from the ferry in his jeep, how Andy had played ball with him, given him candy and chocolate, chewing gum, all new to him as far as he could remember in his short life, with the war having been so long and empty of sweets. Karl-Heinz also wore, in sun and rain, a much-too-big fatigue cap Andy had given him. I suspected he wore that cap even to bed and in the bath.

He was my friend all right, Karl-Heinz was.

And then the fourth week had come and gone, and one morning it was Wednesday of the fifth week.

Early that morning I had left the house to keep my appointment with the Village doctor, waiting for him to assure me of what I had known so tremulously for the past two months.

Doctor Landers had taken my hand in his own and with a warm, wise smile had said, "It's a little one all right. A lucky little one, my dear. It has a strong healthy, young mother taking good care of it already. Come see me again in a couple of months," he had said just before I went home.

Five weeks it was now since Andy had left. Any day now his letter would arrive. Any day now!

I almost missed the mailman's call that morning, what with telling my mother word for word what the doctor had said to me earlier. I heard him only when he called a second time, rattling the front gate, glad to have mail for me at last. He had just shouted for the third time, "Miss Lisa! Two letters from Texas, America!" I came flying through the open kitchen door, nearly falling down the stone stairs.

Before I had even taken the letters out of the smiling man's hand I saw that both had familiar handwriting — but they were not from my darling!

With trembling hands and a wildly pumping heart, I read on one envelope Red's given name. The other letter was from Mrs. Morrell, Andy's mother.

Not taking time to tell my waiting mother I had mail from America at last, I ran over the wetly shining garden path to my father's shack. There I fairly sank down into the pile of cut firewood, knowing deep in my heart that something terrible had happened to Andy.

My skin covered with goose bumps and icy sweat, I tore open the letter from Andy's mother first, my eyes devouring the beautiful handwriting, seeking news of my love.

October 29, 1946
The Morrell Ranch,
Larchmont, Texas

My dearest Lisa,
Forgive me please for not having written sooner. It was only this morning when I realized how very cruel this was to you, how selfish of me. I sat down and began to write — several letters — only to tear each one up. Yet one such unsatisfactory letter must do, to carry to you the immensity of what you must be told.

My dear child, if only I could put my arms around you, hold you close to me while you read this. Please be brave, dear heart. You see, Andy was in an accident. He died only minutes after, never leaving Germany alive.

A sound, inhuman and like the anguished growl of a wild animal, escaped my lips. Then I read on — feverishly — not really comprehending.

It happened just outside of Bemerhafen, the day he was to leave for home. It all happened so suddenly; he was dead minutes later.

We have finally laid him to rest close to his home, in a cemetery for soldiers of foreign wars. The shock of Andy's death left Dad with a heart attack, from which he is still recovering. *As for myself, only yesterday did I find the strength to look into Andy's personal belongings, which the army sent to us. I will keep them for you until the day — may it be soon — I can put them into your hands.*

It is of that I want to speak to you now, of what I've found in this bag. And maybe, it will help you as it helped me, to bear what seems much too cruel.

In a small, carefully wrapped bundle I found many pictures of Andy and you. How he must have treasured them! There is also a small box filled with letters and notes you sent him; he kept them because they came from you. I found pages of his last letters meant for you, headed For my only love — you, dear Lisa. This letter I read — forgive me — and when I finished, I cried. I cried as I had never cried before.

Then I dried my tears, and with my heart wide open, I read it again. My life suddenly took on new meaning when I read my son's happy thoughts for his child. The child you carry. His and your child, my daughter, which he loved so already. Deep inside my wounded heart I began to feel healing grace, this peace touching my soul. I felt trust in the beginning of life anew, reading Andy's testimony of the great love you shared.

Suddenly my hands stuffed the half-read letter into the pocket of my dress, pushing it down deeply, deeply as if by doing so I could hide the terrible truth its pages held.

With ice-cold fingers I ripped open the letter from Red. I could hardly read it; Red's handwriting was strangely shaky.

Nov, 2, 1946
New York
Fifth Army Hospital

My dear Lisa,

Surely you must think me a heartless coward, seeing I am only now writing to you, after Mrs. Morrell has written to you and you know.

Oh, Lisa, Lisa, I am as miserable as a lost soul thinking of you, seeing you in my mind reading this letter. The most difficult letter I shall ever have to write in my life.

What words are there, kind enough, big enough, to tell you that I know your grief. Your love was so special. It was your name Andy called just before he died, with his last breath.

On the train to Bremerhafen he told me of the child you carry. His son — he was so sure it would be a son. . . .

The words were all meaningless to my mind. I would be honored . . . anything for you and the child . . . Please remember I am your friend . . . Write to me soon . . . waiting to hear from you. . . .

I couldn't go on reading. My fingers let go of the paper; it was suddenly much too heavy to hold. The letter slipped down between the logs. It did not matter. It did not matter just now to know how Andy had died, how Red's shoulder and arm were broken. Nor that the intoxicated driver of the other car had been sent to prison.

Andy was dead.

Dead . . . Andy was dead . . .

My empty eyes fastened on a half-eaten apple someone had dropped on the path, evidently finding it wormy. And this ant-eaten, spoiled brown thing now became to me the center of all, the only object existing to me, the beginning and the end of — it did not matter what.

My gaze held it, touched it, circled it a thousand times. Another thousand times. Nothing mattered except this foul piece of apple and the importance to stare at it, closely, exactly, again and again and again.

Perhaps an hour had passed when my father came into the garden looking for me, wondering where I had gone with my mail from America, as the mailman had told him, glad with having at last brought to me the letters for which I had waited so anxiously for so many long weeks — so he had thought.

When my father saw me sitting there so still and unseeing, his face turned ashen. In a soft kind voice he begged me to let him know what the letters said.

As if it were not I who spoke, I heard my voice answering him. "Andy is dead," relating the details of how it had come to pass.

Strangely emotionless, I watched my father's eyes fill with tears. After a moment he grasped my hand to pull me off the wood pile. Wordlessly, dumbly, I followed him through the garden and up to the house, like a small child holding on to the dry, warm hand of the kindly old man. I could not know I had this faint smile frozen on my face, my eyes staring into nowhere, staring to keep out the bad thing, the thing that hurt so much. . . .

What was it again? What had I locked away? An apple? A letter?

No, no, I must not think of it!

Chapter 21

Not once did I cry; nor did I say a word. Not until my father tried to speak to me.

"Child, don't try carrying this all by yourself. We are here with you." And my mother had looked at me with wide, mournful eyes.

For an instant I felt my trance tremble and begin to break open. With sudden fear I quickly made it close again, lashing out at their gift of love. "For God's sake, leave me alone! Just leave me alone!" The crack closed. I was safe once more.

My parents became frightened by my gruff refusal to let them share my loss, by the watchful look in my eyes.

In silence for the rest of the day I made beds, washed floors, wiped dishes. I ate whatever was put before me, my body taking care of itself and the life growing inside me. But all the while I heard this whispering inside me: *The letters,* the letters.

I did not want to listen. I did not want to hear.

It's not true! These are meaningless lies! I closed my mind protecting my inmost self. When night fell, I crept tired and numb into bed.

I slept all night. But when the first arrows of the rising sun came flying into my room, I awoke. And I remembered. Dear God, how I remembered!

And now my magic trance vanished with the night, abandoning me to the truth, to a pain savage like a monstrous black thing tearing me apart, clawing my soul to shreds.

"Andy! Andy! Oh Andy!" I whispered into the silence, the pain sharp now and terrible and real.

"He is dead . . . He is so far away I cannot even follow . . ." I whispered aloud, frantically, while I thought I felt the walls of my room cave in, fall on me, crush me. In a sweat of sheer terror I threw on my coat, my shoes.

I was not aware where I was running to after I left the house and the yard behind me. Blindly my feet found the road that followed the Rhein, carrying me toward the oak, the tree that knew my love, that knew the miracle of our love. I ran to the spot I knew as quiet and peaceful, where the world would leave me alone in my pain for just a little while longer.

There, between the tree's giant roots, I threw myself down; I pressed my face into the unresponding earth, and I screamed. I screamed, but never a sound left my lips. I begged the dark womb of the earth to open up and devour me, to cover me as she covered my love . . .

I cradled my head in my arms and lay still. Oh, to be dead, to have all pain and all words in those letters sink down into the earth with me! To have the world ebb away in fiery rainbows, in ribbons of black and white, merging, becoming grey, dark grey, black . . . Ah, blackness and — what?

I was not dead. I was alive.

I was alive, and Andy was dead.

Why don't you let me die, God? Oh, God, why don't you let me die, too? Don't make me feel all this pain. Please, please. . . .

But the sky only looked on, unresponding and coldly inhuman. The earth never heard me, did not want me yet, would not listen to a wild cry I would not at another time have recognized as my own.

"You! You up there! Yes, you! How can you do this to me? Taking his life away, making him lie in a coffin, dead and cold — cold — when only yesterday he was warm and vibrant with love so alive. Can't you hear me? Are you deaf? Made of stone? Or are you not . . . not . . . anywhere . . . after all?"

For an instant, for an eternity in hell, I was flooded with a strange, satisfying hate.

"Ha! You are not! Not not not! That's it. Now I have found you out! At last I have found out about you! I know now that to love is only to lose! To death — stronger and greater than you! The arrogant victor! Now I know! And I will never love again!"

A great rage took hold of me, gnawing away at me. I saw the blue of the sky now as but the emptiness of lifeless space. The river flowing by was, after all, just a flow of dirty water, swollen with the refuse of the many cities along its banks, spoiled with the stink of their factories, sewers.

And The Village. Ha! Just a dirt smudge, a compost heap of pettiness. The world but a pain in the eyes of God, if there ever was one in the first place.

I was drunk with rage. My eyes could see only what my numb mind let them see: distorted by grief, changed with the blind fear of having been left alone, ready to accuse even the one I loved for having left me so suddenly and treacherously. After a long while, exhausted, at last I became quiet, lying still, spent, my very soul burned to ashes.

The wind in the crown of the tree above went on harvesting purple and lemon-yellow leaves. A family of migrating birds had a last argument with a little red squirrel. The river flowed by as always. And the sun announced to the world below that it was noon, as on every ordinary day of the week.

I did not care. And I did not hear at first the slight rustling through the leaves and dry grass, coming closer, then stopping.

I lay as if frozen, unable to move my head to look up, to see who had stopped beside me. Then, whoever it was, bent down to me, put his hand on my back, gently trying to turn me over. Through spears of grass I saw a pair of black dust half boots, laced to the ankles. Familiar boots. Through half-closed eyes I looked up: grey baggy pants, grey jacket. My father's face, his eyes wide with fear. Then tight muscles relaxing. Relief washing over his face, softening it. Suddenly his arms lifted me up to him, crushing me to his chest. "Thank God I've found you!"

I clung to him, struggling to find voice. At last I mumbled into the folds of his jacket, "I wanted to die. I wished to be dead . . . not to feel any longer. . . ."

"Don't! Oh, my poor child, don't. Your mother and I were terribly worried when we got up and found you gone. It was your mother who remembered your talking about this place here, the giant oak. I thought I would go mad looking for you." Suddenly his voice was a sob torn from his heart. "I couldn't find you."

I, too, was crying, horribly, helplessly. "Andy is dead. He just died . . . died . . . just, just like that. . . ."

"Yes, I know."

"I love him so much, so much. Now there is nothing . . . nothing. . . ."

"Oh, my poor child. Today there seems to be nothing. But today."

I lifted my face from his chest, imploring him with wet eyes. "Tomorrow, too, is empty. My whole life is empty now."

"Today you are blind with grief."

I shook my head at him. "You don't understand. Without him . . . what is left? What's the use . . . ? His child. This child has no father! His child . . . will have . . . nothing."

"It will have a fine mother! And two sets of grandparents."

"It still has no father!" I nearly shouted back at him. Then I turned away from him, to hide my face in the roughness of the tree's bark, warm, and almost alive, seemingly aware of the fierceness of my pain. "I am afraid. I am afraid to death."

"We all are afraid at times," my father said. "But one cannot just escape. Certain facts must be accepted. You must learn to accept. It will take time. It cannot be forced. But the child not yet born . . . you will have this child. And one day, in his child, Andy will not be dead. There is your path to tomorrow!" He put an arm around my shoulders and with his other hand he gently took my face away from the tree. "Come." And he steered me towards the river, where he made me sit down beside him on the embankment.

"When you were a child, we used to sit like this together and talk about many things. You were forever asking me questions then. One day you asked me if I believe in life after death, and I answered you, yes. Yes, I do. In one's children, in good deeds, we live on. So I believed then and so I believe, now. You are my child. And one day there will be your child, then your child's children. You'll see. You will see."

He talked on, and I listened, new thoughts beginning to lift my head, my heart. I thought of how much I wanted this child. How I had always wanted this child, from its very first moment. I wanted Andy's child. He was not to be dead after all.

So I was thinking, with my father's words like soothing music, touching me gently. And once more my eyes found the river, now seeing it wide and rolling along, green with soil, fish, and insects, with life itself. Aloud I said, unable to keep still now with this surprise, "Why, there is a reason for everything! For being alive! For loving someone! Even for dying there must be a reason. Why one has to die and another goes on living. For being born . . . and . . . and. . . ."

My father listened with his heart, answering me once in a while.

When the sun had turned homeward her face, I was ready to go home, too, at last. And it was I, now, who gave my father a hand to help him to his feet, to walk back together, he and I, through the grass to the road and onto the narrow, winding path that led us home through the fields, lying nearly empty under the weak glare of the evening sun. Waiting, like me, for another spring.

I walked on with my head held high, with enough courage for today. Tomorrow — tomorrow I would rise with the sun, and I would let the day take care of itself.

Day by day, from hour to hour, I would go on, walking into tomorrow. And it would be all right. For little Andy and for me.

I had taken the first step.

The first step on the road to the future.

Chapter 22

So I felt walking home with my father that evening.

But, oh, how many days and nights were to follow when I struggled with my promise to myself! When I asked the heavens above, Why? Why us? Loneliness sat in my heart, heavy as a stone, an overwhelming longing tugging at me cruelly. At times I felt my heart as a raw bit of flesh inside me, bleeding.

And yet, despite these dark hours, I felt something of immeasurable value had come to pass; something inside me had changed, come alive, to look around in wonder as if for the first time. And something good and fine it was, though it had not yet a name. Gathered its newfound strength, it opened the gate to my temple of grief and loneliness — to let in peace, to let in life anew.

Many an hour my father and I spent talking together, like before.

"How can it be possible . . ." I began one rainy Sunday afternoon, the two of us sitting in the living room, my mother busy in the kitchen making apple jelly, Uncle Max an interested onlooker, ". . . to question the existence of God and yet somehow, needing to believe? Suddenly finding yourself wanting to believe, needing God to be there for you, after all."

"What makes you ask that, my dear child?" my father asked back, putting aside his newspaper, instantly concerned with the seriousness of my question.

"That morning by the river, I blamed God for Andy's

268

death, for having let him die, while I gloried at the same time in deciding that there was no God at all. I felt righteous, filled with an absorbing hate. But even while I thought all that, I wanted Him to be there. I felt terribly alone. Like the only person left on earth, forgotten and lost, and, suddenly I wanted Him to exist after all."

"How very suddenly you had to grow up, my little one. And much too soon."

I wanted my father to understand what had returned again and again to my mind, making me uneasy, filling me with haunting questions.

"How could I have blamed God, begging Him to let me die — how could I call His name even while I was denying His very existence?"

"Child, my child. How very much you belong to this world. How all too human is your way of thinking," my father began answering me.

"I, too, have felt the torment of such questions, was disturbed and plagued by them." He was shaking his silvery head slowly, sadly. "A lifetime I have lived — to know but as much as you know." He nodded to himself. "You think me an atheist, but do you really know, what that means?"

"When I was a child," I answered, "I wanted to be exactly like you, in every way. I admired everything about you. Even now I remember I was there in the room when Uncle Johannes named you an atheist, perhaps thinking me too young to understand. And one day I heard your sister, Helen, arguing with you in the kitchen on a Sunday morning. The others had just returned from church. She was all in black, looking frightfully severe, kind of scary. You were sitting by the window, and I was just outside, catching flies for my frog, Hansel, which I had won from Philip shooting marbles. Aunt Helen looked upset, because she had wanted you to come to church with them, and you had politely refused. She was angry, blaming you for having married a woman not of your faith. For letting her bring up your child in her own faith — Protestant. In no faith at all, she called it. You answered her so quietly, I couldn't understand too well. Then she attacked you for not going to church, for not going to confession. And you had raised your voice, enough for me to hear outside.

" 'My sins are my own to know and to carry,' you said. And, 'Don't you worry about my soul, about what I will get or deserve to get in that kingdom of ours of yours or in that hell of fire and brimstone. Just let me live my life, and take care of your own salvation whichever way you think best.' So you said, then, turning away from her, thinking it enough. But she had called you a heathen, a pagan. I wanted to run to your side and tell her that you had no sins — none at all. At least none worth mentioning to God. Of that I was sure!"

"You never told me any of this before," my father said to me, seeming quite moved.

"We have never talked of these matters before," I answered him.

As if musing to himself, he said, "I guess it takes more than water and bread to shape a child into a person." For a while he sat as if deep in thought. Then, "You ask what I am. A pagan? A heathen? An atheist? None of those. A stoic believer, then? Again I say no, though I am convinced one's life must be much less complicated if one can simply believe, accept." For a moment he looked at me wistfully.

"When I was a young man, strong and healthy and quite cocksure at times, I never thought much about God or if He existed. I could depend on myself, I could work; I loved what I was doing. Life seemed easy and uncomplicated, and I knew how to keep my nose clean, how to stick to my code of morals, my own sense of values, I thought. Growing older, it became more difficult to do that: I had taken on responsibilities. The world had changed, and I soon found out that she doesn't leave you alone just because you want to be left alone. You see? Sometimes it was all very confusing to me, too. And sometimes, on more than one occasion, I, too, found that I wasn't so brave after all, nor was I strong enough to be so . . . alone. I was scared at times . . . as you were scared."

"You began to believe?"

"I found that I had always believed. After much searching and soul tormenting, after much thinking, living, reading books about the thoughts of great minds, I found . . . yes . . . I found I had always believed."

"In Him? In God?"

"In what He stands for in our human eyes. In what we really mean when we talk about Him."

"But you did not go to church. You still don't go to church."

"No."

"Why not? Does one not learn about God in church?"

"Perhaps one like me can listen to Him better atop a windblown mountain, hear Him more clearly beside a rushing stream. When giving a hand to a neighbor, to a child in need, to a kitten with a hurt paw. Perhaps it is too difficult for an old dog to change directions in mid-river. He might have come to like his familiar old hide, feel comfortable with his fleas."

"You have never been such an old dog — I'm sure of that!" I exclaimed.

"But what about when you have grown so old you can't

climb a mountain to feel the presence of God? What then?"
I asked.

"You still ask these darn, applecart-upsetting questions!
Yes. It could be a problem all right, having to think how
with the failing of one's body one could very well lose what
is to him best on earth, in life. But how very confounded of
you to think the inability to climb a mountain could also
lose one's rights to a pair of wings and a harp in that other
world. Well, no matter. Let's not worry too much about
that just now. I can always still *remember* several such
mountaintops, feel the wind singing in the trees and
brushing through my hair." For a moment his eyes twinkled
at me, mischievous and young. Then he left his chair to
walk to the window and look out. He was silent.

"You are a good man, even if you don't do your praying
in church," I declared.

He kept quiet for some time. Then he said, "No one can
really say what there is for us afterward, no one ever came
back to tell. We can only guess, imagine." He turned to me.
"Better to live one's life well on this earth. Then should
there be another life afterward, one can at least say, 'I have
done my best. I have not wasted what was given to me in
that first life.' "

His eyes were twinkling at me. "Anyhow, this I have
found out for myself: to do one's best saves one from guilt,
in the here and the hereafter."

He looked serious again. "What more is there for me to
say? Sometimes as I listen to you asking questions, answering my questions, I can hear how you already belong to
another time. And I say to myself, it is well for her to belong to this new time. I watch you walking with your head
held high, even when the day is dark, and somehow I
cannot be afraid for you. Not for you nor the child."

"Mountain climber," I whispered. "That's what you are. Oh, I just know you won't ever need wings — not in this world or the next!" I paused. "Perhaps I, too, believe in being alive in the now, alive in this world."

He did not answer. He kept quiet for a long time. Only when I moved in my chair, making it creak, did he go on once more. But now there was a tender smile in his eyes.

"Your mother. Your mother now, as you surely know yourself, has never felt the slightest desire to question God's Kingdom on Earth or in heaven, nor has she ever placed herself into a state of disharmony within herself, being all the happier for it all along. She just left me to my mountain climbing, to my books, while she planted a garden, trusting God to send rain and sun. When it became too dry she would look up, quite unabashed at who might see or hear her, and say, 'Let it rain, Father above!' Meanwhile getting ready with her own watering can, just in case He hadn't heard her! But when it rained too much, as it would every once in a while — and surely without God's permission — she would again not hesitate to look up, fiercely this time, into the clouds too free with their riches and say, 'Don't you think it's enough now? Shut if off already!' I would smile to myself, hearing her address what I thought was an indifferent sky, going back to my books in search of what? The light in the darkness? Or perhaps, what is true happiness? The laws of human existence — while the clouds closed up shop and went sailing off elsewhere. While your mother went back into her garden to get a cucumber for the evening meal, stringbeans already washed by the rain and dried by the wind, just waiting to fill her pot. While she gave a smile up to the once-more twinkling sun. And I'm not entirely sure the sun didn't smile back at her."

"The sun did smile back at her! I am convinced of that,"

I laughed with my father. Then I asked, "She never tried to convince you that her way was the right way? You never fought with her over what you believed to be right?"

"We never fought. Perhaps she felt too that there is more than one way to heaven. Understanding another person has always been enough with your mother. I love her very much, and I have always deeply respected her."

"And I love you both. Very, very much!" I took out my kerchief and daubed my nose and my eyes.

My father's face was filled with tenderness from somewhere deep inside him. It was in his voice when he began to speak once again. "How she, too, has influenced your life, that mother of yours, that good, sensible, loving woman. All her life she knew to add salt or sugar — along with my own spices, of course!" And he laughed, looking at me. "Surely the resulting soup can't be too bad after all!"

Suddenly I was laughing along with him, for the first time since receiving the letters. Coming down to earth again, I asked, "But what will the soup do with a helpless little chicken?"

"They will give flavor to each other, keep each other warm. And together they can't help making a satisfying meal!"

"A meal for no one. . . ."

"The chicken has only just been added to the soup. Give it time. All good things take time."

"Oh, Vater!" I called out to him, sadly shaking my head, calling him what I affectionately used to call him in our own particular slang from this part of the country. "Your soup is cold, and it has no desire to become a meal for anyone, ever."

"Time, my dear. Give it time!"

Time is all I surely have enough of, I thought with a

sigh. "Right now I have nothing *but* time."

Yes, our talks were different now. I had grown up. I, too, had drunk from the cup of life, finding it bitter and sweet but worth holding high to drink it down to its last drop, regardless of what it held at the bottom. The happiness I recognized in my father's eyes was as wonderful as the gladness I heard in my mother's voice, touching me, stirring me away from my grieving.

Then, early one morning, I awoke feeling for the first time the child stirring inside me.

For a moment my happiness had no boundaries, was greater than I could seem to bear by myself. I ran to my father and mother, standing there in the kitchen by the sink, and, planting myself between them, I placed their hands on my body. "The baby! It's moving! It's alive and kicking! I can feel it. Here. Put your hand here. Now here. Here. It just moved."

"It's a big baby!" My mother smiled, her eyes shining with her old love of life, her voice as excited as mine. "Already I can tell!"

My father said nothing at all. He couldn't speak. He seemed unable to get out a single word.

Later that same day, when my small friend Karl-Heinz came to visit with me, as he had so often before, he stood in front of my dresser, before a smiling photograph of Andy, studying it. Then he had turned to me and asked — so innocently and as the young child he was — if a baby was still a father's baby if the baby's father was dead before the baby was born.

I told him that was so. And his eyes had began to sparkle as with old adoration, looking from me to Andy's picture and back again. I knew his thoughts — so like a little angel's despite his marmalade-smeared cheeks and all the patches at the bottom of his trousers.

And one day, I shall never forget, Aunt Ernestine came through fog and rain to visit. She, who had stayed at home for years, never needing to go anywhere. She had simply arrived to take me with her for as long as I wanted to stay.

There, in her friendly little house, she kept me busy, showing me how to bake strudel and lebkuchen, how to knit sweet, cuddly things so ridiculously small for the child, whom she already thought of as little Andy, openly challenging my grief.

One morning — oh, I can see it still so clearly — she came rushing into the kitchen with a baby kitten in her hands, followed closely by Mina, its worried mama. Delighted, I had taken the bit of greyish fluff from her hands, crying out with sudden joy. I had always loved small creatures. Touching its softness to my face, I began crying.

I was crying because I suddenly remembered that day when Andy had called me into the storage room to show me the litter of blind, naked, minute mice he had found there behind the boxes and barrels. Because now, sharply, I remembered the brave mother mouse, her great courage. And Andy, alive and vigorous, trying to feed her a small piece of cheese from a hastily opened box of rations.

Aunt Ernestine stood beside me, putting her hand lightly on my shoulder. "Come and see the rest of the litter," she said, taking my hand. "They are all different in color, and so adorable I could sit down on the floor like an old fool and play with them."

I followed her into the hall, where under the stairs the kittens slept in a willow basket, struggling not to show my emotions. But then, when I bent over the basket, filled to the brim with warm, eager life, I had to smile. Then I had to laugh aloud, seeing Mina surrounded by six balls of fluff, six black snub noses, and twelve little ears pointed up over twelve round penny eyes, wrestling one another to be first to reach the moist pink nubs on her warm, giving body.

I kneeled down, with a sense of wonder that somehow we had much in common, this cat mother and I.

I wanted to go home, to be with my father and mother.

I went back to The Village the following day.

Soon after my stay with my Aunt Ernestine I was to know once more deep sadness, experiencing another loss.

One day, without the slightest forewarning, Sgt. Krauss passed away in his sleep. I insisted on going to his funeral, waving off my parents' concern. It was all I could do for the kind man who had been our friend — Andy's and my friend.

He had never married. He left behind no family, no next of kin.

Blind to the stares of the few Villagers and strangers gathered around the grave, I laid down my spray of white lilies. Inside I whispered, "Good-bye, my good friend. Sleep now."

The wind dried my tears on my way home across the fields. The autumn wind alone knew about them. He blew into my face, tousled my hair, and mischievously pinned an oak leaf over my heart for a brooch.

Almost every few days now the mailman would call my name with a shout and a smile.

He was a kind soul, and I suspected he actually felt guilty could he not call my name and hand me a letter. Most times the letters were from Andy's father and mother; but at least once a week now one from Red came sailing across the Atlantic. He had been released from the hospital and returned to Texas to live and work once again in the city close to the Morrell ranch.

The letters from Mr. and Mrs. Morrell were always warm and hopeful, asking me to come and be at home with them.

> *"Please come. Nothing could make us happier than having you with us, and our grandchild, one day soon. There are rooms in our house standing empty, and there is love waiting in our hearts to share. Our hope lies in the future, for all of us, dear Lisa . . ."*

For Red, however, it seemed impossible to consider that now, with Andy gone, I would not want to leave the familiarity of home, my parents.

He simply wrote:

Your time is coming close, and you must not wait. Explaining to me at great length what I must do and where I must go to get the necessary papers from my side of the Atlantic, while he and Andy's father would press from their side a permit that would enable me to come as soon as possible to the U.S.A.

In yet another letter he wrote: *I have decided against going to Alaska. I am satisfied staying here, working once more in my former job.*

In my imagination I could see him smile, writing this.

I received a letter from Andy's sister, Ann, in which she wrote of her forthcoming quiet wedding, regretting that I could not be there. Her future husband's job made it necessary for them to marry sooner than they had planned; they were leaving that same month to live in Washington. *I very much look forward to welcoming you home soon. All of us are waiting,* she wrote.

One day there came yet another letter, a dear, happy letter in which Andy's mother told me of Capt. Miller's surprise visit to their home.

We found so much to talk about, the dear man missed his train and had to stay overnight with us, to our delight. We called Red to come out to the house. As I wrote to you earlier, Red is with us very much these days and a great comfort to me and Dad. Dad and I could not hear enough about you, about Andy. At one time I found myself laughing, for the first time and it felt good, when Capt. Miller told us a certain girl had once upon a time made herself an unbelievably chic coat from the white fur lining of two arctic army coats, which two certain tall guys had given her and reported as lost afterward paying for them cheerfully.

You should have seen Red's face just then! He had been so sure no one besides Andy and you had known about this.

When we told Capt. Miller of your coming to live with us, of the child you carry, he suddenly had to look away and blow his nose. Then he said, and I will quote you word for word, "There was a time when I wasn't sure at all whether the human race deserved a chance. Or not. It makes me feel downright humble and hopeful, hearing this wonderful news." He had to blow his nose again, so as not to show us how very moved he was, hearing we would be grandparents soon, that life would continue with this most precious gift. "I'm getting to be a sentimental old fool," he said, hiding his bright eyes behind his kerchief.

This letter I treasured greatly, keeping it apart from the others to read whenever I felt in need of assurance. One time I even carried it with me on one of the long walks I took nearly daily along the river, to read it just once more sitting there by the green water hurrying past like a living thing obsessed with a purpose, flowing, pushing on, passing by, always passing by.

But I never went back to the oak again.

I always stopped before the bend in the river, before I could see the empty, wind swept crown of the giant. It was enough to sit by the river.

And one day winter arrived. The sun fell lower each day, the fields asleep under a soft cover of white. My road along the Rhein lay crisscrossed with colored shadows of grey and lilac from the stark trees. The forest stood stiff with frost. The swamp lay quiet, captured by the cold, wearing a collar of ice around its rim.

It was almost Christmas. And the New Year.

January, 1947.

And now I greatly enjoyed the crackling warmth of the pea-green tiled Kachel Ofen: to sit beside it, Uncle Max by my feet, ever so much like a meditating cat Buddha, in the cheerful, low-ceilinged room. Or I would sit with a book in my lap, often one Andy had left behind — "To keep you occupied and out of mischief until I return!" he had said.

With my eyes closed I would sit there quietly, wanting to dream that I could feel him close by, see him in the room with me. How I wanted him to be there, even as a ghostly presence drifting with shadowy magic, touching me with ghostly hands.

Feeling my mouth tremble with sadness, I would open my eyes, returning unwillingly to the present, where time spun on relentlessly, the future never stopping. Aware once more of the here and now.

One day, leafing through Melville's *Moby Dick*, I found between the pages one of Andy's black hairs. I touched it, and it seemed to come alive with my touch, making me sharply remember a bright afternoon but one summer past: how Andy had looked, lying there on an olive-green army blanket, reading this book, his hand coming up every once in a while to push back from his face his thick black hair. I had playfully pinned it back with a bobby pin out of my own hair. He had not even felt it.

On another day, sitting there by myself, I suddenly got up to worry the drawers of my clothes chest for items belonging to Andy, just needing to touch them, to hold them in my hands for a little while.

And many times I just sat there looking out the window, not even pretending that I was reading or knitting, watching the snowflakes, like beautiful tiny stars, appear on the glass, seeing them melt away again very quickly. Sitting there, watching the clouds, the restless, ever-changing clouds, while I thought of the future — the future Andy and I had dreamed about. And sometimes I felt enormously sad, that forever had become only a dream.

Then I thought how it would be to live in The Village, to bring up our child there, where I still felt like a stranger. I thought of what Willi Holzer had shouted after me that day down by the river. I shuddered just thinking how his face had looked, glaring at me.

I thought about many things indeed. And at times it was as if I could hear Andy's voice speaking to me. *I know you will like my family. Be happy there. One day you will call it home!*

And suddenly I knew beyond a doubt how very much I wanted to go to Andy's country, to Andy's home and family. Where surely some of our dreams were waiting where our child would have a future.

Clearly I knew now. And I was ready to try. For little Andy. For myself.

That same evening my parents and I spoke of my going away.

With heavy hearts they listened. Hiding her tears, my mother said bravely, "Yes. Not only for the sake of the child but also for your own future, you must go."

"But what about you? You're getting on in years. How can I leave you?" I worried, my heart heavy.

"We have each other," my mother assured me. "You can write often. And when the child is a little older, maybe you can come and visit." She smiled at me, putting her arms around my shoulders holding me to her for a moment.

Then, later that evening, my father spoke once more to me about my going away. He, too, needed to assure me — though it seemed to me that he had to assure himself even more.

"Yes, you must leave here. Find life. It won't come to you here in The Village." He put his hand over mine. "Go and find your place in the world. Choose for yourself where to be happy." Then, closing his eyes, he mused, "Go out into the world and shape your own life. Dare destiny to ignore you. Remember that for the future. The brave are not afraid to begin again. Remember that well, my daughter."

He swallowed a shadow of a thought and his lips trembled for an instant. As if to himself he murmured, "How many times have I wanted to be so brave."

Oh, how sorrowfully well I knew what it meant to them, my going away, their only child, the grandchild they would not see when it was born. For they would stay, their roots in the earth that had borne and nourished them, like old trees not to be transplanted, trusting into the wind their seed, setting it free to find a place of its own.

Then, at last, Andy's father sent me a visa and the permission for me to come to the U.S.A., to stay as a future citizen. Much later I learned of his untiring spirit and of the many hours he had spent getting me these papers, anxiously making sure I could be with them before the child's arrival. I also learned later how he had fought for us — for his son's child, his grandchild's name and birthright. How he had found the highest places and finally returned home with my permission granted.

On a windswept February morning I left The Village.

It was now 1947. Almost two years had passed since that day when Andy first came into my life. I was nineteen now, a young woman. I walked tall.

But, oh, how different was this day from the one Andy and I had dreamed of!

I almost felt a sense of relief when the bus pulled away from the curb, for it was suddenly unbearable for me to see the pain in my mother's eyes, the tight cheekbones under the thin skin of my father's face, telling of a battle of emotions raging inside him.

When the bus whizzed by the stand of pines at the halfway point, I could only see through a veil of tears. I wanted to see two tall soldiers and a girl with long, waving-in-the-wind hair. I wanted to hear them laugh together, alive and young as they had been just two short years before.

But the trees stood in silence, their roots buried deep in dark soil, covered with a carpet of last year's pine needles and fallen cones. The stage remained empty of humans or ghosts, the characters faded away.

The bus rolled on, leaving behind the trees and some of my dreams. Not all, though. Most I carried with me!

For the last time I showed my good-for-one-crossing-only stamped permit on the bridgehead to Mannheim. For the last time I said a silent good-bye to the park by the

Schloss, the buildings and the streets flying by my window. For the last time did I see the neatly patched uniform of a German policeman, a French soldier in a too-large overcoat, a young Pole — or was it a Jewish man? — dressed in boots down at the heel, in a jacket that had seen better days.

My Europa . . . where all detested one another, where all needed each other in a blind mish-mash of frenzied hate and love.

My world. My cruel, kind, ugly, beautiful, wonderful world.

An hour later the train had pulled out of Mannheim's Haupt Bahnhof, and now at last I could sit back and close my eyes. Suddenly I was very tired. I had said too many good-byes.

By nightfall I arrived in Frankfurt. And there, in the large, bombed-out city on the Main, I spent my last night in Germany in a small hotel close to the airport. Away from all the noise of the big city, I huddled on the edge of my bed, a small bird waiting for the morning. With a sudden need for comfort, I took out the letters I had received that last week, reading them over in the impersonal atmosphere of the hotel room.

I'll wait for you at the airport in New York, Andy's father wrote, *Happy to take you home with me at last, thanking the good Lord above for his mercy.*

Soon now you will be here with us, and with you our grandchild. You can't possibly know how anxiously I am waiting for you, my child's grandmother wrote in her last long letter to me.

Smiling, I opened Red's letter, knowing well already every sentence on that one page.

I can't say how very much I wanted to go with Dad Morrell

to New York to bring home a very special person! However this time it seems impossible for me to get away from my work in the city. One thing I promise you: day or night, when you arrive at the Morrell Ranch, I'll be there waiting.

I was still smiling when I shut off the light.

Chapter 23

The passengers on the plane were mostly army personnel, a few war brides and their soldier husbands. The occupation laws now permitted American soldiers to marry German nationals two months before their discharge from the armed forces and their return to the U.S.A.

Only once did I feel a passing sadness, and almost enviously I thought this should be Andy and I, seeing the excited, happy faces all around us. It took much strength to remind myself that I was alone, yet not alone. I had small Andy right there with me. And soon there would be Andy's father and mother, his sister, and Red, dear Red. And all were waiting for us at that very moment!

When we flew over the Rhein I whispered one more good-bye to the winding glassy-green stream below. To the fields. The vineyards, which looked so straight, so clear-cut, as if painted on the picture postcard.

Adieu, lieb Heimatland. Adieu.

I looked down, down to where Europa was rushing away from under the plane — away from me — away from the child I brought away with me, so promisingly alive to the future.

In a wild surge of emotions I had to close my eyes.

From now on I would think about what is. Stop thinking for what is not for what might have been. And I was ready now, as never before, the keeper of our tomorrows.

This I promised myself, while I thought my heart must burst, it was so full.

The plane was steadily flying northeast.

Lucky bird made of iron and steel. You do not have to look back, you do not have to remember.

"Wherever you go, go with your whole heart, my child," my father had said upon my departure.

"I'll remember," I had replied.

"You have chosen," the wind sang outside the plane, giving it a lift and playful bounce. "You have chosen well!"

It seemed only a short while after that my neighbor, a middle-aged prematurely bald army officer, pointed outside and said, "Look down. That is the west wall, the Siegfried Line. And those fields beyond, they are France."

We landed twice for short intervals in Paris and in the Azores before our plane took on the long empty stretch of the Atlantic.

Ever closer to home my neighbor became more talkative, almost excited. "Two years I haven't been home! I must seem a stranger to my family, to my children. Especially to my youngest son. He is about five now, almost six. He certainly has little to remember me as his father, that man who was never around, the face in the photo on the wall." He paused, then went on "Heidelberg was nice, but Boston — Boston is my home!"

Two bright spots appeared on his cheeks, making him look years younger. Then, almost dreamily and as if he was speaking of a beautiful woman, he repeated softly, "Ah, Boston! The Charles. The Common. Harvard and Cambridge. White sails on the Charles under a ruddy sky." For a moment I felt dreadfully homesick listening to him.

"Where are you bound for?" he wanted to know a little later, looking at me curiously.

"For Texas," I heard myself saying.

"That is where your husband is?" he asked with a quick look at my loose navy-blue frock which covered in delicate pleats the presence of my son already very much alive and lustily kicking.

"I am going to stay with his family. My husband is dead these past six months," I replied.

He nodded, and not knowing what to say he kept quiet for a while.

Night came.

The plane steadily droned on over the Atlantic.

Morning came.

We landed and took off again from Newfoundland. Next we touched down in Massachusetts, the United States of America at last.

I'll never be able to tell anyone exactly how I felt just then, how deeply moved I was when for the first time I put my feet down on American soil. Remembering suddenly Sonia, gentle, courageous Sonia who had found a new home and happiness continents away. Sonia, who must have felt as I did now.

In the small military airport, for the first time I wrote a postcard to my parents knowing they waited to hear from me. I wrote to Sonia, to the Hoffmanns, to Aunt Ernestine. And I wrote to my young friend Karl-Heinz, who was surely waiting to hear from me as I had promised.

When the announcer called all passengers for the flight to New York my heart gave an excited lurch: I was actually on my way to New York! I was in the United States of America!

Back on the plane I could think for the longest time of nothing but how it would be to see for the first time the father of Andy, my child's grandfather. I began to worry will he like me? What do I say to him first off? How shall I address him, Mr. Morrell? Sir? He had signed his letters Dad. Hello Dad Morrell? Would that be all right?

By the time the plane landed in New York I had talked myself into a state of fright, my heart beating in my throat. My knees actually felt weak as I followed the smooth strip of tar to the low building and the gate ahead — my gateway into whatever waited beyond.

I gave the official my passport, my papers, taking all back without a word, walking into the imposing building beyond as if in a dream.

There was a large crowd milling about; from somewhere in that crowd a voice began calling, "Lisa! Lisa!"

Looking up and ahead I saw a tall well-dressed man running toward me. I felt my heart almost stop for one short second, the world around me reeling in a moment of wanting to believe . . .

Until the tall figure whipped off his grey hat and I saw the red golden hair, the eyes more grey than blue.

Red!

Dear, dear Red who was openly crying. Who folded me into his arms so very gently, crying unashamedly, "You're here! Everything will be all right now!"

I blinked my own tears away. To see a man standing behind Red. A strangely familiar-looking man.

In a flash I took into my heart the powerful, tall figure, almost instantly recognizing the strong arresting features. The blue eyes, the salt and pepper hair. The blue eyes damp with emotion. The kind face alive with warm welcome. Then my child's grandfather, my Andy's father, opened wide his arms to me.

Like a leaf driven by the wind I found myself running into those outstretched arms glad to be caught and held, forgotten in an instant the worries and doubts of earlier. Hearing him murmur, "Welcome home, dear Lisa," his voice tremulous. I felt him trembling when he held me to him for a moment, then held me out to look into my face, to gaze deeply into my eyes, taking me back into his arms saying simply and with great emotion, "God above, I thank you!" And to me, so very gently he said, "I always knew you would be just like you are, so very young and so very dear."

Tears running down my face I looked up into his eyes. But now his gaze found and included Red, sensitive warm-hearted Red who with wide shining eyes said quietly, his voice vibrating with hope, "Let's go home. Let's all go home."

About the Author

Erika M. Feiner was born in Ludwigshafen am Rhein, Germany. She came to the U.S.A. in 1948 as a war bride. Four children and five grandchildren later, she began writing and painting land and seascapes, flowers and still lifes. She exhibited twenty-five of her oil paintings in the Milton Museum of Arts, Milton, Massachusetts and fifty-five in Quincy, Massachusetts. Writing is her true love, she admits. She has written thirty-four short stories and articles.

Erika lives in Quincy, Massachusetts with her husband of fifty-four years, and her two Siamese cats, Micky and Sam. She is currently writing a sequel to "Yesterday's Enemies."